Also by Ja

THE DUKE'S ESTATES
The Duke Who Loved Me
Earl on the Run
Blame It on the Earl
A Gentleman Ought to Know
The Duke's Best Friend

THE DUKE'S SONS
Heir to the Duke
What the Duke Doesn't Know
Lord Sebastian's Secret
Nothing Like a Duke
The Duke Knows Best
A Favor for the Prince
(prequel)

THE WAY TO A
LORD'S HEART
Brave New Earl
A Lord Apart
How to Cross a Marquess
A Duke Too Far
Earl's Well That Ends Well

Once Again a Bride
Man of Honor
The Three Graces
The Marriage Wager
The Bride Insists
The Marchington Scandal
The Headstrong Ward
Married to a Perfect Stranger
Charmed and Dangerous
A Radical Arrangement
First Season/
Bride to Be
Rivals of Fortune/
The Impetuous Heiress
Last Gentleman Standing
Earl to the Rescue
The Reluctant Rake
When You Give a Rogue
a Rebel

THE DUKE HAS
DONE IT AGAIN

JANE ASHFORD

sourcebooks
casablanca

Published by Sourcebooks Casablanca, an imprint of Sourcebooks
P.O. Box 4410, Naperville, Illinois 60567-4410
(630) 961-3900
sourcebooks.com

Printed and bound in the United States of America.
OPM 10 9 8 7 6 5 4 3 2 1

One

SIR GAVIN KEIGHLEY STOOD AT THE TOP OF A SWELL OF ground and looked down over Yerndon Manor —house, stables, outbuildings, and a bit of fenced pasture in the midst of lands that flowed out over the Yorkshire moors. The place had a grim look. Dark and weathered and overgrown, it had been untended for years. The former owner had willed the manor to a distant cousin, who had received it with indifference and left it to rot. The waste and arrogance of it made Gavin grit his teeth. Estates, and the people on them, should be cared for by those who knew how. He felt this as strongly as anything in his life.

He looked at the landscape stretching out all around the dip in which the manor lay. Some said the moor was lonely or barren, even frightening, but he didn't see it. He'd lived here all his twenty-six years. He'd run free on his pony as a boy, camped out under the stars as a stripling, done his duty to his heritage as a man.

Gavin loved this country in all seasons. Now, in late March, it was stirring. Not the sweeping purple bloom of the heather that came with summer, but smaller wakenings. Secret flowers and hidden dens. Asphodel near the bogs, bracken on the slopes, juniper and cloudberry, nesting birds and wild ponies. He didn't see how anyone could call it empty and bleak. He and this land belonged to each other. No outsider would ever understand that sort of bond. That was why willing Yerndon to some sneering southerner had been such a calculated insult.

And then there it was—a luxurious traveling coach was driving slowly up the bumpy lane. As Gavin's mother had heard, the fellow was arriving today, the absentee owner deigning to show interest at last. This was not the sort of vehicle they usually saw in this area, where one might break an axle on a stone. There was a crest on the door panel. A liveried coachman drove with a man sitting beside him. Did the usurper think he needed a guard in Yorkshire? Well, maybe he wasn't far wrong. Gavin had to admit he had a fine team of horses, though.

The vehicle stopped before the house and a richly dressed lady got down and went in. The carriage continued to the stables. Gavin watched and waited. He'd been here all morning. A bit longer wouldn't hurt.

After a while, a tall figure appeared, walking up from the stables—the wrongful owner as Gavin's mother put it. The man was dressed as if this was Bond Street, London, and not Yorkshire, ill-gotten wealth dripping off him. He moved as if he hadn't a care in the world or a thought in his head. Show him he's not wanted here, Gavin's mother had urged, her outrage whipping up his temper. Give him a taste of the north country. Let him know we won't be patronized. Gavin strode down the hill, all her goads simmering in his head.

The newcomer stopped and waited when he saw Gavin approaching.

"We heard you were arriving today," Gavin said when he reached him. The frippery fellow blinked at this abrupt greeting. No doubt he expected bows and scrapes and empty palaver. He wouldn't be getting them.

"Have you been waiting long?" the man asked. "I wanted to be certain the horses were made comfortable. I am…"

"I know who you are. The Duke of Tereford." Gavin made the title a sneer. "Of the family who cheated mine out of Yerndon Manor."

"Cheated?"

"That's what we call it."

The city fop gazed at him. "I understood that the place was left to my great-uncle by a cousin of his."

"Third or fourth cousin. Barely a relation at all. Done just to spite my kin, who had a far better right to the place."

"Indeed?"

The word was spoken with one raised eyebrow and a brush of skepticism. The smug arrogance of it hit Gavin's roused temper like a lightning strike in dry brush. Before his brain could catch up with his primed emotions, he'd lunged forward and thrown a punch.

The southerner blocked it with a raised forearm, moving startlingly fast. Gavin automatically followed up with another. The fellow leaned aside, dodging the blow without apparent effort. His fists were now raised in fine boxing form. He did not seem to be the effete bumbler Gavin had been pushed to confront, begging for a touch of home truth.

Gavin hadn't intended to fight this duke. He wasn't some rude brawler. He was a respected man of property. But now, somehow, here he was, in the midst of a bout. The man's expert evasion of Gavin's blows—with no return, as if Gavin wasn't worth hitting—fed into his anger. He would just knock the fellow down, teach him a lesson as his mother had urged, and then stand back and walk away. Gavin launched a huge roundhouse right designed to lay the fellow out.

But he wasn't there. Gavin's blow spun through thin air, leaving him flailing off-balance. He lurched to keep his footing, tried to recover. Then something struck his cheek with stunning force and a cutting sting. Gavin fell hard onto his buttocks and then flat on his back.

For a moment he had to lie there, even though the duke was stepping closer, possibly to give him a kick. Gavin's head spun. His senses reeled.

A female figure pushed in front of the interloper. "Don't touch him!" she cried.

Gavin groaned aloud. Of all the people in all the world, it had to be her. Of course it did. She was always just where one didn't wish her to be. Now here she was, to add to the humiliation of being knocked down by his enemy. "I do not need your help, Rose Denholme," he said from the ground.

"It appears that you do, Gavin Keighley, since you're lying on the earth bleeding."

"I am not bleeding!"

"You are," she insisted.

Gavin sat up. His whirling head protested a little. Red drops fell onto the front of his greatcoat.

"I believe the edge of my signet ring caught your cheek," said the duke. His tone was dry, his accent like cut glass.

"I don't wear it when I box. But I wasn't expecting a bout just now."

Was the man mocking him? Did he dare? Was that a glint of amusement in his dark-blue eyes? Gavin wanted to spring up and throttle him, but his head still rang from that—impressive—blow. He was not quite ready to get to his feet.

Rose put her hands on her hips. "What did you think you were doing?" she asked Gavin. "Why are you here?"

"Why are you?"

"I happened by…"

Gavin scoffed.

"If I might…" began the duke.

"You may not," said Rose. "I have nothing to say to those who cheated my family out of Yerndon Manor."

"*Your* family." He looked from her to Gavin and back again. "Are you related then? You do seem to have a good deal in common."

"No!" exclaimed Gavin. Rose said it at the same moment. They could agree on that, if nothing else. He had to stand up. He couldn't sit here looking up at the two of them like a small child.

"Ah." The duke adjusted his fancy overcoat. Feared he'd mussed it with a little action, Gavin assumed. "So, if I understand you, both of your—unrelated—families believe they have some claim to Yerndon Manor?"

"Hers doesn't," snapped Gavin, lurching to his feet and swaying a little once erect.

"His doesn't," said Rose simultaneously, predictably.

And then, like any two members of their families when

they happened to meet, he and Rose descended into the
morass of cousins and intermarriages and promised legacies
and sly betrayals. It had been going on all Gavin's life, the
never-ending dispute, though the wrangling had been growing worse in recent years, it seemed. The Denholmes never
gave an inch. They just spoke louder and poured on more acid.

The duke cleared his throat. "Excuse me."

Gavin did not jump. He hadn't forgotten the fellow was
there. Of course he hadn't. Rose had just distracted him.

"I cannot apologize for defending myself," Tereford went
on. "But if you and your friend would care to start again, you
might come up to the house and..."

"She is not my friend," said Gavin.

Rose crossed her arms and frowned at them both.

"You and your, ah, adversary then," the duke added.

He *was* amused. Gavin couldn't help seeing it. And that
made everything worse. He'd lost his temper, which he'd
been trying not to do lately. He'd been knocked flat. Rose
Denholme had come to stand over him like a dog defending a bone. And now this Londoner was laughing at him. He
clenched his teeth.

"Or just you, if you like," the duke continued, looking at
him. "We should see to that cut on your cheek."

"I'm not leaving him here in your clutches," Rose declared.

"Clutches?" Gavin nearly groaned again. He'd stumbled
into—no, admit it, he'd instigated—a Cheltenham tragedy.
"Go away, Rose. No one wants you here."

"I don't take orders from you. And I think you require the
presence of a responsible adult."

"I'm older than you!"

"Only chronologically."

Rose was three years younger than Gavin. They'd known each other all their lives. As children, before they were dragged fully into the feud that consumed their families, they'd roamed the moors as part of a gang of carefree youngsters and shared a host of adventures.

"You never can control your temper," she said.

Which goaded Gavin, as she'd no doubt meant to do. "And you always can, which is by far more infuriating."

"Only to someone who is always infuriated."

Gavin wrestled with his irritation. He'd been trying to learn how to master his anger, which came so hot and fast. Today had not been a success in that regard.

"Remember that time you fell in the bog and shouted at the loose boulder that dumped you in? For ten minutes at least?"

"I did not shout at a boulder." That was ridiculous.

"Yes, you did. And after you crawled out of the muck, you tried to blame me for pushing you. When I'd been *feet* away."

"I…" Gavin didn't recall this particular incident. But she was probably right. Rose had a memory like the proverbial elephant. It was one of her many annoying traits.

"You smeared mud on my face," she added.

"You Denholmes certainly know how to hold a grudge."

"A statement of fact is not a grudge," Rose replied with a raised chin.

And the family dispute started up all over again. It pulled one in like a raging whirlpool. They went at it hammer and tongs.

At some point, Gavin realized that the duke was gone. He and Rose stood alone in the space before the manor house, visible from its windows, arguing like fishwives. This was outside of enough. And all Rose's fault. "You've made us look like fools," he said.

"*I* have?" But she glanced uneasily at the building.

"If you hadn't barged in…"

"Or *you* hadn't."

"What are you even doing here?" he asked her again. "You didn't *happen* by."

"My father wanted to know…" She closed her lips on the rest of that sentence.

She'd been pushed to come by the older generation, Gavin concluded, as he had.

"And I'm not the one who attacked a stranger," Rose added. "Like some sort of rural footpad."

Gavin's temper flared again. But damnably, she was right. He hadn't behaved well. Even though his cause was just, he should not have thrown that punch. He'd just been so agitated about the fellow's arrival. And his condescension. Gavin wrestled with his annoyance and managed to pull it back a bit. "I suppose you brought a horse," he said.

"Of course I brought a horse." She indicated her riding habit as if he was an idiot.

"I will escort you to it."

"It's more likely I will have to help you onto yours. There's blood all over your coat."

"It's nothing."

"Not to your laundress."

His mother would see the stain, Gavin realized. And she would require the whole story. And she would call him an idiot straight out. Not for fighting. For losing. "I'm leaving," Gavin said. He stalked away.

Rose followed. They didn't speak again but separated, returned to their mounts, and rode off in different directions.

———

Inside the Yerndon manor house, after abandoning his two unexpected visitors to their wrangling, the Duke of Tereford found old furniture, faded wallpaper, the smell of mold, and other hallmarks of his great-uncle's neglect of the many ducal properties. Like the others, this place was in a shameful state. He'd been doing his best to mend matters since he'd inherited the title and properties a year ago. It was a monumental work.

He found his beautiful, golden-haired wife sitting on a sofa in the front parlor. She was ending a talk with a skinny woman of fifty or so. "Thank you, Mrs. Gorne," she said as he entered.

With a curt nod and a sidelong look at him, the woman went out. Tereford sat beside his duchess and met her celestial blue eyes.

"The housekeeper," she said. "Or caretaker, rather, I would say. Defensive and resentful. Can't be expected to keep a place up without help or money. Cannot take responsibility for the state of the linens. Might have been given more warning about our visit. Though I wrote her three weeks ago. She is not well suited to her position, I think. As usual, your great-uncle Percival let a place go to rack and ruin."

Though he nodded, the duke said, "Not quite as usual. Apparently, on this last estate we need to restore, we are the villains of the piece."

"What do you mean?"

He told her what had just occurred. "From their extended and practiced argument, I gathered that the gentleman and lady are scions of prominent local families. Both the Keighleys and the Denholmes apparently see themselves as the leaders of society hereabouts. Their estates border Yerndon, and both families claim they were cheated out of it."

"But I have seen the records," said the duchess. "The previous owner's will was quite straightforward. There was no entail or any such thing. He named your great-uncle clearly as his heir."

"Our visitors seemed to think that was an act of spite aimed at them."

"Both of them?"

"Well, their families."

"They are related to the old owner?"

"Through a labyrinth of descent and marriages that I did not really follow, Cecelia. Apparently. Or merely in their family lore. You know how deceptive that can be."

"How strange." She looked intrigued. "What were they like?"

"The fellow who wanted to knock me down had black hair, eyes as gray as the skies hereabouts, rough-hewn features.

Looked like he spends much of his time outdoors. Midtwenties, I would say. He's strongly built. Pugnacious obviously. He might develop a punishing left with better training. Gentleman Jackson would have a few things to say about his boxing form."

"No doubt that is the important thing, James," replied the duchess with a fond smile.

"It was when he was trying to flatten me." He returned her smile. "The lady looked a little younger. In fact, she said she was, I remember now. Red-brown hair, blue eyes, what I would call soft features. Pretty-ish."

"Ish?"

"Well, no one can hold a candle to you. But she might have had an engaging quality if she had not been declaring me a monster."

The duchess's blue eyes twinkled. "You observed them very closely."

"I had ample opportunity. They were too busy bickering to pay me any mind. It was like watching a play. One of those ridiculous French farces where people go on and on about lord knows what."

"I wish I had seen it."

"Seen the fellow who tried to put my lights out and his… Not friend. They were both very clear about that. Hereditary rival, shall we say?"

"And our neighbors here, it seems."

The duke looked around the shabby room, then out the window to the bleak sweep of moorland beyond. "I doubt we will ever spend time here, Cecelia. Let us just hire some workmen to make repairs and leave this place to itself. We have done enough over this last year. We can find a tenant from London."

"But we are so close to finishing the job."

"The baby is coming in three months. You can't tell me you aren't tired."

"I am a bit fatigued from the journey," she admitted. "But that will pass. You know I have been perfectly healthy since the stomach upsets ended." She put her hand to her gently curved midsection.

"I know that I *will* get you back to London well before the birth." The duke's dark-blue eyes were full of concern.

His wife nodded. "I would prefer that. We will see what can be done here in a limited time."

He hesitated, then said, "Very well."

"I wonder what would happen if we invited those two… callers to come for a visit?"

Tereford blinked. "You want to ask the fellow who attacked me to stay here?"

"I'm sure he wouldn't do so again. Besides, you beat him."

"Which often goads a man to try again," the duke replied.

"Does it?"

"Yes, Cecelia."

"Well, I'm sure he would not do so if he was our guest. And now that you have met them…"

"I wouldn't call that…melee an introduction precisely."

"And they seemed interesting," the duchess continued without acknowledging his objection. "They will provide some diversion as we set things to rights." A sudden gleam lit her eyes. "Indeed, as they seem to have such an interest in Yerndon, they can help us."

"That is a rather outrageous idea."

"I know." Her eyes gleamed. "And yet curiously appealing, isn't it? We had travelers in Essex, a hermit in Cornwall, and international intrigue in Leicestershire and London."

"You're saying we've become accustomed to an... excessive level of excitement?"

She replied with a musical laugh. "That is one way to put it."

The duke opened his lips to protest.

"You know it will amuse you," said Cecelia.

He couldn't deny it. The pair's bickering had been entertaining. "I doubt that they will come."

"When they each discover that their rival has been invited? Of course they will."

He frowned, reconsidering. "You don't think that attitude will make for a good deal of unpleasantness?"

"If it does, we will send them away. But wouldn't it be splendid if we could end this neighborhood feud as well as restoring Yerndon?"

The duke gazed at her with fond resignation. "You would think of that."

"I did," she answered with a saucy smile.

He conceded with raised hands. "At least it's not matchmaking."

Hoofbeats sounded outside. They turned to the windows. "There are the coaches with the servants and household things." The duchess started to rise. They had learned their lesson at other ducal properties and now provided their own help and amenities. The bare necessities at least.

"I'll see to them," said the duke, waving her back.

The duchess nodded. "I'll write the invitations."

"You expect to find usable pen and ink in this place?"

"I will make do."

He looked back over his shoulder with a grin that made him look quite boyish. "Of course you will."

Two

Rose Denholme sat at a small table beside the hearth in her bedchamber and opened a thick tome of eighteenth-century sermons. She'd appropriated the book from her parents' library some years ago. It had not been missed. It never would be, as none of the Denholmes cared for such reading matter. She placed a sheet of thick parchment paper on the page and arranged the wildflower she'd gathered on the moor upon it, spreading the pink blossom and gently flattening the leaves. Careful not to disturb the delicate petals, she laid another piece of parchment over the plant. Holding both papers steady, she slowly closed the book.

She set it near the fire, but not too close. It should be warm, not hot. Then she put three other heavy volumes on top of the sermons, all of them equally unlikely to be wanted by anyone here in her parents' house. The stack would remain in place for ten days or so, until the flower was thoroughly dried and she could transfer the specimen to one of her notebooks. She looked over at the row of such records on a bookshelf in the corner. Its presence made her room a bit cramped, but her parents had refused her request for a workroom, scoffing at the idea that her collecting was worth the space. Nevertheless, the sight of those notebooks filled her with pride.

It was Rose's ambition to catalog the full range of plants on the moors—sturdy and delicate, familiar and strange—so that people could understand and appreciate its many beauties. One of her greatest pleasures was coming upon a hidden dell and a variety she'd never seen before. To preserve such discoveries, in all their lovely, intricate detail, was profoundly satisfying.

A knock at the door heralded one of the housemaids. "You're wanted in the parlor, miss," she said.

Rose hid a grimace. If her mother had found out about her dawn foray onto the moors, she would be in for a scolding. She was not supposed to go walking alone, even though she knew the landscape as well as the hallways of her home and was perfectly safe there.

But then, it might not be that. Any summons from her parents was likely to be a complaint. Papa and Mama were habitually disappointed in her. She checked her hair and gown to be sure they showed no signs of her outdoor ramble, then walked slowly downstairs.

Her reception was almost ceremonial. Her parents sat side by side on the sofa in the comfortable parlor. This was not a good sign.

"You have received an unusual invitation," said her father.

This was unexpected.

"You've been invited to visit the Duke and Duchess of Tereford at Yerndon Manor," added her mother with more enthusiasm.

Rose thought she couldn't have heard correctly. "Visit? But we are not acquainted."

"It is rather irregular," her father acknowledged. "But they mention that you have met the duke?" He raised his eyebrows sardonically.

"I told you I saw them arrive," Rose replied. Her father had wanted that rumor verified, after all. Hadn't he sent her there? She'd thought so. She hadn't given them any details about the scene at Yerndon. The memory was embarrassing enough without adding their dismay.

"But not that you spoke to him," said her mother.

"A few words, in passing," Rose answered. She'd talked mostly to Gavin. With the usual annoying results.

"Saying something odd, I suppose," replied her father. "That you should still be so awkward in company! It's no wonder you're on the shelf. Twenty-three and no sign of becoming settled."

Rose set her jaw and said nothing. It was no use.

Her mother made a placating gesture. "It was not a proper introduction, true. But we may let that pass. The Terefords wish to know their neighbors."

"But do we wish to know *them*," grumbled Rose's father.

"They move in the highest circles of society," said her mother. "It is a real opportunity for Rose."

"You want me to go?" Her parents had condemned Yerndon's alien inheritors in the strongest terms for as long as Rose could remember. And now they proposed that she visit them?

"I would refuse," said her father. "But Gavin Keighley has also been asked."

Rose's mouth fell a little open. Gavin had been invited? After attacking the duke as he had?

"And we can't let Keighley worm his way into their confidence and perhaps snatch Yerndon out from under us," Papa continued.

"Gavin? Worm?" If there was anyone on earth less likely to be ingratiating, Rose couldn't imagine them.

"Why else would he be going? Of course he intends to pull some trick. As the Keighleys always do." Her father bared his teeth. "And so you must go to prevent him. Little as I care for the idea."

Rose tried to envision this scene. What sort of trick did Papa mean? And what did he expect her to do about it? Her imagination failed her.

"That young man has an evil temper," said her mother, apropos of nothing.

"Just like his shrew of a mother," Papa added.

Rose didn't comment on this judgment, though she silently admitted the latter accusation was deserved. Lady Keighley had always been sharp-tongued, but since the death of her husband nine years ago, she'd grown exceedingly quarrelsome. "You've told me I'm never to speak to Gavin…"

"Don't talk of him so familiarly," said her father.

"Sir Gavin then," replied Rose, not pointing out that she'd known their neighbor all her life. "I would have to converse with him if we were staying in the same house." And since their encounters had become an everlasting argument, the prospect did not appeal.

"You aren't understanding, Rose." Her father looked impatient. "Don't be thickheaded."

"I am *not*," she answered before she could censor herself. Her father defined anyone who disagreed with him, or had different interests, as stupid.

"Of course not," said her mother. "Rose simply hasn't had time to think."

"This is a chance to win our rights," said her father with exaggerated patience. "Tereford can't really want Yerndon. I understand he has properties all over England. Larger and more prosperous." He looked bitter. "Fat, rich southern land where profits make themselves."

Her father found estate management a burden. Rose suspected he wasn't terribly good at it, but he didn't share the details with her.

"You must concentrate on the duchess. Make friends."

"Friends?"

"You are capable of making friends. I suppose."

His cutting tone was unfair. The feud between the Denholmes and the Keighleys filled local society with pitfalls. People didn't want to take sides.

"Get them to hand Yerndon over to us, as is only right," her father added.

Once again, Rose wondered if she'd heard correctly. "Why would the duke do that?"

"I just said. He can't want it. He has better places." Her father's tone was peevish.

"I don't believe, Papa, that..."

"Belief is not required," he interrupted. "Only a bit of effort."

"But why have they invited us?" After the scene at their arrival, it remained incomprehensible.

Her father waved a dismissive hand. "Who knows why such people do anything? I suppose they are bored. You must amuse them."

The sinking feeling that had been growing in Rose increased. She had very little experience with society. In their isolated neighborhood, there were no assemblies or formal parties. She'd never been to London. How was she to amuse people who were accustomed to sophisticated, witty conversation? They might laugh *at* her of course. Most likely they would. Perhaps that was the real reason for the invitation. Rebellion sparked. Why should she care for the opinion of those she'd been taught to hold in contempt? "I don't see how I can do that, Papa."

"You are not refusing to help your family?"

"Well, but…"

"You will exert yourself and win them over to our cause. Surely you can be of *some* use?"

He was not going to listen. Indeed, listening was a rare commodity in Rose's life. Most of the people she knew preferred the sound of their own voices.

"Are *both* my children to be a complete disappointment to me?" asked her father.

This had become a common theme since her older brother, Daniel, son and heir, had gone off to Oxford and basically never come back. Daniel had a scholarly bent, and he'd won a fellowship at his college. This had increased his frictions with their father, which had been painful before.

Daniel now spent his holidays elsewhere and hardly ever even wrote. Rose knew this was distressing, particularly for her mother. She missed Daniel too. And not just because she now had to absorb all of her father's discontent.

Her mother was gazing anxiously at her.

"Very well, I will go," Rose said with a sigh. She would do her best to…accomplish whatever it was her parents expected.

"Good!"

"So we will definitely accept the invitation," said her mother.

"What else have we been discussing?" Her father stood and moved toward the parlor door. "We are counting on you, Rose," he said as he went out.

Was it ill-natured to be rather tired of that sentiment? Rose wondered.

When he was gone, her mother rubbed her hands together. "We must get you ready for this chance," she said. "So much to do! You will take your maid and another servant. I thought young Ian."

"Another?" Did visiting a duke require a personal footman? Even at a small country manor? Did they stand on such ceremony?

"The duchess requested it," Mama replied. "Quite prettily, I thought. Yerndon has no staff, you know. Just Mrs. Gorne and her son in the stables. The Terefords have brought a cook, I understand. Which I must say is fortunate for them. Edith Gorne would feed them on gruel. And halfburnt at that."

"Do you not see how odd all this is?" Rose asked.

"Well, yes, but the opportunity…"

"You don't really think they would give us Yerndon?" It was like something out of a fairy tale.

"Oh, that." Her mother waved the idea aside. Having come from another county, Mama was much less engaged in the dispute with the Keighleys. "No, Rose, this is a chance for you to form a connection with a *duchess*. Did you ever imagine? If you get on, she might ask you to visit in London. Only think, you could have a season, just as we always dreamed."

As Mama had dreamed. Rose had different aspirations. She thought of the rows of botanical notebooks in her room. "I'm twenty-three years old, Mama. As Papa pointed out, firmly on the shelf. Past any thought of debuts."

"Don't say that! If you wouldn't always be grubbing in the dirt…"

This was not what she did, but Mama looked near tears. Still, Rose could not quite abandon her doubts. "Must I go, Mama?"

"It is decided."

"Without even asking me?"

"Your father has written to accept." She clearly considered this question closed. "Now what are you to wear at Yerndon? If only we had known in time to procure some new gowns for you." Rose's mother reached for a magazine on the table beside her.

Mama subscribed to all the leading fashion periodicals. She loved to pore over them and dissect the latest modes. She'd never found a local seamstress capable of reproducing their complex lines and embroideries, however, or a milliner who could create the intricate hats in the illustrations. She was particularly fond of hats. Now she looked Rose up and down with a critical eye, comparing her to one of the illustrations. "You have a good figure. And you are pretty enough. Particularly when you smile. You must take care to smile at Yerndon."

Rose sighed. Even Mama did not seem to realize how irritating this admonition was. Urged to smile for no reason, she always wanted to snarl instead.

"You only need to make a little effort. You are charming when you try to be."

Rose didn't think this was true. She knew she had a number of good qualities. And she was proud of them. But she didn't see herself as charming.

"You can't spend your life wandering the moors, mooning over weeds."

How very seldom one could have what one really wanted, Rose observed as she followed her mother upstairs to look over her wardrobe.

———————

"Go and stay at Yerndon," Gavin Keighley was saying to his mother at that same moment. "Why would I do that?" He didn't care to spend time with the supercilious duke. And he had plenty to occupy him on his own estate.

"To advance our position," replied his mother. "And prevent that milksop Rose Denholme from coaxing some advantage out of the Terefords."

Gavin snorted. Rose might coax a moorland thrush to her hand. He'd seen her do it. But she didn't bother much with people. She'd be a social disaster. And after the scene he'd enacted at Yerndon, he didn't want to subordinate himself as a guest. "Why have they invited the two of us?" It made no sense.

"The invitation said they wished to become acquainted with their nearest neighbors and hoped we would pardon this unorthodox step." His mother sneered. "Unorthodox. What a ridiculous word. I hope you punch the fellow again."

"As a visitor in his house, impossible," Gavin protested. He'd had to tell his mother about the fight. She'd launched him at Yerndon and had been waiting to hear the result when he came back, spotting the cut on his cheek immediately. He'd shaded the truth a bit to avoid a great fuss. If she heard that the effete southerner had knocked him down... Gavin shook his head.

"You will convince them that Yerndon is rightfully ours. And tell them their infamy is well known in this area. They will never be received."

"A duke and duchess, Mama? Many of our neighbors will fall over themselves to host them."

His mother's face reddened, and she scowled. As she did when faced with a truth she didn't wish to accept, she raised her voice. "Yerndon killed your father!"

She had begun saying this not long after his father's death. Papa had been out tracing the boundary between their land and Yerndon's to make some legal point. He'd fallen from his horse, perhaps due to a sudden illness, and not been found for hours. Far too late to help, if help had in fact been possible. In the sudden shock of grief, his mother had put all the blame on the Denholmes. She often said the dispute had ruined her life.

"You will go there and wrest our land away from these pirates!"

Gavin had never been afraid of his mother, despite the intensity of her rages. He had a hot temper himself and knew how one could be carried away by anger. He opposed her when necessary, even though Mama would not give up or be swayed from a position she'd taken, no matter what arguments one mustered. When a matter wasn't critical, it was easier to go along. And he supposed this visit wasn't critical. Only inexplicable and irritating. He would make it brief. "Very well," he said. "I will go."

"You will expose their crimes and shame them into making amends."

That seemed doubtful. But he could state his family's case. These strangers seemed to know nothing about it.

His mother bared her teeth. "Show them we are not some paltry family to be lorded over." She huffed. "Descending like monarchs, despising all they see. Laughing at the ignorant rustics."

Gavin felt irritation spark in him. The Keighleys were an ancient line, not to be discounted. He recalled the duke's too-handsome countenance, and the way the man had walked away from them at Yerndon. In contempt?

"You will wipe their sneering smiles off their faces."

Was this invitation part of a plan to complete Gavin's

humiliation? Some townsman's sneaking jest? Was he to be presented to his household as an uncouth bumpkin? Like a dancing bear?

"We will show them all," growled his mother.

He *would* show them, Gavin decided. He would prove that he was a civilized man and not a crude brawler. He would make this duke swallow his condescension. And then he would return home and forget the fellow existed.

Sir Gavin Keighley and Miss Rose Denholme arrived at Yerndon Manor two days later, within minutes of each other. Gavin was on horseback beside a small carriage, and Rose rode in one. Though this arrival was more sedate than their previous visit, it was not harmonious. They eyed each other warily as they approached the front door. And there was fierce, silent jostling among their servitors, with an audible clashing of trunks. Keighley and Denholme servants generally took on the loyalties of their respective families, and the feud extended through the ranks of both households. They took offense at slights, real or imagined, and stood ready to defend their employers' interests at every turn. Toes were stepped on. Elbows were bumped. Disparaging comments were muttered.

Rose had brought her maid, Sue, and Ian, a youthful footman in training. Gavin was accompanied by Phelps, a taciturn fellow who could act as his valet, though that was not Phelps's job and Gavin had little use for such service, and a housemaid chosen by his mother. "Edith Gorne is useless," Lady Keighley had said. "Housekeeper. *Pfft!* Yerndon must be filthy. You will take your own linens."

In the front hall, they were greeted by the duke and duchess and offered words of welcome. The Terefords smiled and chatted and made no reference to the fistfight. Rose had wondered if it was to be a joke or an embarrassment. Apparently, it was to be wiped from memory altogether. Their hosts' fashionable dress and polished manners were intimidating.

It was odd, Rose thought, that she had never been inside Yerndon before. Her family talked about the place constantly. It was a motif of their lives. But none of them had ever visited. Disagreements and the previous owner's reclusiveness had kept them away. She realized that she had been imagining a dwelling out of a fairy tale. It was just a house though—stone built, foursquare, and shabbily furnished. It smelled of beeswax and had obviously received a thorough scrubbing recently.

Greetings completed, they were taken upstairs to settle, in bedchambers just a few doors apart. It was so strange that she would be sleeping close to Gavin Keighley.

Rose removed her bonnet, gloves, and cloak and contemplated her reflection in a somewhat cloudy mirror set above a dressing table. Her auburn hair was flattened. She fluffed the ringlets Mama had crimped around her face just an hour ago. Her high-necked, long-sleeved gown had been designed for warmth as much as fashion. Or more so really. She'd always enjoyed wearing the cozy garnet wool. But her mother's laments had convinced Rose that all her clothes were dowdy and likely to be viewed with contempt by a duchess. It was true that the Terefords were exquisitely dressed, in clothing far too fashionable for the neighborhood, and so good-looking they were like a pair of lovely porcelain figurines. A neighbor who had relatives in London had spread the news that they were leaders of the *haut ton*, absolutely top of the trees, as he put it.

Gazing at herself in the mirror, Rose shook her head. These were the people she was expected to charm. She hadn't the first idea what to say to them. Beguiling conversation was just another item on the list of things she never thought of, or cared about—fashion, society, flirtation. She frowned at her reflection. She hadn't had the chance to sample those things. Not with the way things were in this neighborhood. She *might* have grown adept, in other circumstances. Who could say? But her life had left her ill-suited for the mission she'd been given.

Rose sighed and wondered if she should have fought harder to refuse the invitation. But her parents would have nagged and complained and criticized until she gave in.

She would make this visit brief, Rose told herself. And having done her duty, however clumsily, she would go home. There was a soft knock at the door, and Sue came in to unpack her trunk.

Gavin threw his greatcoat, hat, and gloves over an armchair in his assigned bedchamber and went to stand at the window and gaze out at the moor. He was keeping a close watch on his temper. It was rather like riding an untrained, headstrong horse who continually fought the reins and was always ready to turn and bite. Gavin smiled slightly at the comparison. He was a superb rider. He would not be overborne. The door opened, and Phelps came in. "Am I to stow away your clothes?" the man asked with absolutely no enthusiasm.

"I'll do it," Gavin replied. "You chat with young Gorne in the stables and any of the other servants who seem likely. Find out the lay of the land."

"To what end?" Phelps asked.

"So that I know what I'm dealing with."

Phelps frowned as if he didn't quite understand this. Well, Gavin didn't either. He'd brought the man, a gamekeeper rather than a personal servant, because he wanted the feeling of having an ally at his back. Someone who could handle himself in the event of…trouble. Not that there was going to be any. Gavin would play the vapid chatterer, however the role might gall. "Just see what information you can pick up about these Terefords," he said.

Phelps nodded and went out.

Rose donned her best gown for dinner to make a strong start before the inevitable disappointments of her other clothes. It was another conservative garment, this one of fine striped cambric. Neither the custom nor the weather encouraged low-cut gowns in Yorkshire in March. She draped a cashmere shawl over her arms for greater warmth and took a breath.

"You look fine as a fivepence, miss," said her maid.

Rose smiled at her, opened her bedchamber door, and went out with a slightly lighter heart.

There was a bright fire in the dining parlor. Rose appreciated the heat even as she wondered about the state of the chimneys. Had anyone looked at them during the years of neglect? Mrs. Gorne was not known for competence. The chimneys were probably in dire need of cleaning, choked with soot, and in danger of catching fire. Rose started to mention it, and then decided this was not the sort of sparkling remark she was expected to provide on this visit.

Ian and the housemaid Gavin had brought along were serving the meal. Rose didn't recognize the girl. She must be new to the Keighley staff. She saw Ian bump the maid's elbow, trying to make her spill a pitcher of gravy. The girl gave the young footman a glittering defiant glance and trod on his toe. Ian bared his teeth and pushed her away with one broad shoulder. The maid only just caught her balance. Going out of the room, the two jostled in the doorway. She'd have to speak to Ian and Sue, Rose decided. This sort of thing was unnecessary and might lead to catastrophe.

"This is a very good dinner," said Gavin. He sounded rudely surprised.

"We brought our cook and some supplies," said the duchess.

"We have fine foodstuffs here in Yorkshire."

If this was her competition, she might actually manage to appear charming, Rose thought.

"Of course," replied the duchess. "We didn't know the local merchants. Perhaps you can recommend the best ones?"

Gavin frowned. Rose knew that these wouldn't be right at the top of his mind, as his mother oversaw the household purchases. She spoke, listing the purveyors her family used.

"Berwick overcharges," grumbled Gavin.

"He has the best quality," replied Rose. "One has to pay for that."

They fell into a dispute. The usual wrangling over next to nothing, Rose thought. Must he contradict everything she said? She struggled to bring it to a close.

"You've known each other for a long time," commented the duke. "Most of your lives?"

"How do you know that?" Gavin asked. He seemed poised to take every remark as an insult.

"There was mention of an incident at a bog. An offending boulder?" The duke smiled.

He'd heard that, Rose thought. And what else? She couldn't remember all they'd said on that first visit as the duke stood by. It might have been anything. When a Denholme and a Keighley argued, they didn't hold back. Memories and insults far older than she was just came tripping out, like old songs learned in childhood. Under the gaze of these polished newcomers, it was embarrassing. Was the duke mocking them? It didn't quite seem so, but Gavin was gritting his teeth. He was going to lose his temper. Couldn't he see that would just make matters worse? "You should have the chimneys cleaned," she said.

Everyone looked at her.

Rose pressed on. "I daresay it's been years. You wouldn't want the soot that's built up to catch fire."

"A good point," said the duchess. She was smiling as if she understood Rose's diversionary tactic. "We will see to that. Perhaps you know of someone?"

Rose did. She said so. She ignored the fact that Gavin
Keighley was glowering at her. For no reason whatsoever.
She was used to that. At least he wasn't about to throw a
punch.

"We mean to put Yerndon in order," the duchess continued. "Your opinions are welcome."

"Why should we give them?" Gavin asked.

"You seem to have an interest in the place," said the duke.

"Interest?" Gavin's tone had gone sharp.

"You know it and care about it, shall we say."

"Shall we say," Gavin echoed sarcastically.

She should have endured the nagging and refused to
come, Rose thought. This was excruciating. She wondered
how soon she could escape. The duke and duchess looked
at each other. They had to be regretting their quixotic invitation. But watching them, the chief thing Rose noticed in
the glance was affection. This pair was clearly in love. There
was a gleam of humor too. Rose searched again for mockery. No, it wasn't quite that, she decided. They were amused,
certainly, but not in a cruel way. The Terefords weren't what
she'd been led to expect.

"What are the chief amusements hereabouts?" the duke
asked.

"Nothing you would like," Gavin replied.

Really, thought Rose, did he ever listen to himself?

"There must be some pleasant rides despite the sameness
of the country."

Gavin bridled at the description.

"The moor is very beautiful," said Rose.

Tereford turned to her. "Do you find it so?"

"Oh yes. It is full of interest when you know it well."

"We will go walking, and you can show me," said the duchess.

"Not too far," put in her husband. "You must take care of yourself."

Rose had naturally noticed that her hostess was expecting a child. She liked the duke for his concern.

"Not too far," the duchess agreed.

"And perhaps we will try a ride in the morning," the duke said to Gavin.

Rose's fellow guest agreed without visible enthusiasm.

The evening continued in the same vein. Rose tried to produce interesting information about the neighborhood, without great success. Gavin contradicted nearly every remark she made. It was a reflex. She knew he had no strong opinions about Mrs. Rennie's spaniels. He couldn't have cared less about Letty Ferris's skill on the harp. He only felt he had to disagree with a Denholme. It was ridiculous. And certainly anything but charming.

When at last the socializing was over and Rose could withdraw from her trial, she left the front parlor in a rush, picked up a lit candle at the foot of the stairs, and hurried up. She was free! But somehow she found herself walking upstairs beside Gavin. Was there no end to her bad luck? He looked relieved as well as dour. Must he always look dour? Suddenly, Rose was fed up. In the middle of the staircase, she paused one step above him, so that their eyes were on a level, and blocked his way. "We must stop arguing in front of the

Terefords," she said. "We're making a spectacle of ourselves. And it's extremely uncomfortable."

"I don't argue."

"Gavin. You tear at me every time we see each other." Which had not been often before this, as she had been forbidden to speak to him. And now they would be forced to converse for the length of this stay at Yerndon. Had that not occurred to her parents?

"Well, you are wrongheaded," he said. "Fuzzy-minded."

She was not. In fact, she was one of the few people who could hold their own against him. Rose suspected that this irritated him the most. "And you are always right?"

"Not always. But I know this visit is a mistake."

"Perhaps you should go home." If he did, she could. What a relief! She would find some excuse that was not horridly rude.

"And leave the field to you?" He shook his head.

"There is no field. This is not a military campaign."

"It is a contest, and the Keighleys *will* be represented…"

"It is not a contest."

"No? What do you think it is?"

"A penance."

"For what?"

"Not being able to resist my family's orders," said Rose bitterly.

There was an arrested look in his gray eyes at this, but he said, "Ridiculous."

"You are arguing again."

"No, I am not. I am merely expressing an opinion. I suppose I have the right to do that."

"You certainly have a great many of them."

"And you do not?"

Rose wasn't sure whether she had opinions or simply too many admonitions crammed in her head. "Do you want to keep on amusing the duke with our wrangling?"

"What?" Gavin stiffened, his eyes snapping.

"The duchess too. They find us curious, I think."

"They can take their…"

"Not in a malicious way. It seems to me. The duchess is rather charming."

"She's all right," he replied grudgingly.

"And the duke seems a pleasant enough man."

"He is an affected, supercilious fop."

Rose thought they both knew this description wasn't accurate, but she said only, "Whom we do not wish to entertain with our endless disputes. Because it is embarrassing."

Gavin gritted his teeth. It took him a moment to say, "I suppose not."

Was it so very hard to agree with her? "*I* don't. So I suggest… I propose for your consideration that we *pretend* to get along in order to stop amusing them."

For the first time in this conversation—the first time in ages actually—Gavin really looked at her. His gaze was riveting. Rose found she couldn't look away. They had been…comrades once, ranging across the moors with their youthful gang. And even after that, there'd been a few months when Rose was sixteen that she'd thought… A load of twaddle, Rose told herself.

"Pretend," he repeated, as if he'd never heard the word before.

"Yes. You will not disagree with everything I say."

"I don't…" He stopped. He almost, very nearly but not quite, smiled. "Nor will you, with everything I say."

"I…" It was true that *she* didn't do this, but there was no sense saying so. Rose nodded.

"We make a treaty," he said slowly. "Give the illusion of amity."

"Yes." For some reason, Rose found the phrase disheartening.

The wavering light of their candles played across the strong planes of his face. Finally, he nodded. "Very well. I agree."

"I suppose it will be difficult for you," said Rose, the words slipping out.

"For me?"

"You are so accustomed to saying whatever you like. And to getting your own way."

"If you think that, you have no idea about…anything," he replied, surprising her.

How had he come so close? Neither of them had moved. Yet here they were, inches apart, in the silent house. Rose hadn't noticed how close until now. His gaze was intent. She felt as if she could fall into it. Rose swayed just a little.

Gavin put a steadying hand on her arm, then snatched it back as if she'd burned him.

Gray eyes should be cool, but his had a flame in them. And his lips. She'd never properly considered the shape of his lips. They…lured. Rose felt hers part a little. Somehow, they'd come closer still.

They both flinched. Gavin looked…aghast? Was that the expression? Not as if his senses were reeling, Rose thought. Well, neither were hers. She absolutely insisted on that. This was something else entirely. Perhaps a reaction to the rich dinner. She wasn't used to such fine food. She turned, gripped the stair rail tightly, and resumed her walk up the steps. He moved beside her. The silence was fraught. It had to be broken.

"Why did you bring Phelps with you?" she asked.

"We were instructed to bring extra servants." He snorted. "The cheek of it!"

"But Phelps isn't a valet. I thought he was a kind of huntsman."

"He's very good with a gun."

Rose stopped again and turned to look at him. "What? You mean to send him out for rabbits? For the cook pot?"

"I mean to have someone I can trust with me here."

"On a country house visit."

"So they call it."

"It is not a foray into enemy territory."

"Is it not?" Gavin asked.

"It is *not*." Rose insisted on this.

"I thought we weren't going to argue." He seemed to enjoy the irony of his point—arguing about not arguing.

"When we are alone, I suppose we will behave…as we always do." One couldn't quite call it normally, Rose thought.

"Ah, that is a relief." They'd reached the upper floor. He strode along the corridor and into his bedchamber. Just two doors away from hers. The door closed with a snap.

Three

GAVIN WAS ALWAYS HAPPIER OUT OF DOORS. AND SO when the duke was up and ready for an early morning ride the next day, Gavin felt slightly more in charity with him. Very slightly. The quality of the fellow's mount was another recommendation. Grooms had brought Tereford's riding stock up to Yorkshire in easy stages, it appeared, and the animals were among the finest Gavin had ever seen. He had to admire the ease with which the duke sat on the spirited mount too. He was obviously at home in the saddle.

Gavin led him down a track through the moor where there was no risk of rabbit holes. Whatever he thought of the man, he wouldn't risk the horses.

There was no need to talk if they kept up a brisk pace. But Gavin found that the absence of conversation left him free to think about his encounter on the stairs last night. The flash of… He decided to call it intense awareness. That was a tolerable label. Unlike some others that…did not apply. He wouldn't think about those. It had been surprise, mainly. He'd been taken unaware. Suddenly, there had been Rose, inches away and so softly pretty. Some sort of startlement in her blue eyes. She'd swayed. He'd reached out instinctively. And then they'd come to their senses and shaken off…whatever. It had been very strange.

In recent years, he hadn't thought of Rose as Rose, the girl who'd roamed the moors with him and lent her vivid imagination to their group's adventures. They'd grown up. She was a Denholme as he was a Keighley, members of families who were fiercely at odds. He seldom saw her. When they did meet, they exchanged barbs in passing. Many of them were remarks they'd more or less inherited from their elders, Gavin realized now. His mother was very free with those. But last night, there Rose was, as lovely as her name...

"It's an odd landscape," said the duke at his side.

"Eh." Gavin's mind swam back from far away.

"It's as if a great dun carpet had been thrown over uneven ground."

"If you look more closely, you'll see a marvelous design worked into that 'carpet.'" Not that an outsider would ever understand the moors.

The duke looked startled. Clearly, he had thought Gavin was a brutish dolt and would not be capable of extending his comparison. "Design?" he asked.

"And in June..." Gavin's voice broke off. He wasn't here to describe a sea of blossom, the lazy hum of bees, moorland ponies outlined by a crimson sunset. He'd been sent to gain an advantage, not teach the Duke of Tereford to love the moors. Better that he didn't actually. Aversion would keep him away. "It's not your kind of country, I suppose," he said instead. "You won't spend much time here. At Yerndon, I mean."

"Probably not," the duke replied.

That was honest at least. There was no affection in his tone for the place Gavin loved.

"You mainly raise sheep here?" Tereford asked. "For the wool?"

"Aye," replied Gavin. "Best quality."

"They must be a hardy breed."

"They're fine for those who tend their lands."

"As Yerndon has not been tended," the duke said.

"It has not." This could be his opening. Gavin searched for the right phrase.

"I should find a responsible tenant. Perhaps you know of someone?"

Gavin's temper rose. "Are you mocking me?"

"No." Tereford smiled. "Perhaps teasing a bit. I beg your pardon. I had no right."

Wrestling down his irritation, Gavin said nothing.

"So the tangle over this property began several generations ago? I didn't quite understand the...debate between you and Miss Denholme when I arrived."

Here was his chance. Tell the duke the whole story, his mother had commanded. Make him see the justice of their claim and the Denholmes' deception. Talk him around. As if Gavin had any skill at such things. He liked to do, not debate.

He pushed aside his doubts. "It was 1715, or thereabouts," he began. The tale was very familiar, at least. It was like a fairy story, though real, of course. "Laura Keighley—my several times great-aunt—went down to London and contracted a grand match. The son of a duke—Lord Edwin Cantrell."

"Edwin," said Tereford. He shook his head. "I don't recall any mention of him. But I believe there were a number of sons in that generation of Cantrells."

"He was a younger one," Gavin replied. "I don't think the Keighleys understood how insignificant that made him." Gavin's mother had much to say about their stupidity.

The duke gave him a wry glance.

Gavin ignored it. "The family expected every kind of benefit from the marriage. A touch of nobility," he sneered. "The land around Yerndon was given as her dowry."

"All of it?" asked the duke.

This was a tricky point. Gavin had hoped it wouldn't be raised. "A large part of the acreage," he answered.

"I seemed to hear that some of it came from the Denholme family."

The fellow had sharp ears, damn him. "Laura died young," Gavin continued. "And Cantrell married again. Dora Denholme."

"And she brought the rest of the land as her portion?"

"Yes." Gavin rushed on. "Cantrell turned out to be a wastrel, an aristocratic idiot." Realizing that his companion was a Cantrell and might not appreciate this label, Gavin faltered briefly. "The connection meant nothing in the end. The Keighleys had given up their land for nothing. And we *never* give up our land."

"This Edwin sired a son who inherited Yerndon?" the duke asked.

Gavin nodded.

"By which of his wives?"

Gavin looked away. "Dora."

"I see. And this line has managed the estate?"

"If you want to call it managing." Gavin didn't. More

often they'd pulled money out and gone off to visit their grand relatives.

"And it endured up until the last Cantrell, who willed it to the previous duke? My predecessor."

"A man who cared nothing about the place and left it to rot," Gavin replied contemptuously. "He never even came here." It was an unforgivable lapse, to him.

Tereford nodded. "My great-uncle was not a good steward."

Gavin snorted agreement.

There was a pause, and then the duke said, "Tell me, Sir Gavin, when you marry, if your wife brings you a dowry, will you feel it remains the property of her family? Even after her death?"

That was not the rule of law, Gavin acknowledged silently. His mother always argued fairness over legality. "The land was meant to stay with the Keighley line," he replied. "And Laura Keighley had no children."

The duke nodded. "So you feel that your family made an…investment, more than a century ago, which did not pay off. And now you would like to have it back."

When it was put that way, it sounded a bit dodgy, Gavin thought. His parents and grandparents never stated things so baldly.

"I'm not really persuaded by that argument," added the duke.

At this point, his mother would have flown into a rage and shouted, Gavin thought. And that wouldn't have done any good either. The duke would have simply stared at her, with his maddening self-possession. Her idea that the duke would hand over Yerndon was daft. This visit was not only burdensome; it was a waste of time.

Gavin urged his horse into a gallop. Riding hell for leather was a good way to drive problems from one's brain. And if he went hard and fast enough, perhaps the duke would take a spill. He'd like to see him, and his lamentable logic, tumble into a thorny thicket. Nothing serious, just a few humiliating scrapes.

But his wish was not granted. He simply discovered that Tereford was a bruising rider, perhaps better than Gavin himself. There seemed no challenge he couldn't rise to, the pillock.

———

Rose left the house with the duchess soon after breakfast. Cloaked and gloved, they walked out into a dew-covered late March morning. Drops sparkled on budding branches and in the long grass. Mist drifted over the heather in the distance, and long shadows crossed their path. Rose carried her specimen box on a strap. Taking it along was so automatic that she didn't even think. When the duchess asked what it was, however, she regretted that habit. Some of her friends, and particularly her mother, found her dedication to preserving moorland plants eccentric. A fashionable Londoner would probably find it bewildering. Still, Rose explained her method.

"How interesting," said the duchess. "These samples last well?"

"If they are properly dried and handled carefully," Rose replied. "I mount them in notebooks."

"I should like to see some of them."

Rose nodded, taking this for mere politeness.

They strolled along, dawdled really. Left to herself, Rose would have tramped off for a long, brisk ramble. But she wasn't here to please herself. She was supposed to be charming and to press the Denholme land claim, wresting Yerndon away from the duke. Had no one considered that these were contradictory aims? But careful consideration was not a hallmark of the neighborhood feud. "When will your baby arrive?" she asked the duchess.

"Early summer."

"That's a lovely time of year here."

"Is it? Not much has been done with the garden."

Rose looked back. A low stone wall surrounded the patch of land near the house. Some scraggly plantings showed above the grass. Rose preferred the wild parts of the moor, but she enjoyed a fine garden as well. This was not one.

"You'd think they might have planted a shrubbery to provide some shelter," the duchess went on. "I expect it is terrible when winter storms sweep in."

Rose wouldn't have said terrible, but it could be cold and windy. "Will you be here in the winter?" she asked.

"No."

There was no equivocation in the word, no hint of doubt. Rose examined her companion's lovely face. She seemed daunted by the sights before her.

"The moor looks grim now," the duchess added. "I can't think what it must be like in January."

"It isn't grim," said Rose.

"You don't think so?"

"It's beautiful."

"One's home country is always dear, but..."

"There are tiny streams with hidden waterfalls," Rose said. "And ravines full of flowers. Look there." She pointed to a bloom at the side of the path. "Asphodel."

"It is pretty."

"I could show you some lovely spots," Rose said, her enthusiasm for the moor surfacing. She enjoyed showing it off.

"Are they far away?"

Rose hesitated, doubting they had the same definition of *far*.

The duchess smiled as if she understood this. "I would like to walk a bit. Let us see what we can find."

They left the confines of the house and went along a winding sheep path. Heather rose on each side, cutting the wind and muffling sound. Rose took a breath. Something deep inside her relaxed.

They moved slowly along the beaten earth. "Stay away from places like that," said Rose when they passed a patch of bog. "Never walk where it is so green."

"Why?" asked the duchess.

"You will most likely sink in. And might find it hard to get back out again."

"Ah." The duchess edged away from the boggy spot.

"That is cloudberry," Rose said as they moved on. "When they're ripe, you can use them in jam and juice. Liqueurs too."

"You know this place in your very bones."

Surprised and flattered, Rose smiled at her.

"You know, that's the first time I've seen you really smile." The duchess smiled back.

It was a kind smile. She was a pleasant woman, Rose thought. Not some rapacious interloper. Not pretentious either, despite her beauty and status. The things Rose's parents had been saying about the Terefords weren't true.

Rose gazed over the moor as they walked along. The Cantrell family had become mythic villains to the Denholmes. And perhaps the last resident of Yerndon had deserved some of their criticisms. From all accounts, he'd been a sour, spiteful old man. But the current duke and duchess were nothing like that. They were treating her well, and the *feel* of their household was warm and accepting. The pair obviously loved each other. Their servants seemed contented as well as efficient, which was always a sign. Rose still didn't understand why she'd been invited to visit, but the stay was making her think.

High-pitched voices sounded from the path ahead. They came around a clump of gorse and out onto a wider track where they discovered two shaggy moorland ponies plodding toward them. The animals had thick sheepskin pads on their backs and carried a whole gaggle of pale, brown-haired children. "Goodness," said the duchess.

The ponies slowed and then stopped a few yards away.

"Hello," said the duchess. "Are you out for a ride?"

The child who seemed oldest—a girl—nodded. She couldn't be more than eight or nine, Rose thought, but she looked self-possessed and in charge. She held a little boy and a tiny girl before her. On the other pony a girl of perhaps six or seven supported another a year or so younger. They were well dressed and seemed at ease despite the absence of any adult. Rose was surprised not to recognize them. She knew all the families hereabouts.

"My name is Cecelia," her companion continued. "And this is Miss Rose Denholme."

The eldest child examined them carefully. Their appearance apparently satisfied her because she said, "I am Maria Brontë." She indicated the children before her on the pony. "This is my brother, Branwell, and my sister Emily." Pointing at the other mount, she added, "Those are my sisters Elizabeth and Charlotte."

"Anne isn't here because she's just a baby," said the boy. He looked not more than four, but he spoke quite clearly.

They all seemed like babies to Rose.

"How do you do," responded the duchess. "Are you lost?"

"No," Maria declared with unusual assurance. "We are learning our way about the moors." She seemed to feel this was a perfectly reasonable activity for five small children on their own.

"We are engraving the pathways on our memories," said Elizabeth from the other pony.

"Indebly," added Charlotte.

"In-del-ibly," corrected Maria. Charlotte mouthed the syllables silently.

They all seemed to be unusual children, Rose thought. She couldn't understand where they'd come from. Then she remembered a piece of news. "Brontë," she said. "Have you recently come to live at Haworth parsonage?"

Maria nodded, grave and thoughtful far beyond her years.

"Your father is the new curate at the church in the village," Rose said.

"He deserves a finer post," said the younger girl on the other pony. "He is far better educated…"

"Charlotte!" Her eldest sister glared at her.

"I heard him tell…"

"And you know you are not to repeat all you hear."

"But Papa said…"

"That wagging tongues are the devil's tools."

Charlotte looked subdued.

"What about your mother?" asked the duchess.

"Mama is ill, and we are keeping the children out of her way," said the older girl on the second pony. Elizabeth, Rose remembered. She spoke as if she wasn't a child herself.

"Except for Anne," offered the boy. "She can't sit up properly, so she had to stay home." He appeared to savor his superiority in this regard.

"She is just a few months old, Branwell," replied Charlotte.

"That's what I *said*," he replied.

"My cook is making treacle tarts today," said the duchess. "Will you stop in for a visit with us and have some?"

"No, thank you," said Maria without hesitation.

Branwell turned in his seat to glare up at her. "Why not?"

"What is treacle tart?" asked the tiny Emily before him.

"A sweet," answered her brother. "You've never had one. Why can't we, Maria?"

They were all thin and delicate-looking. Ethereal as elves, Rose thought. One wanted to give them any number of treats.

"Greed is a sin, Branwell," said Maria.

The boy made a rude noise.

"Branwell! What would Papa say if we indulged ourselves?"

"Piggishly," said Elizabeth.

"We needn't tell him," suggested the little boy.

Rose wondered what it was like to be the only son among so many sisters.

"We cannot lie!" Maria looked scandalized.

"Not telling isn't the same as lying."

Maria gazed down at him, more in sorrow than anger it seemed. "I have grave concerns about the state of your soul, Branwell."

He was a toddler, Rose thought. Would his father really begrudge him a bit of pastry?

Emily stared back at Maria with great haunted eyes. On the other pony, Charlotte looked wistful.

"Besides," said Maria. "We are not to be speaking to people or going off with strangers."

This sounded like something their nurse had told them, Rose thought. And good advice, of course. "We are not strangers but neighbors," she said. "My father called on yours when you first arrived. Perhaps you saw him. Mr. Denholme."

"I remember," said Charlotte. "Because it sounded like where foxes would live. He was the man with no hair."

Rose bit her lip. Her father's baldness was a sore point with him.

Maria nodded in recognition.

"And we are neighbors of your neighbors," said the duchess. "So practically acquainted already. I think you might stop in for refreshment."

"Mightn't we have just a bite?" Elizabeth asked Maria. "We could divide a tart between us all. Would that be greedy?"

Branwell started to protest and then pressed his lips together.

Under four pairs of hopeful eyes, Maria gave in, with one parting shot. "You are not to stuff your faces, mind."

Rose thought it was a phrase Maria had heard at home, and that the speaker must be an irritating person.

They walked back along the path with the ponies trailing behind them. Rose tethered the animals in the overgrown garden to crop the grass, and they took the children into the front parlor, where they shed their coats and hats. A bit later, when a plate of tarts and glasses of milk had been served, Rose took it on herself to divert Maria with gentle questions so that the others could devour as many sweets as they dared.

That turned out to be most of them. Tarts slipped off the plate and were passed along with a magician's sleight of hand. Blissful expressions followed each bite. Emily in particular grew sticky and covered in crumbs. Branwell experimented with pushing a whole tart into his mouth at once. His eyes danced as he chewed with bulging cheeks. Rose was exchanging a look of enjoyment with the duchess when footsteps sounded in the entryway. Maria Brontë started, and when the parlor door opened, she jumped guiltily to her feet.

The duke and Gavin came in, dressed in their riding clothes. Maria sank back into her chair. She didn't look relieved, however. She glanced at the ravaged plate as if the men's arrival had roused a sense of their transgression.

"Who is this?" asked Tereford with a smile.

"Some neighbors," his wife replied. "The Brontës from Haworth parsonage." She pointed as she named them. "Maria, Elizabeth, Charlotte, Branwell, and Emily."

"Anne is too little to go out," said Branwell. He seemed fixated on this fact.

"Is she?"

Gavin was surprised when the duke waded in and sat down amidst the children. On the floor!

"But you are not," Tereford went on.

"I'm nearly four," the little boy declared, as if this was a perfectly reasonable age to be paying calls.

"Where are your parents?" asked Gavin. The oldest child flinched, and he regretted his tone. He hadn't meant anything by it.

"The children have been out riding on their ponies," said Rose. "They've been telling us they love the moor." She gave Gavin a look that suggested he should understand this sentiment. Well, he did.

"It's glorious," exclaimed the smallest girl, flinging out her arms with a surprising wealth of emotion.

Gavin wondered that a child so small knew the word. She had something sticky smeared on her chin. And were those crumbs in her *hair*? He met young Emily's eyes and discovered an ardent spirit behind them. "Brontë," he said. "Your family arrived here recently. I have met your father." He had called on the new curate, as was polite.

The children all looked at him. They showed a range of expressions, from apprehensive to mulish to…prepared to judge? That didn't seem possible.

"He is a learned man, I believe," Gavin added. He'd found the man pompous, but he thought it better not to say so.

"Papa studied at St. John's College, Cambridge," said the eldest child. "He has been a school examiner."

That one was Maria, Gavin recalled. She looked like a miniature schoolmistress herself. The strict kind who did not tolerate levity.

"Quite a scholar then," said the duke.

Maria nodded solemnly.

"He writes poetry too," said another of them. Elizabeth, Gavin remembered.

"Does he?" Tereford sat among them as if he was an indulgent uncle rather than a peer of the realm. The man kept on flouting expectations.

Elizabeth folded her hands, sat very straight, and recited.

> *"The sun shines bright, the morning's fair,*
> *The gossamers float on the air,*
> *The dew-gems twinkle in the glare,*
> *The spider's loom*
> *Is closely plied, with artful care,*
> *Even in my room."*

Gavin was not impressed, except by the little girl's feat of memorization. He might have commented on that accomplishment, but she went on before he was required to give an opinion.

> *"See how she moves in zigzag line,*
> *And draws along her silken twine,*
> *Too soft for touch, for sight too fine,*
> *Nicely cementing:*
> *And makes her polished drapery shine,*
> *The edge indenting.*
>
> *Her silken ware is gaily spread,*
> *And now she weaves herself a bed,*
> *Where, hiding all but just her head,*
> *She watching lies*
> *For moths or gnats, entangled spread,*
> *Or buzzing flies."*

Nothing for the flies here, Gavin thought, as he watched the last of what had seemingly been a plate of treacle tarts disappear during this recitation. He tried not to regret the loss, though he was fond of treacle tarts. These children were ethereally slender. They needed the sustenance more than he did.

"You have memorized a good deal of it," said the duke at the pause.

"I know lots more," Elizabeth replied. "Papa says learning poetry is good exercise for the mind."

"And the act of creation emulates God's work," said Maria Brontë.

"Emulates, does it?" The duke glanced at his wife. He seemed oddly nonplussed. The duchess was clearly amused.

"Exploring the heights of imagination," said... Which was it? Charlotte, Gavin recalled, who couldn't be more than five years old. If that. She must be parroting a phrase she'd heard at home. All of them were, Gavin decided. He thought the new curate must have an unusual household.

"'Ars longa, vita brevis,'" said Branwell.

"You know Latin?" the duke asked. And why he should be daunted, Gavin did not know.

"Only a little. Papa is teaching me."

A very strange household, Gavin thought, if the toddlers were spouting ancient tags while the little girls repeated singsong poems. The picture was a bit disturbing.

As if she might have sensed his reaction, Maria stood up. "We should be going," she said. She gathered her siblings with an admonitory glance. "Thank you very much for your hospitality. And the..." She looked at the empty plate, blinked, glanced at her brother and sisters, and shook her head. Hadn't they given her any tarts? Gavin wondered.

The other children rose to their feet in a hurried mob.

"I hope you will visit us again," said the duchess with a smile.

"Do you ever have plum cake?" asked the little boy.

"Branwell!" His mortified eldest sister took his hands,

discovered their stickiness, wiped them on a napkin, and pulled him away. They all began putting on the coats and hats and gloves that had been piled on a chair in the corner.

The duke escorted them out. Watching through a window, Gavin saw him laughing as he lifted the smaller children onto their ponies. It didn't seem the sort of thing a leader of the *haut ton* would do. He lifted a hand in farewell too, when they waved goodbye. And he kept at it as long as the children did.

"I wonder if I should have sent someone with them?" Tereford asked when he returned to the parlor.

"They seemed self-sufficient," replied the duchess. "But young." She turned to Gavin and Rose. "They're not in any danger riding on the moor?"

"They're being careful," Rose replied. "I spoke to Elizabeth about the bogs, and she said they'd been warned to keep away and would do so."

"Those ponies would hurry them away from danger if they gave them a kick," said Gavin. "Or on their own if they sensed anything." Moorland ponies were clever creatures.

"We rode over the moors when we were small," said Rose.

"We were older than that," Gavin replied.

"Not than the oldest ones."

"We didn't take babies along."

"I began tagging after my brother when I was four."

"Your brother was not a good…" Gavin realized that he was arguing with Rose. Again. It just happened. The words came out before he thought, as if they were some script he'd memorized for the stage. But he had promised to resist.

They were to pretend to agree. Or at least not to *dis*agree. "Ah, Daniel," he said. "He's, uh, still at Oxford, isn't he? I heard that. Is he doing well?"

Rose blinked. "He doesn't write often. He is certainly happier there than here."

"He doesn't care for this place?" asked the duchess.

Rose looked as if she wished she hadn't spoken. "He is very scholarly, deep in his books. He and my father...have rather different views."

Gavin found that he didn't like to see her so uncomfortable. "As young men and their fathers tend to do," he said. "Wouldn't you say, Tereford?"

"Oh yes." The duke shook his head. "More than sometimes."

When Rose's expression eased, Gavin discovered that he appreciated her relief. He didn't care to see her unsettled by these outlanders, he decided. They had no right to poke their noses into local affairs. "Those were curious children," he said.

"They were terrifying," said the duke, which seemed extreme.

The duchess smiled.

"Are they typical of the neighborhood?" Tereford asked.

"Not in the least," said Gavin. "Our youngsters are more likely to be pelting along the moor tracks waving sticks as sabers and covered in mud."

"Or lying in ambush behind a crag and jumping out with a great shriek," said Rose.

Gavin remembered that occasion. His mount had leaped

straight up, all four feet leaving the ground. He hadn't fallen off though. "You screamed like a banshee," he told her.

"I certainly did." She looked amused by the memory.

Rose was always rather pretty, Gavin noted, but when she smiled... It made a man wish she would smile more often.

"The oldest, Maria, was unusually assured for her age," said the duchess.

"Spookily so," said Gavin.

"Did you think that as well?" The duke looked relieved. "I felt as if I was talking to a schoolmistress. And being marked down for dullness."

Gavin was unsettled to find they'd shared the same thought. He and this duke had nothing in common.

"You are too harsh," said Rose.

"Not harsh. Apprehensive." Tereford grimaced. "I am making a study of the young, since we will soon have one of our own, and more often than not I find myself quaking in my boots."

Tereford kept being...not what he expected, Gavin thought. He wished the fellow would stop it. It was confusing.

"I suspect Maria's parents rely on her too much," said the duchess.

"They said their mother is ill," replied Rose.

"It must be serious. Perhaps we will call and see if there is anything we can do."

"That would be kind," said Rose. "They are new to the neighborhood and have no friends as yet."

"Not if this illness is contagious," began the duke. He frowned. "The children looked all right."

"We will take care, James," said his wife. "As I have been doing all along."

"I know."

The looks they exchanged were full of tenderness. They were less and less what he had expected, Gavin thought. Nothing like it at all, in fact. The duchess *was* kind. The duke was tolerable. He'd endured no mockery in this house, no sly digs or arrogant dismissals. In fact, even in the brief time he'd been here, Yerndon had begun to seem like a…home. More than his own did, at times, when his mother was on a rampage. The idea made him feel strange. He didn't know what to do with it. It had to be wrong. So he simply set it aside. "If you visit the Brontës, you might have to endure more maudlin verses," he said.

"As long as they are not about spiders," replied the duchess with a small shiver.

The duke laughed.

He had a warm, free laugh, Gavin thought as the two of them departed to change out of their riding dress. Not the least sarcastic. Tereford might be hiding any amount of ill nature, but Gavin didn't think so. The villain of their property dispute seemed anything but. Which made matters more awkward rather than less so, he decided. He wasn't sure just what to do about that.

When he left his bedchamber a bit later, he encountered Rose in the upstairs corridor.

"You did well," she said.

"Well?"

"Not arguing," she explained. "I hope it wasn't too difficult." She smiled.

Such a lovely smile, Gavin thought. She ought to smile. She ought to *have reason* to smile. "It was the greatest strain imaginable," he answered. "I made Herculean efforts." He relished the spark of amusement in her blue eyes.

"You were going to tell me that Daniel was a poor rider and a worse adventurer, not worth tagging after."

"How do you know…"

"You've said it before," Rose added. "He was often ill as a child, you know."

Gavin had heard something about that. He hadn't paid attention. Why not? "I didn't mean…"

Rose waved this aside. "Daniel wouldn't care. He doesn't pretend to ride well. And he has told me that his scholarly explorations suit him far better than muddy rambles on the moor. He's quite healthy now too."

"That's good."

She nodded. "And you didn't lose your temper even once today. As yet."

"That is the sort of remark that makes me more likely to do so."

"Consider it retracted." Rose turned away toward the door of her bedchamber.

He didn't want her to leave. He wanted… He had no idea. "Why do you never get angry?" Gavin asked her, surprising himself. She started to speak, and he added, "Almost never."

Rose cocked her head. "I'm not prone to it."

Gavin knew that he was. He'd been told so all his life. His mother relished this resemblance between them.

"Also, my grandmother once told me something when I was visiting her in Wells. My Naismith grandmother."

Gavin nodded. He had never met her mother's mother. If she'd visited, he'd never heard of it.

"I was in a flame about something. I can't remember now what it was, and she said that she managed her temper by being grateful a thing was not worse."

"Worse?" asked Gavin.

"If she was splashed by a passing carriage, for example, and angry at the driver, she would be glad that she had not taken one more careless step and been ridden down by the team. Or if a friend was stubborn or heedless, she could be grateful that they did not live in the same house and she didn't have to endure those moods more often."

"And that helped?" Gavin asked.

"Once she was grateful, she was less angry," Rose replied.

"Grateful," he repeated. This plan seemed unlikely.

"So she said. She had quite a quick temper. But she didn't often give it free rein." Rose gazed up at him, her lips a little parted.

He had come closer to her as they talked. She hadn't moved away, but she was standing almost against the corridor wall. One more step and he could slip his arms around her, press her into the paneling, take those lips for his own.

Rose stared into his eyes. She looked uncertain. Curious? Dubious? Willing?

Gavin's senses swam. His pulse spiked. Did she feel the same...allure?

She blinked. Reality snapped back into place around

Gavin. What was he thinking? What was happening to him? He stepped back. "Er."

She turned and moved quickly into her bedchamber, closing the door with a snap behind her.

Four

ROSE LEANED ON THE DOOR TO HER ROOM, HER PALMS flat against the wood. She was not panting. These quick breaths might seem like panting, but they were not and could not be. Panting would signify unsuitable emotions that she was *not* feeling. She was simply... She had no idea.

She heard Gavin's footsteps retreat down the stairs.

What was so unsettling about Gavin Keighley being kind and listening to her and cordially conversing? Despite the criticisms and complaints from her parents, she'd known he wasn't an ogre. He was a good landlord and had been a staunch friend to some mutual acquaintances. His mother... Well, Lady Keighley was a difficult person. His twin sisters, just turned eighteen, not an age when admiration was automatic, revered him. He was widely respected. It was just that he had constantly argued with *her*.

If he stopped... He had stopped. Or begun to stop. What would they do instead?

Rose recalled the warmth in his gray eyes in the corridor just now. He'd made a joke. He'd asked about her brother. She hadn't known when she proposed their treaty that she would like the change so much. When this visit was over, and they went back to feuding...

She didn't wish to think about that.

She'd come upstairs for a shawl. The duchess would be wondering what had become of her. Rose fetched her wrap, pulled it around her like a shield, and left her bedchamber.

At the bottom of the steps she came upon the young footman she'd brought along to Yerndon. "Hello, Ian," she said. "Are you getting on all right?" Rose was aware of the rivalry between her servants and Gavin's. She'd done her best to discourage it, but she knew that subtle jostling went on.

The tall blond lad nodded. "I have been learning a good deal from the duchess's staff. They're prime." He frowned. "A long sight better than the Keighley lot."

"Just do your best to—"

"What's that fellow Phelps even doing here?" Ian interrupted.

He must be upset to do that, Rose acknowledged.

"He doesn't do any work," the footman continued. "Not even for Sir Gavin. He hangs about the stables or wanders off onto the moor. Says he might bag a rabbit or two, but he never does. What's he up to?"

Rose didn't know. And repeating Gavin's remarks about the man would only enflame matters. "Just ignore him," she said. "And get along with everyone else."

To her surprise, Ian blushed crimson. "But there's the other one," he said.

"Other?"

"That flibbertigibbet maid that came along."

"With Sir Gavin, you mean?"

Ian nodded.

"I hadn't seen her before. What is her name?"

"Lucy Trent," the footman replied in a constrained tone.

Rose didn't know any local family by that name. "Has she made difficulties for you?"

"Not to say difficulties, beyond a few silly tricks. It's just..." Ian shuffled his feet. "I never seen anyone like her before. She's full of daft notions, grand as you please, for all she's only a housemaid."

"What sort of notions?" This didn't sound like the kind of servant Lady Keighley would hire.

"Speeches out of Shakes-pear. They go on and on. You can't understand half of it." He shook his head, looking puzzled and perhaps a bit admiring. "I don't know how she remembers it all."

Definitely not Lady Keighley's sort of servant. Rose wondered if Gavin's mother had sent the girl here to be rid of her. "Well, just let her be."

"Oh, I let her be. But what will she do, eh? Pester the life out of me, belike." Ian turned and made his distracted way to the kitchen door, more uncharacteristic behavior.

His reaction was so striking that Rose consulted her maid as she was dressing for dinner that evening. "Is Ian having some trouble here?"

"Oh, him," replied Sue. She shook her head as she fastened Rose's auburn hair into a knot on top of her head, letting curls fall at the sides. "He's all right. He's just never been anywhere but home."

Neither had Sue, Rose noted, though she was taking the

tone of a world traveler. "He said something about the house-maid Lucy Trent."

Sue grinned. "Lucy's an odd one, no mistake. She could talk the birds out of the trees." She held out Rose's pearl earrings, and Rose put them on. "She's taken to teasing Ian. He's an easy mark, miss. And nobody else pays much heed to Lucy. Which she don't like."

"If she's bothering him, I could speak to Sir Gavin." Rose didn't really want to undertake that conversation, but she would if there was unpleasantness in the household.

"No need. Lucy's not bothering exactly. More confusing young Ian." Sue's grin widened. "She's a pretty lass, you see. And not one Ian has known all his life."

"Ah."

"Yes, miss." Sue straightened the folds of a sleeve. "This blue becomes you. It's a fine gown."

Rose surveyed her reflection in the dressing table mirror. She did look rather well. There was a flattering color in her cheeks, and her expression seemed more at ease than those she sometimes glimpsed in mirrors at home. Which was odd. "My dress is nothing compared to the duchess's toi-lettes," she had to say.

"Ah, well she's something else again. Paris fashions, I'll be bound. And no expense spared."

As well as wholly polished, Rose thought. And yet the duchess was not at all toplofty. She didn't flaunt her beauty. Because of that, Rose could be amused at being consigned to a lesser category, not to be compared with her flawless hostess.

"Edith Gorne's gone," Sue added as if this followed from her previous remarks. "The tale is, her sister's ill and needs help, but nobody believes it. They're letting her say that so as not to admit being dismissed." The maid shook her head. "There were mouse nests in the pantry. A regular village of them, running right under your feet."

Mrs. Gorne had been a lax housekeeper, though it was true she'd had no help, Rose noted.

"Saying there was nothing to be done about them." Sue made a disgusted sound. "She might have gotten a cat. Or two." Sue put a shawl around Rose's shoulders and stepped back, finished. "She took her great lump of a son along with her."

Mrs. Gorne had liked living alone and not really exerting herself, Rose thought. She hadn't been pleased when the house filled up and had been sour and discouraging whenever Rose encountered her. She wouldn't be missed. "Does that leave Phelps in charge of the stables?" Rose asked.

Sue shrugged. "Not him. There's the duke's coachman and the grooms who brought his riding horses. I don't know what Phelps finds to do."

No one seemed to, Rose thought. It wasn't really her affair, though she still wondered about Gavin's characterization of the man. Good with a gun indeed.

Downstairs, she found there was to be another guest at dinner. Richard Milsome had called to welcome the Terefords to the neighborhood and been invited to stay. A gentleman of fifty, he had an estate some miles north of Yerndon, of middling size but very well managed. Gavin came into the parlor as she was greeting him.

"Miss Denholme," Milsome replied with a bow. "And Sir Gavin." His tone suggested that this was a surprising combination.

He couldn't be blamed for that, Rose thought. Denholmes and Keighleys were not invited anywhere together. The risk of upsets was too high. Most recently, there had been a public argument between Rose's father and Gavin's mother in the village—raised voices in the churchyard, rude gestures and cutting insults exchanged. A spectacle for all to see. And yet here she and Gavin were. It was no wonder the visitor looked brightly curious.

"Hello, Milsome," said Gavin. He liked the man. Milsome had pleasant manners and a genial line of conversation. Tonight though, his eyes were lit with interested amusement as he looked from Gavin to Rose. Anyone who hadn't heard about their unprecedented visit soon would, Gavin thought. It would be a wonder to the whole area. The Terefords had upset the apple cart for good and all.

They went in to dinner and were presented with another savory meal. The duchess's cook really was first-rate. Milsome complimented the food, and Gavin agreed. The group chatted about the weather and the market for wool. And all the while Milsome observed the scene like someone waiting for a play to begin. Finally, it seemed he didn't wish to wait any longer. "I hope your parents are well," he said to Rose.

"Very well, thank you," she replied.

"And your mother, Keighley?"

"Also well." Mention of both naturally recalled the shouting match in the churchyard. Gavin frowned at him. The

Terefords knew nothing about that. He hoped Milsome would refrain from mentioning it.

Milsome gave a half shrug, half smile, as if he could barely resist. "All pleased about this visit, are they?"

"How could it be otherwise?" asked Gavin.

"Rebellion in the lower ranks?" murmured Milsome with a sly, sidelong glance.

Rose's musical laugh startled Gavin. "I didn't know you were such a humorist, Mr. Milsome." She spoke lightly, but Gavin caught the spark in her usually mild blue eyes.

"No?" Milsome replied.

"Nor did I," said Gavin. His tone was a bit too sharp. Rose did irony better. He tended more toward smoldering ire, which was less effective. Rose could carry the flag on this sally. He felt an odd flash of happiness. It was the first time he and Rose had made common cause since they'd stood side by side defending a moorland redoubt as children. He'd forgotten the...pleasure of it.

"Who doesn't appreciate a good joke?" Milsome seemed to imply that they didn't.

"Indeed," said Rose. "*Good* ones are a rare treat." Gavin gave her a silent bravo and, when she looked at him, a private wink.

The duchess, who clearly missed no nuance, changed the subject. "I understand you were a friend of Charleton Cantrell's, Mr. Milsome."

The guest turned to her with a smile, relinquishing his probe without obvious regret. "'Friend' is probably too strong a word. I did spend an evening with him now and then in his last years."

Gavin realized that Milsome was the only one among them who'd known the former owner of Yerndon. Charleton Cantrell had died when Gavin was ten years old. And the man had not been fond of youngsters. He'd called their group vermin once when he ordered them off his property.

"How did you meet?" their hostess asked. "I understood that he was rather a recluse."

"At the village blacksmith's," answered Milsome. He enjoyed the group's surprised reaction before going on. "By chance, each of our horses had thrown a shoe while we were out riding. We talked as we waited for repairs. He seemed an interesting old fellow, and I was new to this neighborhood. And so we scraped an acquaintance."

"Interesting?" Gavin had only heard Cantrell described as spiteful and venomous.

"In a chat on the street or over a glass of wine," replied Milsome. "We had no...issues to resolve. And so he was amiable enough. He could be quite crusty when provoked."

"Most people can, I suppose," said the duke.

"And Cantrell endured quite a bit of it," said the guest with another of his sidelong glances at Gavin and Rose.

Gavin felt his temper rising. "He did some provoking himself."

"It's a trial having hostile neighbors," replied Milsome.

"Or sneaking, vengeful..." Gavin stopped and gritted his teeth. He did not want to descend into that old argument in front of the Terefords. He was here to win them over. And more, he had an agreement with Rose. He would not break his word. He wrestled with a spate of angry objections. What had Rose said about her grandmother's methods? The idea seemed silly, but he had no other.

So. How could this situation be worse? Well, Milsome could be staying here with them, a constant irritation. But he was not. He'd be leaving soon, while the moon still lighted his path home. He could have told the story of the church-yard altercation, made a real drama of it. But he had not, though it had clearly been tempting. Gavin could have railed at him here at the dinner table, a travesty of hospitality. *That* would have been well worse. But he had managed not to let fly, a satisfying success. Surprisingly, Gavin felt his temper begin to subside.

"You live near Haworth, Mr. Milsome," said Rose. "Have you met the Brontës?"

She was following the duchess's example in turning the subject, Gavin noted.

"The new curate?" Milsome nodded. "Yes. He seems an odd mixture of stiff manners and oversensitivity."

"How so?" asked the duke.

"Well, I called on him because, as you say, I live nearby. The family has just arrived in the neighborhood, you know, and I thought to help make them welcome. But Brontë didn't appreciate my visit in the least. I caught him in the throes of creation, he said, writing a poem. He made me feel like a dashed inconvenience." Milsome frowned. "'Throes,' what sort of word is that? And he's the curate of St. Michael's. A reverend is meant to be available to his parishioners, isn't he?"

It was a fair point, Gavin thought.

"I begged his pardon," Milsome continued. "Though it went against the grain. I started to leave, and then he sat me down and told me how very ill his wife is. Unable to rise from her bed, the poor lady. And what was he to do? Apparently they have a packet of children."

"Six," said Rose. "We met most of them on the moor."

"Six! Good lord." Milsome shook his head. "I suggested he get some relative to come and help, and he liked the idea. Said he'd ask his wife's sister. I felt as if *I* was the parson making sick visits."

"Perhaps not the time for poetic composition," murmured Rose very softly.

The duchess heard. Gavin saw her throw Rose a speaking look. He didn't think the others noticed.

After the meal, they moved from the dining room to the front parlor. Milsome didn't stay long, as he had a distance to ride before the moon set. When he had gone, the duchess declared she was tired, and the duke gave her an arm up to bed. Rose followed. Gavin, not quite ready to retire, stayed on, considering the evening. It had been quite pleasant, one of the most enjoyable he could recall. The Terefords were very good at setting a festive mood and encouraging conversation. But Rose had done her part too. He was feeling... mellow, not a familiar state. He liked it, he realized.

Upstairs, Rose had removed her ornaments and started to unbutton her gown when she realized that she'd left her book in the parlor earlier in the day. She was not sleepy and wanted to read. Before she put on her nightdress, she must slip downstairs to fetch it.

The hallway was silent, the stairs empty. The parlor was dim and quiet, still warmed by the dying fire. Rose was walking across to the table where her book lay when a voice from the shadows made her start.

"I beg your pardon," said Gavin. "I thought you hadn't seen me, and I wanted to let you know I was here."

She turned, lifted her candlestick, and found his dark figure in a chair by the hearth. "Why are you sitting in the dark?"

"I don't know. I felt like putting out the candles."

"Is something wrong?"

"No. It just seemed peaceful."

Rose stared. This was not a Gavin sort of word. And he sprawled, looking utterly relaxed, in a not-Gavin sort of way. There was her book. She picked it up. She should hurry off now. Her mother would disapprove of these circumstances—alone with a man in the dimness, no trace of a chaperone. With Gavin Keighley of all people! But she was curious.

"We got on well when we were young, Rose. Didn't we?"

"Umm." Her fingers tightened on the book as her heart sped up. She started to say that they had—casually, as he'd sounded—but she couldn't get the words out. She'd been ambushed by a memory.

On a hot summer's day when she was sixteen, Rose had been out on the moors alone. She was not supposed to tramp those beloved paths on her own, an unaccompanied young lady. That had been forbidden for a while. Not quite since she'd been told, at twelve, that she was too old to roam on her pony with the gang of local children, but soon after. She'd been terrified to feel her world constricting. It had made her into a sneak.

That day she had muddy patches on the front of her gown. She hadn't noticed the dampness when she'd knelt to peer into a crevice of rock. A grasping briar had caught her hair and pulled out the braid. Wisps stuck to her cheeks. Her mother would say she looked a fright if she was caught when she returned home. Her specimen box was full, though. As was her spirit. She'd found a hidden nook well off the path, taken off her shoes and stockings, settled on a dry rock, and thrust her naked feet under a tiny waterfall. It felt wonderful.

She hadn't worried when she heard voices and the clop of hooves. No one could see her through the thicket. She was very careful about things like that, lest someone tell her parents they'd spotted her. She knew this landscape. She could hide like the shyest wild creature. There was no angle from which she could be spied. Branches arched over her head too.

"You must be bored silly in this place," said a young male not far away.

"I am never bored on the moor," replied another. Rose recognized Gavin Keighley's voice.

"You can't say you prefer it to Leeds?"

"I can and do."

Sounds indicated that they had paused at a place farther down the tiny stream to let their horses drink. Rose stayed still and silent. She'd heard that Gavin had a school friend visiting. Neighborhood gossip said he was the son of a wealthy merchant and "divinely handsome." Some girls expressed hopes of attaching him even though he was only nineteen.

"And the females," said the stranger. "What a pack of country dowds! Gawky, no conversation. I'd hardly call any of them pretty."

Rose had become more conscious of her dishevelment, her bare feet in the water. And glad to be invisible. She'd thought it unfair that she hadn't met the visitor because of their family dispute. Now it seemed no great loss.

"You haven't met the prettiest," said Gavin.

"Aha! And why not? Are you keeping her from me?"

"Our families are at odds."

Rose's mouth had dropped open, there on the stream bank. Only one local family was at odds with the Keighleys.

"I doubt she can compare to Miss Williamson."

"I think she could," said Gavin.

"What, match the toast of Leeds? You must show me this paragon."

"I don't think I will."

They'd laughed and moved on. Rose had lost herself in whirl of fantasy. But the next time she'd encountered Gavin, a number of mooning months after the incident, he'd been curt and distant. She'd decided he'd been joking. Or merely making himself interesting to his friend. He hadn't meant it at all. He'd been rude to her at every opportunity since.

"Rose?" Gavin frowned at her in the dim dancing light of her single candle.

The memory had flashed by, but she had been silent too long. "We got on as children," she said in answer to his earlier question.

"This Yerndon dispute has worsened since we were young." He spoke slowly, as if he was just noticing this.

"Like a cart rolling downhill," replied Rose. "Gaining momentum."

He nodded. "But why?"

It was easier to ask the question, and to observe the change, here, away from their homes, which was ironic since they were at Yerndon itself. The answer was more obscure.

"The positions haven't changed for years," Gavin added. "But the intensity…"

It was true. Rose found she had sat down. She placed her book and candlestick on a small table.

"I suppose the disputes have become a habit," Gavin went on. "What Denholmes and Keighleys talk about. And then time goes on and the annoyance of never getting anywhere grates on people."

"Never convincing the opponent that you are *right*," said Rose. "Everybody seems to want that. And when they can't, they curse them." It occurred to her that his mother was the one who mostly fanned the flames. Not that her parents didn't leap upon every provocation Lady Keighley offered.

Gavin leaned forward in his chair. "Yerndon belongs to Tereford. Legally willed away. There's really no question about that. We are all helpless."

"Not a comfortable state."

"I've never cared for it."

"No, you go to great lengths to find a way forward. I remember you spent weeks charting a path through the Grimsden mire."

He smiled. It gave Rose a sense of unreality. She was sitting here with Gavin Keighley, in the cozy dimness, and he was smiling at her. "I did, didn't I? I became rather obsessed with it."

"And constantly muddy."

Gavin laughed, lightly and freely. It was a deep, warm sound that seemed to caress Rose's skin. "The focus of a fourteen-year-old boy."

"You managed it though." Their little gang had used that secret path to astonish several adult moorland residents.

"I did." Gavin's smile faded. He looked puzzled. "But to keep on doing a useless thing, like flogging this property dispute. More and more fiercely. That is stupidity."

"Like shouting at someone who doesn't speak English," Rose agreed. "Thinking that higher volume will get your meaning across."

He looked at her. "I'd forgotten how quick you are, Rose."

She didn't feel quick. Quite the opposite. The atmosphere in the room seemed thick and dizzying.

"It seems that being away from home changes one's... perspective." Gavin gazed at the coals of the fire.

Rose watched the strong planes of his face. She'd known the boy. She didn't really know the man. Yet the one was the foundation for the other.

"What I've always hated was the neglect," he said contemplatively. "That was the real sticking point for me. A fine old place falling into ruin right next door to me. Nothing I could do. It drove me mad."

"But the duke is remedying that," said Rose.

"Yes."

"What issue does that leave?"

"What indeed?" He paused again, for several long moments. "Do you remember our last summer holiday out on the moors?"

Of course she did. It was after she'd been warned it was time to become a "young lady," and she'd clung to every moment of that precious time. "I'd been told I couldn't go out with the group any more when the summer ended."

"I was off to school then."

"We built the castle." They and their friends had chosen a hillock and shifted an impressive number of stones into a wall around the top with a sort of platform in the middle.

"Our last-ditch redoubt," said Gavin.

It had felt that way to Rose, the collapse of her life of freedom. They'd all spun tales of heroism for each other. They'd hurled spears over the wall at imaginary invaders. Romans, Saxons, Picts, Danes, depending on the story. They'd triumphed again and again. Until the holiday ended, and they'd separated for what turned out to be the last time.

"It must be there still," said Gavin. His eyes lit. "We should go and see."

"But Gavin."

He turned to look at her.

"We've been sent here to battle each other," said Rose. The memory of that youthful fortress had brought it back. Had he forgotten they were opponents? "You can't tell me you weren't ordered to make your family's case to Tereford. Against mine. And to win."

His gaze was steady.

"I certainly was," Rose added. "My parents expect... unreasonable things."

"Single combat warriors," he said. "Sent out to resolve the war? But if it is left to us..."

"Us." Rose repeated the word because of the way he'd emphasized it.

"What would our solution be?"

The room couldn't be hot. The fire was down to embers. But Rose felt flushed all over. He'd never spoken to her in that soft tone before. It was...seductive. Had she ever truly understood that word? His voice reached inside her and...stirred. What would he say next? What would she do? Rose felt the need to stand up. Sitting in a chair, as if she was awaiting events, seemed unsupportable. She very much wanted... What?

Gavin mirrored her. He stepped closer. He was tall, powerful. Of course she knew that. Candlelight flickered on his rough-hewn features. There was the scar on his cheekbone, small but more noticeable with the way light slanted across his face. Their friend Collin had caught the skin with a cast fishhook when he and Gavin were fifteen. The wound had bled all down Gavin's shirt. Collin had been horrified, but Gavin shrugged it off. As he tended to do. That scar was matched now by a scratch caused by the duke's signet ring during their fistfight. Without conscious thought, Rose's hand came up to touch the first scar.

The skin was warm, a little rough under her fingertips.

Somehow, they drifted down his cheek. It was smoother there, near his lips. Which parted.

"Rose," he breathed, a nearly inaudible question.

The obvious answer was to lean closer. So that she could...

The kiss started out slight, barely there. It trembled on the brink of ending, a sheer impossibility. Unthinkable. But once again Rose's body acted without consulting her mind. Her arms went around his neck, and her mouth yielded to his. In the next instant, she was crushed against him and swept away.

Rose was pliant and fragrant in Gavin's arms. She kissed as wholeheartedly as she did everything. He felt as if he'd been dipped in fire. Between them the kiss grew deeper, more urgent. His head spun. He was losing himself in longing.

And then she pulled away and gazed up at him with wide, wild eyes.

"Rose," he repeated hoarsely.

"You... I... Kissed."

"We did."

"How could we do that?"

He had no answer. They *had* done it, and it had been stunning. But with all that lay between them, it made no sense.

"It's been years since we exchanged a pleasant word."

That was true. He couldn't deny it. Why did it seem to make no difference? No, that wasn't right. Their troubled history had made the kiss more intense.

Rose blinked at him. She seemed dazed. She pushed at his chest. Gavin took a reluctant step away from her.

"We were pretending to get along," he began.

"And were carried away by the pretense?" she asked skeptically. "Are we complete fools?"

Gavin struggled with a muddle of emotion. His youth, the recent past, the astonishing present whirled together in a great snarl. Memory, enmity, desire. He could make no sense of it. "I suppose circumstances…" He trailed off, not knowing how to finish that sentence.

"Circumstances?"

"A dark room, no one about…" This sounded idiotic.

"Do you kiss any woman you find alone in a dark room?" Her voice had sharpened.

"No, of course not. I haven't been in…"

"I hadn't thought that the chaperones were right about such things." She'd gone acerbic. "But perhaps they are."

"You kissed me," Gavin said, and immediately knew it was a mistake.

"You're saying I thrust myself on you?" Her tone was icy this time. Enough to freeze a man to his bones.

"I didn't mind. I mean… No!" He should have shut his mouth, Gavin thought. But he went blundering on like a goaded ox. "Only that *I* didn't…"

"Really wish to kiss me?" she cut in.

"No. It wasn't like…"

"Allow me to beg your pardon, Sir Gavin. Rest assured it will *never* happen again." Rose snatched up her candlestick and her book and rushed out, leaving Gavin in the darkness. The seething darkness, he thought. The aching darkness. The unfathomable darkness. What the hell had he done?

Five

"DID YOU SLEEP WELL?" ASKED THE DUCHESS THE NEXT morning as she and Rose sat at the breakfast table together. The gentlemen had gone out riding early, which was becoming their habit.

Aware that she looked heavy-eyed, Rose offered a stunning understatement, "I was a little restless." In fact, she had passed much of the night in an agitated state, in a world suddenly turned topsy-turvy. She had kissed Sir Gavin Keighley! And she had liked it very much.

Which was a vast and desperate problem.

First of all, *she* had kissed *him*. Moved by some inexplicable impulse, she'd leaned in to that impossible kiss. And then she had let herself revel in the sensations—melting, fiery, astonishing. It had been rather glorious. *Until* her mind caught up with her errant body, and she'd jerked back into stark reality.

She had done it. As he'd pointed out! Rose flushed with humiliation. It was like that earlier occasion when she'd thought he admired her and then discovered her mistake.

But had it been?

He'd enjoyed the kiss, an insidious inner voice suggested. His hands and lips had been eager, his response wholehearted. She could not be mistaken about that. But when the…spell had broken, they'd gaped at each other like victims of a catastrophe. He'd stammered out some nonsense she could scarcely remember, and they had fallen back into the impasse of recent years.

The many insults she and Gavin had exchanged over time had come back to Rose in the night. Would she see contempt in his eyes when he returned from his ride? Mockery at his triumph over her? And her family! If they ever found out…

"I am sorry," said the duchess. "Do you need anything to be more comfortable?"

Comfortable! What was she talking about? Rose wondered if she would ever be comfortable again. But the duchess knew nothing of kisses. She was talking about Yerndon's accommodations. For now. Rose had noticed that their lovely hostess was keenly observant. She was intelligent too. She worked things out. If Rose wasn't careful, she would deduce more than she should. "No, thank you," said Rose. "I'm sure I'll sleep better tonight."

"Well, you need only ask."

"Thank you." Rose had begun to like this woman who was supposed to be her enemy.

"I am going over the house this morning to see what needs to be done. Would you care to come along? You know the place better than I do."

"Actually, this visit is the first time I've been inside."

"What?"

"Mr. Cantrell didn't receive our families."

"Yours and Sir Gavin's?"

"Yes." The sound of his name did *not* send a delicious shiver through her. It was a shudder, Rose decided. That must be what it was. It was a wave of regret. That she could never kiss him again? No!

"I must say I don't understand the basis of this feud. Can you explain it more clearly?"

This was the opportunity she had been sent here to find. Rose wrenched her thoughts away from incendiary kisses. "It began many years ago with Mr. Cantrell's great-grandfather. Or was it great-great? One of them. He'd married a Keighley and a Denholme."

"Both?"

"One after the other. Most of the estate's land came in their two dowries. But their fathers regretted giving the acres up afterward, because the connection to the Cantrells..." Rose's voice trailed off. She couldn't tell *this* Cantrell that the line had been judged useless wastrels.

"They had expected the matches to benefit them more than they did," said the duchess.

Rose nodded. "Also his mother—the most recent Mr. Cantrell's—was related to both our families. Second and third cousins. So there were more connections. And people began to believe that the land should be returned. Particularly when Mr. Cantrell had no direct heirs."

"So Yerndon seemed...available?"

"Yes." And the feud had grown more heated as a result.

"I see," said the duchess. "I wonder why he didn't will things that way? He could have split the acres between the families. It seems reasonable."

"There was a final break long before I was born," said Rose. "I know the Keighleys tried to get Mr. Cantrell to marry a daughter of theirs. He refused, and there were insults. On both sides, I think. And Mr. Cantrell expressed contempt for a Denholme niece as well. He was very puffed up about his grand lineage. Thought he was above the people here in Yorkshire." Or so Rose had been told over and over. "He went to London many times when he was younger. But he never brought back a noble bride."

"I wonder if he met Great-Uncle Percival."

"Who?"

"The previous duke." The duchess shrugged. "If he had, I don't think he would have left Yerndon to him." When Rose looked inquiring, she added, "Percival was not a likable man."

There seemed nothing to say about that.

"Perhaps Mr. Cantrell enjoyed playing people off against each other over his will," her hostess continued. "Some older people are like that. They enjoy the power."

Rose was doubtful. "I don't think he saw enough of either side to do so."

"So do you think Yerndon should belong to your family?"

The direct question startled Rose. Her parents would expect an emphatic yes and cogent arguments in favor. But the matter seemed more complicated than Rose had ever realized. "I…er…"

The duchess smiled. "You and Sir Gavin accepted our invitations in order to argue your cases, didn't you?"

Of course she'd worked this out. Or known it from the beginning probably. It might even be the reason she'd invited them. Rose was beginning to realize that her hostess's motto might be, "let's see what happens." It was a fascinating approach to life.

"What is *your* opinion on the matter?" she asked.

No one had ever asked for Rose's personal view. She was young, and female, and expected to be biddable. Everyone just told her what to think and what to do. She didn't always obey, of course. Now she took a moment to gather her thoughts. "I'm weary of the fighting," she replied. "I wish it would just *stop*."

The duchess nodded encouragingly.

"Yerndon should be cared for," Rose continued, working out her position as she spoke. "Everyone hated to see it neglected, and it shouldn't be. But you are here to remedy that. People needn't be so...grasping."

The duchess cocked her head, waited.

"If they would just let the past go, we could make amends with each other. We could have good neighbors in the house here. Exchange visits and be...a normal neighborhood."

"A pleasant picture. We must see what we can do."

The duchess spoke as if it was a task that could be ticked off a list. Simply and efficiently. She didn't know about the shouting in the churchyard, the continual sniping like ancient border raids. The weight of all those clashes dragged at Rose. Things were too far gone. Amity was a pipe dream.

The duchess got somewhat laboriously to her feet. "I must get to work." She picked up a small notebook and pencil that lay beside her plate. "Are you coming along?"

She would be happy to help this cordially reasonable

woman, Rose thought. Her attitude, and her peaceful house-hold, were a balm. She stood, and they set off on their tour of the house.

They began at the top in the attics, examining the state of the walls and floors and windows and listing needed repairs. As they moved through the rooms, Rose was more and more impressed with the duchess. She was clearly an exceedingly capable person. She was not some lazy aristocrat who left responsibilities to others. No problem seemed to daunt her. She knew just what to do to solve it. Though by the time they reached the ground floor again, she looked quite tired. She stood with a hand on the newel post at the foot of the stairs in the entry hall and breathed deeply. Standing beside her, Rose said, "You are worn out."

"I am a bit fatigued. I will leave the basements for another day."

"You should sit," said Rose. "Or go and lie down? Wouldn't that be better?"

"A comfortable chair and a cup of tea will set me right." The duchess gave her a sidelong glance. "Ah, there's no need to mention the full extent of our labors to the gentlemen."

In other words, Rose was not to tell her husband she'd tired herself. "I won't. If you rest now." She offered an arm to support her.

The duchess gave her a sweet smile as she took it. She really was charming. There'd been no trace of the haughty noblewoman Rose had been led to expect.

They'd turned toward the parlor when there was a rap on the front door. It sounded like the blow of a riding crop, and Rose wondered why the duke would knock on returning from his ride. But he wouldn't, of course. It must be visitors. As she was standing right there, she let go of the duchess, went over, and opened the door.

Jillian and Janet Keighley, Gavin's identical twin sisters, stood on the threshold. They wore smart riding habits, peaked hats, and satirical expressions. In tandem, they raised dark eyebrows. "Do they have you playing footman, Miss Denholme?" asked one of them.

Rose could never tell the twins apart. It was always slightly surprising to see them, two young ladies who looked exactly alike. They had black hair and square faces like Gavin's. Their features were far more delicate, however, and their eyes light blue rather than gray. They wore their hair alike and enjoyed confusing people over their identities.

"Are you doing the cleaning as well?" drawled Jillian, or Janet. "Is that why they invited you?"

Rose became aware of the dust on her gown, especially around the hem. She'd done some stooping and crawling during their inspection as her companion couldn't. Her hair was probably festooned with cobwebs as well. Her hands showed dirt. She no doubt looked a fright. It was just her bad luck that the Keighley twins had caught her in this state.

"Good morning," said the Duchess of Tereford, her exalted status suddenly evident in her cut-glass accent. With just two words, she'd somehow pointed out that it was not customary to call without an introduction, or acceptable to subject a guest of hers to sarcasm.

Rose hadn't heard her speak so imperiously before. The phrase *blistering setdown* drifted through her mind. One didn't become a leading light of the *haut ton* without being able to administer one, she decided. She was glad not to be a potential target. "May I present Misses Jillian and Janet Keighley, Your Grace," she said, adopting the same formal tone. "They are Sir Gavin's sisters." She didn't try to differentiate between them, as she couldn't.

"We were out riding, and we thought we would stop in and see Gavin," said one of them in a more subdued voice.

Placing a claim of connection, Rose thought, braver than she would have dared to be at eighteen. Of course there were two of them, automatic allies to bolster each other.

The duchess let them hang for a long moment, then coolly invited them in.

Thus it was that when Gavin walked into Yerndon's parlor a bit later, he found his sisters sitting there and the atmosphere fraught.

It was like returning to a different household from the easygoing one he'd left. And like a splash of icy water in his face. The fact that he had kissed Rose in this parlor in the dimness of evening was one thing when he considered just the two of them. Unsettling enough, but it was quite another in the harsh light of sisters. Not to mention his mother, whose outrage would be epic. A man might be called head of the family, but in Gavin's experience this was a courtesy title. He lived with three females who liked authority as little as he did. Including his. He saw the duke and duchess exchange a look filled with some sort of information. Rose was looking at nobody.

"There you are," said Janet as if he'd been missing for days.

"Mama wondered how you were *getting on*," said Jillian.

Gavin heard his mother in the emphasis. She expected results that he'd already concluded were impossible. The duke would not be handing Yerndon over to either the Keighleys or the Denholmes. He'd made that clear as they talked on their rides. He had no intention of choosing one family over the other. He saw no reason why he should. And he thought it would only make things worse if he *did*.

"Gavin?" prompted Janet.

"I am well," he said.

His identical sisters stared at him, waiting for something more satisfying.

"We had an enjoyable ride over the moor this morning," he added. "As you did too, I suppose."

Jillian looked irritated. He felt annoyance rising to meet it. Why had they stuck their noses in? He didn't need their... help. If that was what they were calling it.

"Did you ride the duo?" he asked. The twins' favorite horses were also sisters. They joked about that together.

Not today, however. Jillian gave him a disdainful glare.

"The duo?" asked the duke.

"Our horses are nearly twins," said Janet. She was frowning at Gavin too.

The urge to tell his sisters just to *go away* was rising. Gavin struggled to subdue it. It wouldn't do. He didn't want to drag argument into the Terefords' formerly serene parlor. Yerndon had come to feel like a refuge.

He remembered his new exercise. What could be worse

than this? he asked himself. He might have missed a jump out on the moor and hurt himself or his mount. But he was too good a rider for that. He might have returned to find Rose and his sisters shouting at each other like their parents in the churchyard. But Rose was still and silent. That wasn't actually better. "It's a fine morning to be out," Gavin added doggedly.

"Not at all *dusty*," said Janet, flicking a scornful glance at Rose.

Rose did have quite a bit of dust on her dress, Gavin saw. Why? Had there been some sort of tussle before he arrived? He imagined his sisters and Rose grappling on the floor as he and the duke had done at their first encounter. No, of course that hadn't happened. Was he going mad?

"It was kind of you to call," said the duchess.

Gavin nearly jumped. He hadn't realized their lovely hostess could speak with such steely dismissal.

"Indeed," said the duke. "But we mustn't keep you from your ride any longer."

He had it too. *Imperious* didn't begin to describe that tone. Gavin realized then how kind the Terefords had been to him and Rose. Because they wanted to be, not because they couldn't be otherwise.

His sisters rose together as if drawn up by strings. Gavin wondered if the duke could teach him to enforce social obedience in a few words. He envied the skill.

"Have you heard about the Milsomes' ball?" Jillian asked as they moved toward the door.

She was not much daunted, Gavin noted. More annoyed.

His sisters did not take reprimands well. He could see thoughts of revenge simmering in their blue eyes. Then her actual words caught up with him. "Ball?" he asked incredulously.

"Well, a dancing party."

"The invitations have gone out," said Janet. "I know one is coming here." She looked at Rose. "Won't that be lovely?"

His sisters had teeth like predators. Gavin had never noticed this before.

"Lovely," Rose replied.

She didn't sound cowed. Gavin couldn't decide *how* she sounded, exactly.

"Will you go?" asked Jillian with artificial surprise.

"Why not?"

"Oh, well…"

"Good day," said the duchess. The duke held the parlor door open.

Jillian and Janet departed without an escort, another sign of disapproval. The door closed behind them with a definitive click.

"Dancing party," Gavin couldn't help but exclaim. "What can Milsome be about? No one does such things here."

"I expect Mr. Milsome decided that our mutual visit changed things," said Rose.

"For the better?" asked the duchess.

Rose shrugged. She was angry, Gavin realized. Rose didn't often get angry, and she didn't show it in the way he was accustomed to at home. So it was hard to spot. But there it was. His sisters had managed the thing.

"Our presence here certainly roused his curiosity," Rose said.

And he'd talked about it, Gavin thought. Made a good story of their conversation, he supposed. Now everyone wished to see them appearing together, like a carnival attraction.

"I must go and shake out my *dusty* gown." Rose stood, caught up her shawl, and went out.

Oh yes, she was angry. Gavin found he was on his feet. "I must just… I have a …" He strode out without a vestige of an excuse. He had to speak to Rose, though he didn't know what he was going to say. He'd been trained to insult Denholmes. Snide comments tripped off his tongue. Other sorts of conversation didn't come easily. But that was ridiculous. He was a civilized man. He could converse. He spoke with friends, with near strangers such as the duke and duchess. He didn't deride them—any longer.

But Rose had moved into a unique category—a Denholme he'd promised to treat politely. A Denholme he had passionately kissed! What were they to say? They had found plenty to talk about as children. Years ago. They couldn't do the same now. Could they? He strode after her in determined confusion.

The Terefords remained in the parlor, side by side before the crackling fire. "It would be something to see them dance together," said the duchess.

"But what sort of something?"

"Don't sneer, James."

"I wasn't. I've given that up. Especially in this case."

"This?"

"They're so thoroughly accustomed to sneering at each other."

She smiled. "I daresay they'd be well matched on the dance floor."

"And elsewhere, my dear matchmaker?"

"That remains to be seen. I haven't made up my mind."

Her husband said nothing more. He merely looked at her until she turned to meet his eyes. Then he added, "I've learned my lesson, you know."

"Lesson?"

"I don't command or assume or...scold. But I have to say, my darling Cecelia, that you look very tired."

"I'm all right."

"Tired."

The duchess sighed. "I went over the house this morning."

He frowned. "Crawling into attic corners and shoving furniture about?"

"No, no, Miss Denholme did that."

"Thus, the dust," he replied.

"Yes. But even so, it was more taxing than...usual. Just standing on my feet too long seems a big task these days." She shook her head.

"You should have let me do that. I am capable." His smile was wry. "You have taught me all about making lists."

Her answering smile was warmer. "I know."

"Cecelia."

She made an impatient gesture. "I have always been able to work as long as I wished. I am...was hardly ever fatigued."

"You have an important new job."

She put a hand on her rounded midsection. "Yes. Perhaps I need to learn a lesson too."

The duke watched her with tender concern. "I think, when you are more rested, in a few days, we should start back to London. By slow stages."

"Oh, not just yet."

"This place isn't in bad shape. I can find an agent to manage any repairs without difficulty."

"I know, but I think we can make other things right."

The duke raised dark brows. "What things would those be?"

"Those that are burdening our guests."

"Burdening. Such as sly young sisters?"

"They did have the manners of hissing cats. But this feud, James. It's too bad. Something should be done."

He frowned. "I want to take care of you. If you need to be elsewhere, Yerndon and its neighbors can go hang."

"I will change my ways," the duchess promised. "I'll put all the work off on you. Just as you once thought to do with me."

They exchanged a reminiscent smile. "I'll hold you to that," said the duke. "I want to see you lolling on sofas and nibbling delicacies. You can wave a languid white hand, give orders, and send me to fetch and carry."

"Or the slightly bewildered young footman," she replied.

"Or him," the duke agreed with another fond smile.

She wrinkled her nose at this picture. "It sounds very dull."

"I will do my best to amuse you. Along with our oddly

assorted guests." The duke glanced out the window. "Do you think they're coming back anytime soon?"

"I think they've stomped off to their separate corners to revive their spirits."

"Boxing language, Cecelia?"

"I picked it up somewhere. From some sporting fellow. Do you want luncheon? I'm a bit hungry."

The duke rose. "I will hunt down sustenance and bring it to you."

"Pickles," she answered. "Can you be sure there are pickles?"

"If I have to ride to Leeds to procure them," he said with an elegant bow. "I am at your command, as I am at your feet."

"You might rub them while I eat," teased the duchess.

"Yes, my lady," he said with a matching twinkle in his dark-blue eyes.

Outside, in a corner of the garden, Rose brushed the last of the dust from her skirt. There was not really so much. She was not a disgraceful, disheveled hoyden as her mother would no doubt have declared. The Keighley twins had just wanted an excuse to twit her. Drat them and the people who taught them to behave so.

Rose stretched out her arms and breathed deeply. She was so glad to be outdoors, in the fresh wind blowing across the moor, alone. She'd been glad to pitch in this morning. She thought she had been helpful. But this was really her element.

When Gavin appeared, she nearly stamped her foot. "You were out on the moor all morning," she said. "It's my turn now." But the wind was in her face. It blew the words away, and he came nearer.

"I hope Jillian and Janet didn't..."

"It was just the usual chaffing," Rose interrupted. Had she actually kissed him last night? That seemed an impossibility in the clear light of day, after another tussle with Keighleys.

"You might have..."

"Had a shouting match with your sisters? As is our families' habit? Right in front of you? What would you expect to do then?"

He gazed at her, with nothing to say apparently. That ought to be satisfying, but Rose didn't find it so.

"We could have berated each other as our parents did," she went on. "That would have made an edifying spectacle for the Terefords."

"That isn't what I was going to say."

"No? What were you proposing that I might have done?"

He looked pained. "I don't know. But after last night..."

"We wake in the morning and find that nothing has changed," said Rose. The twins had made her feel that even more strongly.

"Something has changed," he said. He stepped closer.

He drew her. She remembered the touch of his hands, the taste of his lips so vividly. And the scorn in his sisters' eyes. And her parents' stern judgment. "I need to get away." Rose turned and moved toward a path.

"Where are you going?"

"For a walk!" The moor always comforted her.

She had no wrap or bonnet, still less gloves. She would be chilled after a while, but she didn't care. She knew the landscape. The sun was bright. It would warm her in some sheltered nook, which she could certainly find. This was where she belonged, Rose thought as she strode along. This was her true home, not some stuffy parlor where silly girls sniped at her for the stupidest reasons. Or no real reason at all, for pity's sake.

She topped a small rise and saw Gavin tramping off in the opposite direction. Good! He had acknowledged her wish for solitude. Rose did not feel the least regret. She did *not* wish to go after him. It was futile to talk about that kiss. To bring it all back. Yearning threatened to rise in Rose's chest. She walked faster, taking long steps, swinging her arms, breathing deeply and slowly. She would not think about last night. She would look for plant specimens, though she did not have her collecting case with her. Her side felt bare without it. She missed her routine of collection and preservation most sorely. That delicate, intricate work soothed her soul. She was walking too fast to spot hidden treasures. She needed to move though, which was not the same as fleeing.

She would think about something pleasant and soothing. This "ball" the Milsomes planned popped up instead, the opposite of those things. It was a dreadful idea. Rose imagined Lady Keighley, sitting on the sidelines, scowling at any passing Denholme. Her parents glaring back. Janet and Jillian on a dance floor, sneering and tripping her if she dared to…dance with Gavin? Rose stopped short. What would it be like to dance with Gavin? Rather…invigorating? She never had, of course. That would be a spectacle for the neighborhood to marvel over.

Why must people create complications? It seemed to be all they were good for. Or bad for. More often the latter, Rose thought.

A breeze ruffled her skirts. A skylark flew up and hovered. Sweet and pungent scents wafted by. As it always did, the moor soothed her. Settled her feathers, she thought, smoothed out her fur. It was strange that a wild place could do that, but it had all her life. She walked on, more peacefully.

She paid no attention to direction, knowing she could find her way back whenever she liked. She watched a hawk float on the wind. The way its wings tilted to catch the air seemed the very emblem of freedom. She bent over a cluster of blooming violets in their nest of moss. She paused for a while in a stony nook where sunlight poured down and warmed her. And then, her mood much better, she walked on. There was no one waiting at home to scold her about solitary rambles. Unless the duchess disapproved? Let her try! But from what she'd observed so far, Rose didn't think she would.

When Rose found that her feet had led her to the hill where her childhood gang had built the "castle," she was not really surprised. They'd been talking about it. When she had no other destination in mind, memory had drawn her there.

Rose looked up the tumbled slope. She hadn't climbed it in years.

She hesitated, smiled to herself, and tied a knot in her skirt and petticoat to hold them out of the way. Using her hands to steady her steps, she ascended the hill, went over the low wall, and surveyed their old construction.

Stone didn't change. Their ringwall was intact, as was the uneven platform in the middle of that circle. Sprigs of green poked through the joints. She could remember their excitement as they gathered rocks and piled them. The memory made her sad, a little, but she was also happy to see the place. They'd had such fun here.

"Is it still the same?" called a deep voice.

Rose turned, and there was Gavin, clambering up the other side of the hill. Their reminiscences had led him here as well. Inclinations drew you along on the moors. She knew that. And the fort was as much his as hers. She could hardly order him off. She didn't really want to. She untied her skirt and let it fall. He stepped over a last rock and joined her.

"It is," he said. "Look, there's Alan's cannon 'emplacement.'"

He stood tall beside her, his black hair tossed by the wind. He looked like he belonged to the moor. Rose's anger had blown away with the wind. Yet her pulse sped up.

"Do you suppose the spears we threw are lying out there on the ground?" Gavin gestured at the surrounding heath.

"The wood would have decayed by this time."

"Yes. How can it have been ten years?"

"Day by day," Rose replied.

He turned to her, his gray eyes penetrating. "You say that

as if they dragged. How can you think so in a place like this?" He gestured at the landscape again.

"Any day on the moor is wonderful, but I have too few of those. Young ladies are not to wander alone. Or older ladies. No ladies at all." That had sounded daft. Rose pressed her lips together.

"But you know the land so well. You are quite safe."

Rose appreciated the sentiment, even though it was not the point. He had no idea what it was like to be hampered by the conventions put on females.

"Surely no one would accost you."

She could evade anyone who dared try, Rose knew. She was aware of every movement on the moor, and she could fade onto next-to-invisible sheep paths and be gone in a moment. But her parents cared more about appearances than actual dangers. Or, that wasn't fair. They wanted her safe, as well as respectable. But most especially the latter.

"You always could slip away, like magic." Gavin bent closer as if he was afraid she would vanish right now.

She was in danger, Rose realized. She had somehow ventured into uncharted waters, and now she was right on the edge of kissing Gavin Keighley. Again. She mustn't want to do that. She mustn't recall the delicious shock that had coursed through her when they touched. But she was, so clearly that she was trembling. It would be some sort of poetic completion to step into his arms right here, where they'd been comrades long ago.

"What are you doing up there?" called a childish voice.

Rose jumped and turned to find the Brontë children

gathered at the bottom of the hill. Aware of every movement on the moor indeed, she thought. Gavin had seized every bit of her attention. A wolf might have leaped on her. If there were wolves left in this country, her mind automatically corrected. There were not.

Five pairs of childish eyes gazed up at them. Once again the children rode two shaggy moorland ponies equipped with thick sheepskin pads. Maria held Branwell and Emily before her. Elizabeth and Charlotte sat together on the other mount. They were warmly dressed, as Rose was not. That was the reason for the goose bumps on her arms, she told herself, not wild arousal. Not the fact that she had been about to thrust herself on Gavin Keighley again. She should be thankful for the interruption. Rose tried, and failed.

Gavin growled.

The sound reached down into Rose and…summoned. She felt like a plucked harp string.

"Why are people always where you don't want them to be?" he muttered.

"Because that is the nature of people," Rose replied without thinking.

Their eyes met. Rose felt she was gazing at a kindred spirit down to their very depths.

"Is it an ancient tomb?" called Charlotte Brontë.

Kindred, Rose thought. All of their kindred stood between them in oppositional lines. She looked away.

Gavin moved over to the edge of the slope. "Come and see," he said in a resigned tone. The children hopped off the ponies and swarmed up the low hill. "Be careful climbing,"

Gavin added. "Some of the rocks will tilt under you." He wondered if he should go down to help. But the two oldest were boosting the smaller ones over the obstacles and holding them steady.

A moment later, they poured over the edge like a troop of invaders. But they had to be welcomed rather than repelled. And he had to stop thinking of Rose in his arms, arched up against him in eager demand. As if that was possible when she stood right there, windblown and delectable.

"What is this place?" asked Elizabeth Brontë. "Is it a relic of former dwellers in this land?"

Small children did not speak this way, Gavin thought. Only these did—apparently.

"No," replied Rose. "We built it, with our friends. When we were a bit older than you."

"Built it!" Branwell looked around in delight. "Like a fort." He picked up a stick and began to brandish it like a sword. Charlotte found another and fenced with him on the rocky platform. Emily danced around them, shrieking with joy.

"Stop acting like barbarians," said their eldest sister, Maria.

The girl had heard that scold somewhere, Gavin thought, as the two lowered their improvised weapons. From some humorless git.

"We used to play at being barbarians," said Rose. "That was just the word the Romans used for the people who lived here first, you know."

Good for her, Gavin thought. Trust Rose to offer kindness.

It was her natural element, he remembered. She'd always been the one who settled their youthful spats. He felt a pang of admiration, and longing.

"The Romans spoke Latin," said Branwell, as if this was not a point in their favor.

"Yes. They marched through here many centuries ago," Gavin said. "You can see the ruins of their camps, and the wall they put right across England up north a ways. We pretended to fight them off." And then sometimes they had played at being a legion besieged by the blue-painted Picts.

"Ha!" Branwell waved his stick at the ringwall. "Take that, Romans."

"We threw—" began Rose, then broke off, pressing her lips together. Gavin met her rueful gaze. With a nod he agreed that introducing the idea of spears was not advisable, particularly with these children. They'd fill the air with missiles. Rose smiled, and Gavin was literally warmed by it. She set his blood alight. "Sometimes we battled Danes," she said. "Or Saxons."

"They came through here too," Gavin added.

"With the Romans?" asked Charlotte.

"After them. This land has had many invaders."

"A place of warring kingdoms," replied the little girl dreamily.

"It was." As if in answer to this statement, the wind came up, sweeping over miles of heather in a great whispering rush. "Do you hear that?" Gavin asked the children.

"What?"

"The sound of the wind. Listen."

They all stood still. It was almost as if the children cocked their ears.

"They call that sound 'wuthering' here in Yorkshire."

"Wuthering," repeated Emily. "Wuthering, wuthering." She licked her lips as if she liked the taste of the word.

"It's bringing clouds," said Rose. She pointed at the horizon. "We should go."

There was no other choice, Gavin thought. They couldn't live here in their old stronghold, pleasing as that fantasy might be. The past was gone. The present was tangled. The future was…a mystery.

He stepped forward to help the little ones down the hill.

The Brontë children rode alongside them back toward Yerndon, and so Gavin found no new opportunities to bewilder himself talking with Rose.

Six

"I AM GOING INTO HAWORTH TODAY," THE DUCHESS SAID at breakfast the next morning. Everyone was present. There had been no early ride as the duke said he had things to do. "I want to call on Mrs. Brontë," she continued. "I keep thinking of those children."

Rose hadn't told her about the encounter yesterday. That would have involved mentioning her encounter with Gavin, and though the duchess was a remarkably subtle chaperone, Rose didn't know how far her tolerance would stretch. When Rose had slipped back inside yesterday afternoon, cold and windblown and carefully *not* in the company of Gavin Keighley, the duchess had caught her. She'd clearly been watching for Rose to return, but she only asked if it had been a good walk. There was no litany of questions, even though Rose had been gone for hours. Rose's mother would have interrogated and scolded her. There had been none of that. There had been something else though. Rose had received the distinct impression that she was expected to monitor her own conduct and take responsibility for the standards she would meet. Which ought to be those that earned respect. The exchange had been surprising, and extremely interesting.

Now it almost seemed as if their hostess had sensed the

meeting at the fort without being directly informed. "The children said their mother was ill," Rose pointed out.

Over at the sideboard, the housemaid Lucy was setting down a fresh teapot. Ian the footman, who had just come in with a tray, bumped her elbow. Tea sloshed out of the spout onto the wooden surface. Lucy whirled, eyes flashing, and jostled the tray he carried. Crockery rattled and nearly fell to the floor.

The duchess turned. She and the duke had their backs to the sideboard. Rose and Gavin faced it, and thus had had a clear view of the servants' tussle, perhaps designed to impress their feuding employers. The local war went on, they signaled. Rose sighed.

Under the duchess's eye, Lucy dropped a curtsy, her gaze on the floor, and went out. Ian arranged clean cups beside the teapot, his figure rigid. The duchess turned back. "I intend to leave a card at least," she said. "I shall consider the children a sufficient introduction. Will you come?"

Rose agreed. She was surprised when Gavin did too. Morning calls were not his habit. He seemed determined to puzzle her these days.

Ian departed with his empty tray. There was a clatter and a thud from outside the breakfast room door, followed by a half-audible curse.

A low feminine laugh followed and then a volley of muttering. The words were indecipherable, but the tone was fierce.

After a moment, the sound of footsteps receded.

"Did you hear that?" asked the duke. "Do you think something is wrong?"

"Cook says there is a vendetta in progress," replied his wife.

Of course she would know what was going on in her household, Rose thought. She was beginning to think there was very little the duchess *didn't* know.

"Vendetta?" asked the duke. "What do you mean?"

"Our servants seem to feel they have to…represent us," said Rose.

"Represent?" The duke raised his dark brows. "Further your family dispute, you mean?"

Rose nodded, ashamed that it had spilled over into the duchess's harmonious household.

"Cook is not particularly concerned," the duchess said. "No broken china so far. A deal of heat but not much else, she said."

"Phelps told me that our maid Lucy Trent is daft," said Gavin.

She would check with Ian again, Rose thought. If he was being made miserable here, she would send him home. They could just do without a footman.

"Daft as in…unbalanced?" asked the duke. He looked at his wife with concern.

The duchess shook her head. "I believe she has quite a vivid personality. Which must be awkward in her position."

"Or in any young woman's," Rose heard herself say. The others looked at her. Well, it was true. "And what does Phelps know about it?" she added. "He is never in the house." Gavin might make an effort to manage the Keighley servants, she thought. What was the point of their appearance of amity if the staff made a mockery of it?

Gavin started to speak, then appeared to change his mind.

"Phelps is the one who goes out most days with a gun?" asked the duke.

He noticed things too, Rose thought. Really, nothing got past the Terefords.

"After rabbits, I expect," Gavin answered.

"And yet we haven't seen any on the table." Rose thought Phelps was just sloping off so he didn't have to do any work.

"Hunting is not an exact…" Gavin began.

"Yet Phelps is said to be so expert," Rose interrupted.

He frowned at her.

The duke looked at them, then over at his wife. "We aren't worried?" he asked her.

"No."

"That's good."

They smiled at each other. Both seemed amused and very much in harmony. Rose felt her irritation—automatic over any matter involving Keighleys and Denholmes, or their households—fade away. The Terefords' home was so unlike her own. There was no simmering rancor or constant flow of criticism. Instead, she felt warmth and acceptance and equity. The duke and duchess might have disagreements. They must, on occasion. Everyone did. But they seemed so ready to understand and make allowances. She wanted to live like this, Rose thought. Not always mired in suspicion and disputes. Not worrying about hostile encounters and malicious whispers. It was too bad she saw no way such a change could befall her.

Later that morning the Terefords' elegant coach was brought up from the stables. The duke handed his wife carefully in, Rose joined her, and the men mounted up to ride beside them. They made a small cavalcade to the little village of Haworth six miles away.

Once there, the duke left them to meet with a builder who lived at the edge of the hamlet. The rest of them were directed to the parsonage, a rectangular gray brick house with five windows above and four below, the front door in the center. The unadorned building had a chimney at each end and a graveyard next door. Though she loved the moor, Rose had to admit that this residence was rather bleak.

Gavin dismounted and handed the women out of the carriage. His fingers were firm on Rose's, seemingly reluctant to let go.

They knocked. After a short wait the door opened, and they were greeted by a female servant with a broad Yorkshire accent. She shook her head when the duchess asked for Mrs. Brontë. "Too ill for visiting," she declared.

A small head appeared, peering around the servant's broad hip. "It's the duchess," exclaimed Charlotte Brontë. "And Miss Denholme and Sir Gavin."

"A duchess for truth?" The servant stared. "I reckoned they made that up." She shook her head at the visitors. "They do make things up."

Several small Brontës jostled for position in the doorway. "Stop that," said Maria's voice from the rear. "Behave properly."

"What is this noise?" demanded a man's voice.

"Now you've disturbed the reverend," said the maid. She looked concerned.

A tall man with brown hair and prominent cheekbones loomed up behind her. The children faded back as she stepped aside. "May I help you?" the man asked. There was just a touch of Ireland in his voice.

"How do you do?" said Gavin. "Gavin Keighley. We met soon after you arrived."

"Ah yes."

Gavin didn't think the man actually remembered that brief ceremonial visit. He introduced the duchess, whose title brought raised eyebrows, and Rose.

"We met your charming children walking on the moor," said the duchess. "I had thought to call on your wife."

"She is too ill to receive you." A pained bewilderment crossed Mr. Brontë's features, as if he had no notion how to deal with this misfortune.

"I'm sorry to hear that." The duchess said it as if they hadn't already known.

Gavin wondered if Mr. Brontë was going to leave them on the doorstep. He seemed lost in despondence. But at last the man said, "Please come in. Tabitha, some refreshment in the parlor." He used the word *refreshment* as if it was foreign to him and he had no idea what she would produce.

Gavin signaled the coachman. It had been agreed that he would take the horses to the village inn until they were needed again. They went in and sat down in the front parlor. The house was plainly furnished, the fire a bit meager.

"You are a neighbor, Sir Gavin," stated their host. He remembered that much at least.

"As is Miss Denholme."

"Not parishioners, however. Where do you attend church?" Brontë looked ready to admonish them.

"We are nearer to Burnley and go there," said Gavin.

"Ah." The reverend didn't seem quite ready to ask a duchess about her religious habits. "Is there something I can do for you? As I said, my wife is very ill and cannot receive visitors."

"Might we see the children?" asked the duchess.

"They should be at their lessons. I would not wish to encourage them to neglect them. Branwell in particular is prone to slacking."

"Isn't he young to be worrying about that?" asked Gavin.

"One cannot be too early in subduing the will."

The last phrase galled Gavin. It sounded like the sour platitudes offered at his school, a place he had not enjoyed. "I rather think one can."

"You are not an educator. I am. I was an examiner at Woodhouse Grove, a Wesleyan academy. So you see, I am better able to judge these things." His pompous tone was just at the edge of offensive, though Gavin wasn't certain whether he meant it to be. The Reverend Brontë did not seem very conscious of others' feelings.

Rose could see Gavin's temper rising. It was quite visible, she realized. His cheeks reddened. His hands had closed into fists, and his gray eyes...crackled. That was an apt description. An explosion seemed imminent. "Children are usually given some freedom before going off to school," he said.

He hadn't liked his school in Leeds, Rose remembered. He'd told a friend of theirs that the place made him feel like a sheep in an overcrowded pen, wanting to rampage and knock the fences down. Which hadn't sounded much like sheep to her.

"That is a mistake," replied their host. "It allows bad habits to take hold."

"Habits? Such as?"

"Wandering attention. Back talk and argument." Brontë said the last word as if it applied to this conversation and was a judgment on the nature of Gavin's education.

Rose waited for the inevitable outburst. Not that Gavin would hit the curate as he had the duke, but he would surely utter some savage setdown.

A silence stretched. The riposte did not come, despite the annoyance in Gavin's eyes. As Rose watched, his fists slowly opened.

Tabitha entered with a tray containing a plate of oat cakes, a jug, and four pottery cups. Could it be ale? That seemed unlikely in this house, as well as inappropriate for a morning call.

"Is that the cider?" asked their host.

"Yes, sir."

"I told you… Why didn't you bring tea?"

"We're all out," the maid replied.

Mr. Brontë gave her an impatient look. She set the tray on a table before the fire, filled the cups, offered them around, and went out. Rose sipped. The cider was very strong. It had clearly been fermenting in a barrel since pressing. Brontë tried his and set it aside with a grimace. If he had Wesleyan leanings, he would avoid alcoholic drinks. Suspecting that the cakes were meant for the children, Rose did not take one. Only Gavin drank all of his cider.

"My wife's sister is coming to stay," said Brontë abruptly. "To set things to rights."

"I'm sure Mrs. Brontë will be glad of her company," replied the duchess.

"I wish she would get here," was the petulant reply.

They didn't stay long after this. The children did not reappear, and their father made no pretense of enjoying his callers' company. He escorted them to the door with obvious relief.

"Let us walk," said the duchess when the door had shut behind them. It was not a long distance to the inn where the carriage waited.

"What a smug ass," said Gavin when they had left the house behind. "I pity his children."

"I thought you were going to tell him off," said Rose.

Gavin looked at her, then at the duchess. He started to speak and then paused, perhaps remembering that they both knew how he had flown at the duke on first meeting. "I have been employing your method to curb my temper," he replied.

"Method?" asked the duchess.

"You mean..." Rose was startled.

"Your grandmother's method, rather," he corrected.

The duchess looked brightly inquisitive.

Amazed that he'd remembered, Rose said, "My grandmother managed her anger by being grateful that the situation—whatever was irritating her—was not even worse. She said gratitude was a soothing balm."

"I like that idea."

"It is rather effective," said Gavin, only a little grudgingly.

"What were you grateful for while the Reverend Brontë was speaking?" asked the duchess.

"That I didn't choke on his wretched cider and fall over dead," Gavin replied with a slight smile.

The duchess smiled wholeheartedly. "That would certainly be worse."

"But insufficient," he added. "Even though it would relieve me of the necessity of listening to him. So then I was grateful that the village was not being swallowed up by an earthquake."

"An earthquake?" Rose exclaimed.

"They are terrible things apparently. From what I've read. The ground tosses like the sea and sometimes opens up into a bottomless abyss."

"But they are hardly likely in Yorkshire."

"They are worse though," Gavin said.

There was a twinkle in his eyes. He was actually joking. Rose laughed.

"You laugh like the trill of a lark on the moor," Gavin said, and immediately flushed bright red.

Sir Gavin Keighley speechless? And poetic? The world must be ending, Rose thought. Not in an earthquake but in some less visible revolution.

"I thought it took weeks to plan a 'ball,'" Gavin complained to the duke two mornings later as they walked through the stable block together, examining what most needed repair. The Milsomes' gathering was to take place that evening, and he couldn't quite imagine how it was going to go.

"That depends on the arrangements," Tereford replied. "This is to be a fairly informal occasion, I understand."

At which Gavin would see his mother and sisters as well as Rose's family. He'd confirmed that they were all invited, which made this an unprecedented occasion. The Keighleys and the Denholmes were never asked anywhere together. It was a neighborhood law. Now they had been, and curiosity was running rampant. Combine that with the chance to meet a duke and duchess, and the lure was irresistible. Everyone who could possibly wangle an invitation would be present, Gavin knew. He and Rose would have to face them all.

Only there was no *and*. They were not together. They had simply been planted in the same spot and made an agreement to appear to get along. Appear, Gavin thought wryly. He'd agreed because it was sensible and perhaps more…restful. Had he thought that? It hadn't turned out to be restful at all! Who would have imagined that kiss? Had Rose been shaken to the core, as he had? He'd thought so, from the way she'd gripped him, the look on her face. And then there'd been a moment at their old fort when he'd thought it might happen again. But now she'd gone distant and seemed to want to forget all about it. Gavin gritted his teeth. That was impossible.

He didn't know what to do.

He always knew what to do.

One of the great pleasures of Gavin's life was to put things right when they went awry, to tend. He'd always been that way. The impulse seemed inborn. When his father died, he'd taken up his duties on the estate. He'd watched over his mother and sisters, as much as they wished him to, at any rate. He lent a hand when friends needed aid. That was why Yerndon's decline had eaten at him. A nagging problem that he could not solve nearly drove him mad. And now Rose had become another.

No. She wasn't a *problem*. She was…an old friend, an extremely attractive young lady, an interesting person, labeled a foe of his family. He wanted to draw her closer. He wanted to make things right. She hadn't asked him to take care of her. How would he even do so? What was to be done? Were some matters simply intractable? He could not accept that idea.

Something flickered in the corner of his eye. It was Phelps, slipping around a corner toward a side door. He ought to send the man home, Gavin thought. The impulse to bring him had been wrongheaded.

"You don't care for it?" asked the duke.

"I beg your pardon?" He hadn't been listening.

"I wondered if you don't care for dancing? You don't seem in favor of this ball." Tereford examined a half-rotted beam and made a note on the small pad of paper he carried.

"I like it well enough." He'd danced in Leeds. There hadn't been much opportunity closer to home. Certainly not to dance with Rose. He'd be able to do that at the Milsomes'. There was an idea.

"Are you worried that your mother and Miss Denholme's father will fall into another...debate?"

Gavin turned to look at his host. "You heard about that?"

"The builder in Haworth mentioned it."

He should have known that someone would have a flapping tongue. "I don't think they will do that in the midst of a crowd, no." Surely they wouldn't. They would have some self-control.

"Or that your sisters will trip up Miss Denholme on the dance floor?" asked the duke.

Gavin grimaced. It was actually the sort of vengeance Janet and Jillian might plan. And there were two of them, so they could flank Rose.

"If there is any chance of a melee, I want to be prepared to keep my wife out of it," the other man added.

A horrifying scene rose in Gavin's mind—shouting, shoving, hair-pulling, an audience all agog. He shuddered. That would not happen. Rose would never stoop to such a scene, for one thing. But his sisters... He'd have to keep them under his eye. "There won't be."

"You did try to knock me down when I arrived," the duke pointed out.

"I am sorry..."

Tereford waved the repeated apology aside. "Is your family all hotheaded?"

"My mother..." Gavin bit off the sentence. Whatever his opinion, he would not criticize her to a near stranger.

"Ah. I don't suppose she boxes though. Does she?"

"Of course not!" Gavin met his host's dark-blue eyes, which were twinkling mildly. The duke was nothing like the soft southerner Gavin had originally expected him to be. Nor was he a disdainful, sarcastic aristocrat. He was more complex, and far kinder. Now he wasn't mocking. But he was laughing a little. And could he be blamed? This feud was ludicrous, Gavin realized. When one moved a bit outside it, the futility and triviality became obvious.

"Perhaps I could be of some assistance," Tereford said. "I've faced far worse than quarreling neighbors."

"What?" Gavin couldn't imagine anything that would embarrass this man. He was a model of assurance.

"Public humiliation before most of the *haut ton*," the duke replied wryly.

"You? I don't believe it."

"It is quite true." The duke paused to examine a window frame, scraping it with a small pocketknife he had brought along. "Worm-eaten. This will have to be replaced."

Drawn in, Gavin bent to look. "It's only the window. The wall is all right."

"Yes." Tereford folded the knife. "I would be happy to, ah, join forces with you at this ball. To see that it goes smoothly."

"Why would you help? After the way I greeted you."

"Well, I like you," said the duke. He smiled. "Despite the circumstances of our first meeting. Perhaps even because of them. But chiefly I want to keep my wife calm and safe."

Gavin understood that very well. It was a strong motive. He nodded. "Thank you. I would appreciate your advice."

"I don't know that I have advice. More a plan of campaign."

Gavin looked inquiring. Tereford proceeded to explain as they went on evaluating the state of the stables.

Rose had been watching out the parlor window for the gentlemen's return. When she saw them approaching the house, she rose, smiled at the duchess as if she was just stepping out for a moment, and went into the entryway. She put her hand on the stair banister as if she was about to go up and waited for the door to open.

"Oh, hello," said the duke when they came in.

"Hello," Rose replied. "The duchess is sitting in the parlor."

Tereford turned in that direction, as she had known he would. When Gavin made to follow, Rose grasped his arm and pulled him across into the dining room.

"What's wrong?" he asked as she shut the door behind them.

"Nothing is wrong. I simply wished to talk to you. We must discuss this supposed ball."

"Supposed?"

"It is far too grand a word..." Rose brushed this irrelevance aside. "You know it will be difficult. We must have a plan."

"The duke has offered—"

"I have been thinking," Rose interrupted. She'd been doing little else. "We will have to dance together. Once. Early in the evening. The first dance would be best. Exhibit ourselves and get it over with."

"Will it be such a trial?"

She gazed up at him in exasperation. "That is not the point. Everyone will be watching us. Like hawks. To see what we will do. How we will act. Just waiting for a reason to stoop and sink in their talons."

"You are exaggerating."

"How can you say so? After all these years of feuding? We must establish the...tone. Show people that there is nothing to see. At once. Before anything unfortunate can happen." Rose hoped he was actually listening.

"Unfortunate?"

"There is no need to growl at me. Or pretend that you don't know what I mean." She wrinkled her nose. "The scene in the churchyard? We must present the neighborhood with a perfectly commonplace country dance."

"As if we were actors on the stage?" Gavin asked.

"Exactly. We will smile and converse. The picture of amiability. And then we need not bother for the rest of the evening."

"So I am a bother to get over with as quickly as possible?"

"Why are you being obtuse? This has nothing to do with you. Or me."

"Dancing together has nothing to do with either of us?"

"In this case, no. It is about preventing some sort of... social debacle."

"A melee," he murmured.

Rose had a sudden horrible vision—her father and Gavin's mother faced off and shouting, his sisters and *her* mother staring daggers at each other, the twins doing something outrageous that she couldn't even imagine. "If only our families will restrain themselves."

"As they never do."

"That is singularly unhelpful."

"What do you expect? They never listen."

Rose's heart sank. It was true that her parents paid no

heed to her opinions. She wasn't meant to have any. But this was action, not argument. "We can set an example. That is my point!"

"Oh, is that it?"

He was behaving as he used to, contradicting whatever she said. He wore the mulish, offended expression that was so familiar. She'd thought they would work together. But the kind or complimentary things he'd said to her—the kiss!— were another illusion, broken when the outside world intruded. Underneath, things were just the same. She swallowed painful disappointment. It had been foolish to think years of acrimony could disappear. And she was not a fool. "Did you say something about the duke?"

"Oh, am I allowed to speak now?"

"You have been speaking all along. There is never any stopping you."

"Never? Really?" His eyes were blazing.

"Why are you angry? You know everyone will be looking at us. We must make a plan."

"Which you have done, it seems. You don't appear to need anything from me."

"Beyond your agreement? I would like to know that you will do your part."

"I agree," he replied in a cold, clipped tone. And he turned and walked out.

Rose stood in the entryway, alone. She had thought it was a good idea. She'd even imagined that they would…conspire together to make the ball…not a disaster at least. Perhaps she was a fool after all.

Gavin strode down the lane that led away from Yerndon. He hadn't even taken off his coat before Rose...pounced. "A bother to get over with," he muttered as he moved out onto the moor. Was that how she saw this whole visit—a trial, a strain, a performance? Had she decided their kiss was a mistake?

Perhaps it was time to end this farce and go back to his regular life.

Oddly, the thought of his old routines did not comfort him. Living outside them at Yerndon had revealed certain flaws. There was the good. He was competent, effective. He found satisfaction in his work. He loved the place where he lived. Gavin took a deep breath of the Yorkshire air as he walked. It was his heart home.

But then there was the other side. He was often angry and had to grapple with his temper. He had periods of boredom, which he viewed with impatience. He was...lonely.

Gavin's authoritative stride faltered. He stumbled slightly before recovering and walking on. That made no sense. He had his mother and sisters at home, people he liked in the neighborhood. He thought most of them liked him as well, setting aside the Denholmes. Moreover, he enjoyed being alone, as he was now, out of doors. It was one of his chief pleasures. How could all that add up to lonely?

And yet he felt it now as a deep pang. Being at Yerndon— with Rose, yes, mostly it was Rose—had exposed some primal need. Not just the physical yearning, though that was strong. It had made him see a void at the center of his perfectly adequate life. Rose had done that somehow. Rose, to whom he was a bother to be gotten over with. Gavin gritted his teeth and fought his temper and...hurt. She had hurt him with her cool proposal that they perform for the neighborhood. She had not sounded like someone who...cared.

With a pain in the region of his heart, Gavin asked himself what would be worse than this hopeless longing.

He couldn't think of anything.

He stopped and looked about him. His feet had brought him back to their old childhood fort, the place where she had nearly kissed him again. Or so he had thought. He didn't know the truth of anything anymore. There was someone up there, atop the tumbled stones. Two someones, actually.

Gavin moved closer and stationed himself quietly behind a gorse bush.

A young woman was perched on the highest boulder. It was the housemaid Lucy Trent, Gavin realized. And the young footman who had come to Yerndon with Rose stood before her, gazing up at her face.

She waved her arms in a grand gesture. "'This day is called the Feast of Crispan,'" she declaimed, her voice carrying out over the moor. "'Him as lives and comes home safe will stand on tiptoes when ere this day is named and show his wounds.'" She swept her hands down her body as if exhibiting scars.

The young footman watched her, transfixed. Gavin was impressed by the girl's intensity, though her speech made no sense to him. What were they up to?

"'All shall remember the feats we did this day,'" she continued with one raised finger. "'With drinking and tales, right till the end of the world.'"

She brought the palms of her hands together and held them as if in prayer. "'We happy few, we band of brothers.'"

It was from a play, Gavin realized. Shakespeare. He didn't remember which one. And the language wasn't quite right, was it? It seemed skewed.

Lucy spread her hands and extended her arms. Her voice rang out even stronger. "'Gentlemen in England shall curse they were not here to fight with us on Saint Crispan's Day.'"

She folded her arms over her chest, waited a moment, then bowed.

The footman clapped enthusiastically. The girl straightened, grinning, and leaped off the boulder into his arms.

Gavin edged slowly away, keeping heather and gorse between him and the embracing couple. He felt a little envious at the sheer joy of the scene, and also concerned. His mother would dismiss any housemaid who slipped out for an assignation with another servant. Lucy would be sent away without a character if she was found out. Which seemed a pity after the girl's unusual, exuberant performance. Not that he intended to tell his mother about any of this. But the pair were not being discreet. They had probably been missed at Yerndon. Someone else might inform on them. And he didn't see what he could do about that.

Rounding a hillock, Gavin walked back toward the house. His thoughts went automatically to Rose.

He would follow the duke's lead, as they'd agreed. He would prance across the dance floor as Rose had commanded. And then he really had no idea.

Seven

ROSE ENTERED THE MILSOMES' HOUSE WITH HER HEAD held high and a quite natural smile on her face. She'd practiced it in the mirror until she got it right. She knew she showed no outward sign of nerves. She also knew that she wore a stunning gown beneath her cloak. Only the duchess and their maids had seen her ensemble so far.

When the duchess had offered to lend her a dress for this occasion, Rose had refused at first. But the suggestion had been friendly, not the least condescending. Later, when Rose had looked over the gowns she'd brought with her to Yerndon and remembered her mother's laments about their lack of fashion, she'd changed her mind.

This "ball" tonight was nearly unique in her life. It was true they were a scattered country neighborhood with no nearby town to hold regular assemblies. But other such places managed some semblance of society. Here, the Keighley/Denholme feud had put a damper on entertainments. Calls and dinners seemed almost furtive with one or the other family left out of each one. And so Rose had never had the opportunity to make an entrance before all her neighbors. She'd been overtaken by a vision of dazzling everyone she knew. She would be not the quiet, slightly dowdy Rose

Denholme but a polished young lady. In particular, she wanted
to see Gavin's jaw drop. She would show him! When an inner
voice wondered exactly what he was to be shown, and what
she expected him to do about it, she brushed it aside.

And so she'd accepted the offered gown, which fit her
with only a tuck or two of alteration. The duchess's maid had
helped Sue with her hair as well, giving it a more sophisticated touch. Rose hadn't quite recognized herself as she put
on her cloak in her bedchamber. She'd ridden in the carriage
muffled up in it to preserve the surprise.

She and the duchess took off their wraps in a room set
aside for the ladies. A long mirror stood in the corner for last-
minute adjustments. "You look lovely," said the duchess.

Rose examined her reflection. The dress was made of silk
in a shimmering, golden amber shade. It was exquisitely cut
and adorned with three complementary colors of braided
ribbon. The amber enhanced her auburn hair and seemed to
make her skin glow. Her blue eyes looked back at her with sly
wonder. Even beside the beautiful duchess, she looked very
well indeed. "Thank you," said Rose, her tone covering more
than a single compliment.

The duchess smiled and nodded as they went out.

Gavin and the duke awaited them in the front hall so that
they could enter the ball together. And Rose got what she
wanted. Gavin's jaw actually did drop. His gray eyes went
wide. He looked stunned. Rose felt a bubble of elation rise
through her, and she laughed. A wild, carefree, daring Rose
peeked out of the inner shelter where she lurked, away from
critical judgments.

The duke offered his arm. The duchess took it. Gavin forgot to follow suit. He just went on staring. Rose smiled as she moved off behind the Terefords. After a moment, Gavin came along, hurrying a bit to catch up. They followed a footman to the back of the house.

The rooms there had sliding doors that could be pushed back to open the whole space. The Milsomes had moved all their furniture out, so that it was almost like a ballroom, and they stood in the doorway to greet their guests.

The Terefords were welcomed effusively. They passed through, and then Rose and Gavin stood there together, the target of gasps and murmurs. Rose knew that the rising tide of comment was mostly about seeing them together. But some was clearly for her transformation. To her own astonishment, she reveled in it.

Dark-haired, plump Mrs. Milsome looked around the room, openly delighted by the buzz. Rose hadn't realized she was a frustrated hostess. "You look splendid, my dear," she said to Rose when she had greeted them.

"Yes, indeed," said Mr. Milsome.

"That is an exquisite gown."

Rose nodded thanks. She didn't intend to volunteer the information that it was borrowed, though of course she wouldn't lie.

"Good to see the two of you in charity with each other," said Mr. Milsome heartily.

Charity was not what they were in, Rose noted but did not say. More an armed truce. And tonight she thought she had superior weaponry. She showed her teeth and enjoyed seeing the Milsomes blink at her smile.

Other guests came up behind them, and they moved into the room. Rose wondered who would approach them first. She was not surprised to see that it was Gavin's mother. "The first dance," she reminded him, then went on to the circle hovering around the Terefords. She could make introductions. To a duke and duchess. Who would have thought it?

Gavin watched her go. He couldn't tear his eyes away. It wasn't simply the fancy gown. There was something different about Rose this evening. Or was it just the unusual setting? No, Rose *was* different. He'd thought the ball would make her shy and awkward under all these avid eyes, but she was moving through it like a queen.

"What the deuce have you been doing?" demanded an irritated voice.

Gavin turned to find his mother at his side, and a familiar anger crackling in her eyes. They resembled each other in more than looks. Everyone said he'd inherited his quick temper from her.

"I send you off to befriend this duke, and now I find you slinking along behind Rose Denholme like a whipped hound."

"I wasn't slinking." The thought revolted.

"Who has obviously insinuated herself with them, as you apparently have not," his mother continued.

"She hasn't been…"

"Wearing one of the duchess's gowns!"

"Oh." That explained the dress, which hadn't seemed like Rose's customary style.

"She didn't get a garment like that around here." His mother surveyed the crowd. "My God, the room reeks of envy. And what have you done? Let her steal a march on you, that's what."

"I don't know what you mean." He didn't appreciate being spoken to in this way.

"Then you're a dunce, Gavin. But you aren't. We both know that. So how did that milksop Rose Denholme get the better of you?"

His anger was rising to match hers, a familiar sensation. But he couldn't let it. The idea was to prevent arguments tonight, though he hadn't realized they would rise between him and his mother. "What could be worse?" he murmured.

"I beg your pardon?"

He hadn't meant to say it aloud. "There's a way to control your temper," he began.

"Control my temper?" She glared in astonishment.

What was he thinking? His mother enjoyed her fearsome reputation. She treated her temper like a favorite pet. If she let it loose, *that* would be worse than this. "My efforts will be for naught if there is a scene here," he said.

"Efforts?"

"The duke is very protective of his wife." It was more a diversion than an answer, but it worked.

His mother turned to gaze at the duchess. "She does look like she's about to pop out an heir."

Gavin hoped she wouldn't put it like that to the Terefords. "I want to keep on his good side."

"Are you on it?"

"Yes," Gavin replied. It was true, though it wouldn't get them to the goal his mother was pursuing.

The hired musicians began to tune up. "I have to fetch Ro... Miss Denholme for the dance," he said.

"Have to? What do you mean, have to?"

"It's part of the plan," Gavin replied, obviously not mentioning that the plan came from Rose. He walked rapidly away. The depth of his relief was surprising.

Rose was waiting for him. It seemed she had refused both Rob North and Edward Fleming in order to dance with him. These old acquaintances watched with astonishment and what might be envy as he led her out to join the set of a country dance.

Gavin had attended balls in Leeds during his school days and on later visits to friends there. He knew the steps. He could exchange light remarks when he touched hands with his partner and processed down the line. But standing opposite the radiantly transformed Rose, he felt as if he'd entered a whole new world.

The music started. The dancers saluted each other.

"Smile," said Rose. She was, beautifully.

"It is rather irritating to be *told* to smile," Gavin replied.

"You have no idea how well I know that. But it is mandatory in this case. We are giving a demonstration of amity, if you recall."

"I *do* recall." Demonstrating, pretending, he wanted to chuck it all away.

"So smile."

Grudgingly, he did so. They moved apart, turned, and came together again.

"Not as if you want to bite something," Rose said as they circled around each other.

"I *beg* your pardon."

"Not as if you'd been stuffed and mounted on a wall either."

A laugh burst from Gavin.

"That's better." She nodded up at him, smiling.

"Trophy heads don't smile," he pointed out as they skipped hand in hand down the row.

"They're dead. You aren't. And you have stopped smiling."

"The other dancers aren't grinning like lunatics."

"They do not have all eyes focused on them."

"You actually look happy here in...center stage."

Rose met his eyes. Hers were glowing. "I am. Really dancing, rather than just being taught the steps to a pianoforte, is invigorating."

"Is it?"

"Yes! Moving in time with all these others. I had no notion."

Rose was...resplendent, Gavin noted. He'd always thought her pretty, but he would not have described her as vibrantly beautiful, until tonight. Animation illuminated her.

"That's better," she said. "You finally look as if you're enjoying yourself."

"I am." He was. Her joy was contagious.

"It's great fun, isn't it?" She beamed.

Was this her natural state? And why had he never seen it before? But he had, Gavin realized. Years ago, when they and their friends had careened over the moors together. She'd been filled with a similar light in those days. And then it had dimmed. That wasn't right.

"You're frowning," she said. "What's the matter?"

Gavin restored his smile. Rose was happy now. That was the important thing. As the dance drew them apart and brought them together, Gavin realized that he was enjoying himself more than he ever had at any other ball. He could go on dancing with her, and appreciating her pleasure, forever.

But he couldn't, of course. The set ended. The couples dispersed. And Rose was surrounded by a clamor of eager partners. He hadn't been the only one to appreciate her loveliness and her scintillating glow.

Gavin was startled by a fierce desire to pull her away from them, to threaten fellows he'd known all his life, and to claim her for himself. The strength of it shook him.

He couldn't do that. He couldn't stand in a corner and glower at them either, as he'd heard Lord Byron had been wont to do. A gentleman would dance with other ladies. It was rude to leave those who wished to dance without partners. There was his pact with the duke as well. He'd promised aid. Feeling disgruntled, Gavin went off to do his duty.

Rose's father caught up with her after the third set. Her latest dance partner, an old friend from childhood days, had gone to fetch her a glass of lemonade. Rose was wondering where Mrs. Milsome had managed to procure lemons when Papa came to stand beside her. "You are creating quite a sensation," he said. He seemed more surprised than disapproving, which was a change. "Your mother says the duchess must have provided your finery."

It seemed an odd word. Rose brushed a hand down the silk of her gown and said merely, "Yes."

"You look very well."

"Thank you, Papa."

"And clearly you are doing well too. Have you spoken to the duchess about passing Yerndon over to us?"

Rose didn't want to talk about this. Ever, but particularly here in public, where his reaction would be seen. But she couldn't allow him to harbor unrealistic expectations. "The Terefords are not inclined to do that."

"The duke's reluctant, eh? Keighley's probably working on him. Telling his lies. Get the duchess to cajole her husband. He'll want to coddle her in her condition."

Rose had been having such a delightful time. Now she felt a familiar gloom try to descend.

"You should go over there." Her father gestured toward the duchess. She was sitting on a small sofa that had been brought back in to accommodate her. She had danced one dance with her husband and then settled to watch. She looked perfectly content to do so.

"I was going to dance."

"That's not important. The Keighley twins were over there talking to her. Can't let them start cutting a wheedle. Defend your position, girl." He didn't give her an actual push, but his tone was unyielding. They had gone to such lengths to present an amiable facade, Rose thought. She couldn't be seen to argue with her father. She went over to sit beside the duchess.

"You're not dancing?"

"I thought you might want company," Rose said.

"Good heavens, I have been besieged by visitors. I feel like I'm holding court."

She was rather, Rose thought. The duchess was as close as most of her neighbors would ever get to royalty.

"And I'm enjoying the maneuvers," the duchess added.

"The what?"

"Watch." She inclined her head toward her handsome husband.

Rose would have expected the duke to either join the dancing or stay at his wife's side, but he was roaming the room. He appeared to be making urbane conversation with a variety of guests, but Rose slowly noticed that he was actually herding. If her father drew anywhere near Gavin's mother, the duke drifted between them and somehow directed the flow so that they did not meet. Gavin was doing the same, she realized. She saw him bring his sisters together with dance partners when they had been heading for her mother. "Sheepdogs," said Rose, amused and impressed. The duke's maneuvers were as adroit as they were effective. She was sure no one else had noticed them.

"James doesn't want me upset," replied her companion. "He sees me as more delicate than I am. If your families weren't the ones involved, I could enjoy a good social melee."

There was that word again. Rose felt like making one of those old-fashioned gestures to ward off evil. She resisted.

"As long as I am well away at the edges, of course," the duchess went on.

A new set was forming. Edward Fleming approached the

sofa and requested a dance. Rose couldn't help looking for her father. He was deep in conversation with Mr. Milsome.

"Go and dance, Rose," said the duchess. "You were clearly enjoying it."

"I was."

"And I am very happily settled here." She gestured as if she was indeed a monarch. Rose stood and went. And for the rest of the evening, she evaded her father, using the duke as a roving shield, and she danced, growing giddy with freedom.

She was returning from the retiring room after the supper interval, when Gavin slipped from a doorway to her side. "May I have another dance?" he asked.

"Do you really want one?" Rose asked. She'd had two glasses of champagne.

"Really," he answered, his gray eyes gleaming.

She wondered how much he'd drunk. Not that he seemed the least tipsy.

They joined the set forming up. The other dancers acknowledged them with nods, and much less curiosity than they'd exhibited at the beginning of the evening. Rose's plan had worked. Their presence here together was becoming less marked.

The musicians struck up. Rose and Gavin moved through the figures of the dance, circling, touching hands, separating, coming together. The figures included one where Gavin put his arm around her waist and swung her in a giddy arc, the skirts of her amber silk gown fluttering behind them. Each time they spun, Rose grew more aware of the strength of his muscular frame, the intensity of their unison. It was as if he helped her fly. She forgot her own command to smile as they danced. This was too astonishing for practiced grins. For a time, she noticed nothing in the world but him.

Rose was breathless when the music ended, her senses whirling as if they still spun together. That had been like nothing she'd done before. When Gavin looked down at her with an arrested expression, she knew he had felt it too. Their gaze held as the other couples dispersed and the sound of chatter replaced the music. They were left alone in the center of the room—briefly, too long—before they recovered themselves and moved away. Rose took a deep breath and steadied. She caught her father's glare and decided it would be best not to talk to Papa again this evening. She didn't dare look for Lady Keighley. Fortunately an old friend approached to ask for the next dance, and she was glad to accept.

The event was winding down, carriages being called for to take best advantage of the moonlight, when Rose found herself standing with a group of young people. Directly across, Gavin gazed at her with compelling gray eyes. Rob North and Edward Fleming stood beside her. The four of them were the last unmarried remnants of their childhood gang. The others had settled down and started families and seemed to belong to a different category these days. The rest of this present group were from a younger cohort. She didn't know them well. Gavin's twin sisters, Jillian and Janet, who came to join them just then, clearly did. They leaned close to one of the girls, murmuring and glancing at Rose.

She had been feeling like a social success, and not simply

due to her borrowed finery, a new position for her. Now she felt a tremor of unease.

"Remember when we built our castle and repelled waves of invaders?" asked Rob North.

Rose smiled and nodded.

"Castle," repeated Rob's sister Bella. "What do you mean?"

Rob and Edward told the tale. Rose thought Bella North was more interested in charming Edward Fleming than in their bygone exploits.

"We should all ride out there together," said Bella when they were done. "Wouldn't that be great fun? The weather's growing warmer too." She smiled up at Edward.

He smiled back. Bella was a pretty girl, slight and blond. Edward looked ready to be charmed. "Could we even find it now?" he asked the group.

"We went there a few days ago," Rose said, thinking to be helpful to this budding romance.

"Did you?" asked Jillian Keighley.

"Really?" wondered her twin sister as if finishing the same sentence.

"Who is we?" they inquired in unison.

Their identical gazes were sharp, and Rose regretted her words. Had she thought that one evening of dancing erased years of strife? No, she'd simply abandoned thought and let herself enjoy one evening of careless gaiety. Suddenly, she felt tired.

"A foray from Yerndon," said Gavin to his sisters, allowing them to think that the Terefords might have been along. The twins didn't look convinced.

Rob looked from Rose to Gavin. "What's the place like now?"

"Still much the same." Gavin made an equivocal gesture. "A bit overgrown."

"Oh, I must see it," declared Bella. "Won't you take me?" She spoke to her brother but included Edward with a flirtatious sidelong glance.

"Would you show us the way, Gavin?" asked Rob.

"Yes, Gavin," said Jillian. "*Will* you?" Her emphasis implied more than geographical guidance. She sounded almost threatening.

"If you like," Gavin said to Rob.

Bella clapped her hands. "When shall we go? Tomorrow?"

"We could," her brother agreed. "Who's in?"

Eager voices responded. The Keighley twins were particularly vociferous, determined to be part of the expedition. Bella looked thrilled.

It might have been the sort of plan that young people with leisure time made in other places, Rose thought. Neighborhoods not shadowed by rancor. But then Rob gave Gavin one sidelong glance, Rose another. He looked as if second thoughts were occurring to him.

She wouldn't go, Rose decided. Gavin had agreed to show the way. She hadn't. It didn't matter. She preferred walking on the moor to riding, appreciating each detail of the landscape rather than covering distance. She said nothing as the arrangements were discussed.

They'd barely finished when the duke and duchess approached arm in arm. "The carriage is ready," said

Tereford. The pair smiled and made their farewells to the group.

Rose went out with them, conscious of Gavin behind her and many eyes on her back, glad to be departing in their company rather than with her glowering parents. This was probably how Cinderella had felt, she decided as she put on her cloak at the front door. *Her* glittering gown wouldn't collapse into a pile of rushes, but it would return to its rightful owner. Rose wouldn't be seen in it again.

An irrepressible inner voice piped up. Cinderella had triumphed over all adversity and married a prince. Disaster had overtaken her enemies. The tale didn't mention how satisfying that must have been.

Shocked at the idea, Rose told herself she didn't wish disaster on anyone. But she could hope for change. Tonight might have been a beginning.

Back at Yerndon, as Sue was brushing out Rose's hair, the maid said, "Remember when you were asking about young Ian?"

Rose hid a smile. The footman was only a year or so younger than Sue. "Of course."

"Well, I thought you'd want to know. He's gone sweet on that housemaid from the Keighleys. Lucy Trent. And she on him."

"I thought they were playing tricks on each other."

"Not any more, miss. Seems one sort of mischief led on to another. Lucy's taken to saying they're like Romeo and Jeannette. From enemy clans and all. Doomed. She's mooning about the place like a lost sheep. If a sheep could chatter like a magpie, that is." Sue gestured with the hairbrush.

Rose thought the garbled Shakespearean reference was more apt for her and Sir Gavin. Except, no it wasn't. Enemy clans, yes. Star-crossed love, not at all. What was wrong with her?

"Ian wouldn't have thought of being doomed," the maid went on. "His mind's on other things, if you take my meaning."

"Should I send him home?" Rose asked. She didn't want the footman to be hurt. Or to cause a scandal.

"That'd make it worse, miss. As if Lucy was right, you see. And they was pulled apart by fate." Sue seemed to be savoring the story herself. "I'm not sure what young Lucy would get up to then."

"What do you think I should do?" Rose asked.

"I dunno. I just wanted to warn you, like."

"Of what?"

Sue shook her head. "With that Lucy, might be anything."

Rose sighed. "I'll speak to Ian."

Her maid looked doubtful.

Eight

PREPARING TO RIDE OUT THE FOLLOWING AFTERNOON, Gavin was not in the best of moods. Rose had declared she didn't wish to come on the planned expedition. She'd walked away from him to go down to the kitchen and speak to a servant, and then she had disappeared onto the moors on foot so that he couldn't try to persuade her. It was no good searching for her, even if he'd had the time. She could evade him. That had been established years ago. Rose would not be found if she didn't want to be. He had to go without her. He had no choice in the matter.

He didn't like having no choice. No one likes it, pointed out an acerbic voice in his head. Do you suppose Rose does?

She'd had her way, he retorted silently. She'd gone off.

Yes, to wander alone after she'd danced so joyously at the Milsomes', responded the irritating voice.

That had been a wonderful sight to see, Gavin acknowledged as he rode down the lane from Yerndon. And an even better one to join in. He'd basked in the old glow she'd had when they were children, which returned again. Not gone but simply hidden. Given a chance, there it was—that shining spirit. Resplendent, as she ought to be.

But the curtain had come back down by this morning. At breakfast, Rose had gone back to her recent persona, self-possessed, a little distant. Not glowing. She'd always spoken her mind, Gavin thought. She wasn't the least shy about *that*. But she kept the rest covert. It had made him wonder, suddenly, what parts of himself had been eclipsed in those years since they were youths. And why should they have a pall cast over them because of this endless dispute? It wasn't fair.

Gavin met his two old friends, his sisters, and a small flock of their acquaintances at the Norths' house. It was a lovely April morning with bright sun and only a few small clouds. Winds high above sent cloud shadows racing across the moors. At ground level, the air was calmer and the sunshine warm. The landscape raised Gavin's spirits, as it always did. Whatever else was happening, a man could count on the moor.

He led the group along a braid of paths to the old site. Reaching it, they tethered the horses, and people began clambering up the hillock to the stone construction on top. Bella North had taken Edward's arm and was laughing up at him.

The twins came up on either side of Gavin. "I think she'll get him," said Jillian. They had the long skirts of their riding habits looped over their arms, Janet in deep red and Jillian in dark blue. Gavin could usually tell them apart, though most people couldn't. He didn't know exactly how, a lifetime of living together perhaps. "Who will get who?" he asked.

"Edward Fleming," replied Janet. "Bella has decided he will do."

"Do?"

"Don't pretend to be obtuse, Gavin. We know you aren't."

"Where is Miss Denholme?" asked Jillian.

"She decided not to come."

The twins looked at each other, then back at him. "We assumed she would be here, continuing to make a spectacle of herself," said Janet.

"Spectacle?" Gavin felt a stir of annoyance.

"Oh, it was obvious you enjoyed it," said Jillian. "All the gentlemen did."

"Sad to be so...blatant," said Janet.

"To feel the need to be," said Jillian.

Gavin set his jaw. "Are you going up the hill?" he asked. "Or do you prefer petty sniping down here?"

"Petty," said Jillian.

"Sniping," said Janet. "When did you become such a bore, Gavin?"

"Since he went off to visit with the nobility," said Jillian. "I suppose he's above our touch now."

"Hobnobbing with a duke. The man you used to call a soft, sneering southerner."

"An interloper and usurper," said Janet.

"I hadn't met him then," said Gavin. "I know nothing about him."

"Charmed, are you?" asked Jillian. "Most of the neighborhood seems to be."

"But we expected better of you."

"Did you?" Gavin gazed at them. They were repeating phrases they'd heard and expressing attitudes that had been drilled into them. He'd done the same once.

His sisters looked at him.

"Why don't you get angry?" asked Janet. She sounded genuinely curious now, rather than just mocking.

"What has happened to you?" wondered Jillian in the same tone.

"Do you *want* me to rail at you?" Gavin looked from one twin to the other. They gazed back, narrow-eyed.

"It shows that you care," said Jillian.

"Mama says that passionate souls who feel deeply cannot restrain their emotion," added Janet.

Part of that was true, Gavin thought. And part of it wasn't. One part gave his mother license to rage.

"Don't tell me you're becoming one of the muted people," said Jillian.

"Like Rose Denholme," added Janet.

"She isn't muted," said Gavin.

His sisters pounced.

"Isn't she?"

"How do you know that?"

"What have you been getting up to at Yerndon?"

"And at the dance last night. That was just blatant." The twins nodded at each other.

"Mamma thinks you're a turncoat."

"A craven traitor."

"Or perhaps just a bumbler."

"But you haven't bumbled like this before."

These labels stung. Gavin knew that his mother could be carried away by her rants, like an opera singer lost in an aria. Often, she didn't even remember the details of what she'd said. Still, it was difficult to hear such phrases repeated. She and the twins were his family. "That's nonsense," he said, biting off the word.

"Shall we tell Mamma you said so?" asked Jillian. She grinned at Janet. The girls waited for his response with bright eyes, enjoying the battle.

Gavin confronted his temper toe-to-toe. He could give it free rein. The twins would join him in a shouting match. They had been angling for one. His friends up the hill had seen it before, the Keighleys in full voice. Like a pack of hounds baying, Gavin thought. A short laugh burst out of him at the picture that conveyed. "Please do," he answered and walked off.

Rob waved at him from the top as he began to climb the rocks. He could feel his sisters' stares on his back. If he stopped rising to their bait, would they stop dangling it before him? Another laugh escaped him as he envisioned a great fish snapping at the hook. He was a man, not a fish. He could resist.

From the depths of a thicket on another rise some distance away, Rose spied on the riding party. She'd never done such a thing before in her life. She avoided people on the moor. She never lurked and watched them.

She wasn't certain why she was doing it now. But as she sat there, a wistful feeling came over her, and she realized she was there because of the dancing at the Milsomes'. She'd gotten a glimpse of another sort of life during the ball, one where people gathered in amity and enjoyed each other's company. Now, here was another—the younger generation on the sort of outing that might take place anywhere in the country.

She could have been with them. But if she had gone, the mood would be different, the outing less carefree. The Denholme-against-Keighley tension would have shadowed things. Gavin's sisters, not restrained by a crowd, would be ready to join battle. Their gibes would make some of the others uncomfortable, some perhaps slyly amused. Rose would be annoyed. Even more so than usual after the dance, she realized. So she didn't regret her decision to stay away. Rather, she deplored the larger circumstances as she watched the antics of old friends and bare acquaintances as if they were another sort of moorland creature.

The group seemed to be having fun. She couldn't hear their conversation, but Edward's broad gestures clearly described their childhood campaigns. Bella North listened raptly. Gavin left his sisters and climbed up the hillock. Rob balanced on the highest boulder and waved a stick, much as young Branwell Brontë had on their earlier visit.

Jillian and Janet wandered the perimeter of the hill. They would have felt obliged to twit Rose if she'd been there. Yes, obliged. As if discord was their duty. The two families taught their offspring this, along with social forms and accepted conventions—be polite and respectful except to the "enemy." From this distance, the situation seemed so ridiculous. Or from her new place outside her home, Rose saw. The arrival of the Terefords had brought perspective, showing what might have been.

The group stayed at the fort for nearly an hour, but the attractions of the place were less for adults than for imaginative children. Flirting could be done on horseback. And so they drifted down the hill to their mounts. As they rode slowly away, all their backs turned, Rose eased gently out of the thicket.

It was a slight movement, nothing to attract attention, but Gavin turned as if he sensed something. Rose saw him spot her. Or notice something curious at any rate. She'd been careless. Had she wanted him to see? Rose ducked over the lip of her hill and out of his line of sight.

She wasn't really surprised to hear hoofbeats behind her sometime later. A single animal, not a group. She had no doubt at all that it was Gavin on her trail. Rose rounded a head-high boulder and waited in its shadow. After a bit, Gavin rode into sight. He nearly went right past her motionless figure. Then at the last moment he saw her and pulled up. "I didn't know if you would let me find you," he said.

"I didn't have to." She could have slipped between the boulder and the gorse and taken a path his horse couldn't negotiate.

"I know," he said.

Because he acknowledged this, she stayed.

Gavin dismounted, looping the reins over his arm. "I will walk with you back to Yerndon."

"Whether I like it or not?"

He went as still as she had been. "No. If you tell me to go away, of course I will."

Rose held her specimen box against her chest like a shield. Not against Gavin precisely. More against the knowledge that she didn't want to order him off.

His horse nudged his shoulder, wondering why they were standing about rather than returning to its comfortable stable.

"Where have the others gone?" Rose asked.

"Back to Rob's."

"Why didn't you go too?"

"I saw you."

His tone suggested that he could not have done anything else. Unsettled, Rose walked on along the path. He fell into step at her side, trailed by his horse.

"Why were you watching us?" he asked after a while.

Rose supposed she ought to be embarrassed, but she refused to be. "I wanted to see what a commonplace social outing might look like. As one would observe foreigners."

"Foreigners? They were all well known to you. Rob and Edward wondered where you were."

"And your sisters? Did they wonder?"

His silence told Rose all she needed to know.

Gavin seemed about to say something. Then he didn't. Then he gestured at her specimen box. "Have you found anything interesting?"

"As always."

"May I see?"

She opened it. Rose never minded showing her work. If people liked it, that was pleasant. If they didn't, that showed their limitations. The point was creating a record of the life of the moor.

"Bog rosemary! That's bloomed early."

"It was in a sheltered crevice," Rose replied.

He gave the box back to her. "You must have a whole shelf of pressed specimens by now."

"More than one."

"Can there be anything new for you to find?"

"There always seems to be," Rose replied.

"Ah. Yes."

Something reverent in his tone made Rose add, "I want to know every plant and animal on the moor. I want to walk it all my life."

Gavin nodded. "Yes," he said again, with such complete understanding that Rose went on.

"Until I am old and bent, with wild white hair tossed by the wind and needing to lean on a staff."

"Gnarled and wrinkled and scaring the children," Gavin suggested.

Rose smiled. "At first perhaps," she said. "And then, for the ones who will listen, bewitching them with the tales I have to tell of the land they live on."

"An ancient sage. Regaling them with reality, not fairy stories."

"Oh, I think the things I collect *are* the fairies."

Gavin stopped and looked down at her.

"People feel something magical, and so they imagine otherworldly beings. But what could be more magical than this?" Rose gestured at the landscape around them.

"I want to leave my bones here," declared Gavin.

The sentiment, and the way he spoke it, were so exactly what Rose felt. She realized that he had tears in his eyes.

The sight was so surprising, so touching, that she was transfixed. He blinked, embarrassed perhaps. One tear escaped and ran down his cheek. Her hand came up of its own accord to catch it.

And then they flew together into an incendiary kiss, without either of them seeming to decide to do so. They were drawn together like lodestone and iron, like complementary halves of some native mystery. Rose's specimen box slipped to the ground. Her fingers twined in the hair at the nape of his neck as she gave up her lips to him.

Gavin held her like a treasure, as she deserved to be held, even as his body went up in flames. His hands slipped beneath her cloak and ran up her sides. She shivered and pressed closer. They fitted perfectly, as if crafted to be together. The kiss went on, tender, passionate, complicated, like no other in his life before.

And then the softness went out of Rose. Her palms were on his chest, pushing him away. He stepped back, frustrated and bereft.

Rose moved away from him. "That was a mad thing to do." She shook her head as if to clear it. "Again."

"Again," said Gavin with a different emphasis. Couldn't they do it again?

"Obviously not," she replied, not pretending to misunderstand.

"Why?"

"Don't pretend to be naive. With the way things stand between us?"

"Not us. Our families."

"We are not separate from our families, Gavin."

"Perhaps we could be. Maybe that's the answer. You and I…"

Rose gazed at him from an intolerable distance.

"Together," Gavin finished.

Her lovely lips turned down. "Like wars ended by the union of two noble houses?" she asked skeptically. "That seems rather grandiose. And impossible."

"You are too pessimistic."

"You have your head in the clouds. Would you take me home to your mother?" Rose asked. "She despises me."

"Not that. She…"

"She does, Gavin. And my father would knock you down if he knew what we had just done."

"He might try."

"And what? You would fight him? As you did the duke?"

"I would best your father," Gavin let slip. Which was a daft response, he knew.

"*That* would solve nothing whatsoever." She bent to pick up her specimen box. A gust of wind ruffled her hair.

Gavin's horse nudged him again. The wind tossed its mane. "There's weather coming in."

Rose nodded without looking at him.

They could agree on the forecast at least. How could they be so in harmony on the land and so divided in every other way, Gavin wondered.

A flicker of movement caught in the corner of his eye. Gavin turned and discovered that Phelps was standing on a rise some yards away, motionless, a shotgun cracked open over his arm. The man's gaze was piercing even at this distance. Meeting it, Gavin was certain that Phelps had moved just now so that Gavin would spot him and realize that Phelps had seen everything, including the kiss. Every line of the man's frame declared as much. What he thought about it—well, that was unknown.

When it was obvious that he'd been seen, Phelps ducked down and disappeared behind a clump of heather.

Rose looked back from farther along the path. "What is it?"

She hadn't seen Phelps, which was unlike her. Usually she was aware of the least flicker of movement on the moor. She must be preoccupied by what had passed between them. Gavin was glad of that, since he was in a muddle of emotion himself. He wouldn't have wanted to be in that state alone. He moved to her side, and they walked quickly along the ways they both knew well.

Phelps, Gavin was thinking. Technically, the man worked for him now, but he had been employed by the Keighleys for many years, and for much of that time he'd seen Gavin's father or mother as the one in authority. He was all too likely to tell Mamma what he'd seen. In fact, Gavin only just now remembered that his mother had suggested bringing the man, as she assigned him Lucy Trent. Phelps might have been ordered to report to her. No, of course he had been. That was probably where he went when he disappeared for long periods. And though Phelps had no knowledge of what went on inside Yerndon, now he had some explosive news to impart.

If Phelps was on his way to Keighley Manor now, there was nothing Gavin could do. But somehow he thought he wasn't. Gavin *was* in charge of the estate. Phelps wouldn't want to antagonize him openly and perhaps risk his position. So why had he shown himself?

Gavin didn't know what Phelps thought. The man was an enigmatic character, competent but not given to conversation. He might enjoy stirring up trouble. But he would most likely keep his mouth shut about this incident if Gavin commanded it. He would have to find out, as soon as he could find Phelps, which was often not an easy task.

"What is it?" Rose repeated.

He'd been silent too long. "I was just thinking."

"That never does much good."

He'd expected her to ask what he was thinking about. But Rose didn't do the expected. "Why do you say so?"

"Actions change things, not thoughts."

Gavin looked at her. Rose was marching straight ahead, her expression a bit grim. It was true. They had to do something, not just go round and round considering the difficulties of their situation. But what?

———

At dinner that evening Gavin sipped his wine and watched Rose tell her story of the day. She noticed things on the moor that he didn't. And vice versa. That was what made life interesting, Gavin thought. There was no spice in simply having one's observations and opinions echoed back. Why talk at all if that was the case?

She made a graceful gesture. The Rose who sat at the Terefords' opulent dining table was not the Rose who moved unerringly across the landscape, the intrepid one he'd recognized from their youth. This present Rose was more circumscribed, controlled. Yet neither was she the young woman he'd seen when some neighborhood encounter threatened a family confrontation. *That* Rose drew back like a wary wild creature, willing itself unseen. He'd overlooked her at times, Gavin acknowledged, but often it was because she wished it. She had a number of ways to disappear.

But this Rose tonight was newer. She was assured, interesting, warmly responsive, a Rose drawn out by the Terefords' welcoming household. Modeled on the duchess? Or merely encouraged into existence? She spoke and moved with an air of amused exploration, as if she was surprised at herself. An individual was myriad, Gavin realized. He was himself, he supposed. It was true that he felt like a different man at this relaxed table. Not the Gavin he'd worn— worn out?—in a familiar rut. An idea began to form in his brain, feeling very important. One should search for people who could bring out every part of oneself, he thought. Who could encompass them all. And one should *be* such a person as well.

Rose looked at him just then, as if she had somehow divined his thought. He was startled by the shock of recognition that stirred him as he met her blue eyes. Such depths of emotion lay in that gaze. He could look at her forever and not plumb it all. He didn't notice the duke and duchess exchanging an amused, understanding glance. Nor was he conscious of the time that passed in silence. He simply gazed at Rose until a very unusual interruption broke their intense contact.

The duke's valet came into the dining room, which was startling because this chamber was not part of the man's domain. He kept to their host's bedroom and dressing area and seemed to specialize in being utterly unobtrusive. But here he was, interrupting a meal, clearing his throat to speak. Gavin wasn't sure he'd ever heard the valet's voice up to now. "I'm sorry to disturb you, Your Grace," he said. "But something has…occurred. And I have been delegated to tell you."

"That sounds ominous," replied Tereford with a smile.

The other man didn't smile back. Gavin had never seen him do that. In this case, he looked more solemn than ever.

"Unfortunate, certainly, Your Grace." The valet cleared his throat again. "It seems that the footman Ian and the housemaid Lucy have eloped."

"What?" exclaimed Rose.

The valet glanced at her, then at Gavin before adding, "There is a note. It wasn't noticed immediately because it was placed under Lucy Trent's pillow. And some of the household were…given the impression that Lucy had gone to the village market under orders from Cook. When it became clear that no such orders had been given, the missive was discovered." He came over to the duke and held out a sheet of paper.

Tereford took it, read. "This seems a farrago of nonsense. What does it mean, 'Our forbidden love will not be denied'? Who forbade them?" He looked at the duchess, who shrugged and shook her head. "Hobbs?"

"Beyond the rules of proper behavior and their station, I have no idea, Your Grace," said the valet with a complete lack of expression.

The duchess extended her hand. He gave her the note. "Two households divided." She frowned.

"I think Lucy saw the two of them as Romeo and Juliet," said Rose. "Because she worked for the Keighleys and Ian for the Denholmes. My maid mentioned something. I spoke to Ian about taking care." She looked worried. "Oh, I hope that didn't set them off."

"They can't have gone off to poison themselves," said the duke, half rising from his chair.

"Good lord," said Gavin. He remembered the scene he'd observed at their old fort, where Lucy had declaimed a speech he'd recognized as semi-Shakespearean.

"No, I think they have gone to Gretna Green," said the duchess. She pointed at the note and read, "'We have fled to a place where the laws will let us be eternally united.' How far away is the border?"

"A hundred miles to Gretna," said Gavin.

Tereford sank back into his chair.

"How would they get there?" asked Rose.

"They must have found horses somewhere," said the duke.

"None of ours, Your Grace," the valet put in. "I inquired before I came in."

"No, they wouldn't have been allowed to take them." Tereford looked at his wife. "Shall I go after them?"

"They are not your servants," said Rose. "And their behavior is not your fault." She looked at Gavin. "We brought them here."

"And our families put the idea of enmity into their heads." She nodded.

"So do you think I should try to haul them back?" Gavin

couldn't muster much enthusiasm for the task. Why shouldn't they marry if they wished it? Also, they had several hours head start.

"Lucy will be disgraced," said Rose. She grimaced. "More than Ian will."

There was that, Gavin acknowledged.

"Once she's married much will be forgiven," said the duchess. "It's the way of these things."

"Perhaps," said Rose. She looked uncertain.

"If they wish to be together, should we separate them because of a feud in which they have no part?" asked Gavin.

The words seemed to echo in the room, or perhaps just inside his head. No, Rose was staring as if he'd shouted. "It is the way they have done it," she replied.

"I suppose they thought they had no other choice."

"Running away?" Rose's voice trembled. "Leaving everything behind? Causing a scandal."

It was as if the others in the room had dropped away. Gavin was conscious only of her. "Daring to act?" he asked. "Reaching for what they want? They can return afterward."

"Not the same," Rose murmured, very low.

Gavin admitted it with a nod. Still he added, "I say let them go." Once again he felt that the phrase trembled in the air. "And see what help we can be afterward."

"Help," Rose echoed.

He nodded again.

She looked away, said nothing more.

"We are decided then?" asked the duke. "We will not mount a pursuit?"

Gavin suppressed a start. Of course he hadn't forgotten their hosts were present.

Tereford looked around the table, gathered agreement. "Thank you, Hobbs."

The valet went out, looking disgruntled. But he generally did.

The denizens of Yerndon imagined this settled the matter. But they found, in the next few days, that they were dead wrong about that.

When news of the "star-crossed" elopement spread into the neighborhood, as it very rapidly did, the gossip was lively. But their two families absolutely erupted. A parade of messengers brought scribbled notes across the moor, a new one arriving almost before one read the previous missive. Anyone looking at them would have concluded that young Ian and Lucy had committed high treason, Gavin thought. He was berated and belittled since, for reasons his mother *could not* fathom, he had missed clear signs of betrayal and perfidy unfolding right under his nose. His mother actually wrote the word *perfidy*. Without the slightest sense of the ridiculous, it seemed. On the contrary, she appeared to relish the opportunity for an all-out tirade. To accuse him of blind idiocy, really it was too much!

From things Rose let fall, and her distressed looks, he suspected she was hearing the same sort of thing from her parents. They avoided discussing the family communications. Indeed, Gavin avoided everyone for a while after one arrived, taking the time to master his annoyance.

Their neighbors plunged into the vortex of chatter with the air of enthusiastic playgoers. Truth and even the vestige of plausibility flew out the window. The whole situation seemed worse rather than better since he and Rose had embarked on this visit. Things were getting out of hand.

Their noble hosts kindly said nothing about the blizzard of paper showering the house.

As the furor refused to die down, Gavin became conscious of a desire not to return to his childhood home. Which belonged to him now! Never? Surely not never. But no time soon. It was uncomfortable to feel that way.

The sensation was heightened by the fact that he had not been able to corner Phelps for a frank discussion of what the man had seen. He did know that Phelps hadn't reported it, because he was certain that the upheaval would have been immeasurably worse if the matter in question had been him kissing Rose, rather than Ian and Lucy eloping. If the former news got out… Gavin winced at the scenes that rose in his mind. A carriage arriving to haul Rose away. With shouting. Possibly firearms. His mother and sisters railing at him, hanging on his sleeves in a torrent of words. Fists shaken. Absurd, insulting accusations flying.

The pictures made him…angry. Hotly, stubbornly angry. And for once in his life, his temper did not seem an unreasonable response.

Nine

ON A BLUSTERY APRIL DAY THAT PROMISED A STORM
later, Rose walked on the moor and felt a precious sense of
peace descend over her. No scolding note could reach her
here. No chorus of parental blame marred the spreading
landscape. She didn't have to be embarrassed before the
Terefords, tactful and kind as they were. She might continue
wondering if she could have prevented the elopement. But
it truly seemed that efforts to separate Ian and Lucy would
have hastened matters rather than discouraged their flight.
They'd succumbed to their emotions, seized life with both
hands. Rose wondered how that might feel. The thought of
running away had begun to seem more attractive, though
impossible of course.

She rounded a turn in the path and discovered Gavin
crouched behind a stand of gorse and gazing over the top
of a rise. Rose knew there was a fox den on the other side,
and so she wasn't surprised when he signaled for silence.
Quietly, she joined him and looked down on a trio of fox
kits tumbling over each other with mock ferocity, their small
russet bodies rounded and healthy. Their mother was keeping them well fed. There were plenty of mice to be caught
out here.

The wind was in Rose's face, so no human scent alerted the kits. They leaped and played with delightful abandon. Rose felt her shoulders relax and a smile start on her face. She looked at Gavin and saw the same expression. They didn't need to speak to understand that they both loved this place and everything about it. This was a harmony they'd learned very early in life.

A hunting hawk passed overhead, riding the wind. Its predatory shadow sent the kits plunging into their den. "Well trained," murmured Gavin.

"And instinct," Rose replied.

He nodded.

Now there would have to be conversation, Rose thought. And she was so very tired of people talking at her. Or writing at her, which was similar but worse, offering no chance to correct silly assumptions. Gavin wouldn't rail or complain, but what if he brought up the not-so-small matter of the kisses? Those regretted, yearned for, astonishing kisses! Even more fraught after recent events. What could they say? What might they *do*? "I'm going to walk," she said and turned away.

To her great relief, and unexpected chagrin, he didn't follow. Rose told herself that she'd been searching for solitude, was comforted by it. But it didn't seem quite so soothing now. Do not be contradictory, she told herself. This is what you wanted. She walked, breathed, observed, and gradually regained her equilibrium.

The sound of rapid hoofbeats from a branching path ahead made her sigh and look for a place to melt into the bushes. But there was no good spot just here. So it was not to be Gavin but some stranger who interrupted her attempted idyll. Her luck was out.

Elizabeth Brontë appeared around a bend, riding one of the ponies they'd seen with the children before, kicking its sides to hurry it along. She waved frantically as she approached. "Oh please," she called. "We've lost Emily." She didn't look precocious and studious today, but rather like a frightened little girl.

"On the moor?" asked Rose.

"Yes. Papa is away for a few days, and so we came out with a picnic." Elizabeth seemed to realize how this sounded. She ducked her head.

Rose wasn't surprised that their father's absence had freed them to wander. "Come with me." She led the pony back to where she'd left Gavin and found him a little way off, untying his tethered horse. "One of the Brontë children is lost," she said.

"What happened?"

"We were going back to your fort," the girl said. "Branwell wanted to play Roman defender. Maria said we might just... But then we saw a little waterfall. And when we went to look, there was another even prettier one farther on. And another! We followed the stream to a little pond. And then Branwell fell in trying to catch a frog. Which he had been *forbidden* to do. He is very naughty."

Gavin thought he was just a lively boy, but he said, "What next?"

Elizabeth Brontë wrung her hands. "We had to pull Branwell out and try to dry him off. We didn't notice for... quite a long time that Emily had disappeared."

"Disappeared," repeated Rose, as if she thought the child might have wandered into a fairy mound.

"Emily daydreams." Elizabeth shook her head. "She doesn't even hear you calling her sometimes. Papa thinks she does it on purpose to annoy him, but…"

"She's only two years old," Rose pointed out.

The girl nodded. "She loves the moor. She said she would like to live outdoors with the rabbits and badgers."

"I hope she hasn't found badgers," murmured Rose.

Gavin agreed with a nod. Badgers were not friendly creatures. "We must go and find her." He glanced at the sky. Clouds were massed in the east. There would be rain before too long.

"Oh, will you please?" Elizabeth Brontë began to turn her pony. "I can take you to the others."

Gavin mounted his horse. When Rose raised an imperative hand, he took it and pulled her up behind him. She put her arms around his waist and pressed close, and Gavin wondered how he was to think of anything but her as they rode.

Elizabeth headed back the way she'd come. Gavin followed, holding his larger mount to the pony's pace. In the distance, thunder rumbled. He saw Elizabeth wince at the sound.

"Branwell is already soaked," Rose murmured in his ear, sending a shiver of desire through Gavin. "We must get them to shelter."

"Yes."

Their guide had stopped at the branching of two paths. She turned back to them, her face twisted with terror. "I don't remember which one it was. I've lost the way!"

"You said three waterfalls and then a pond," replied Rose.
Elizabeth nodded, biting her lower lip.

"A small pond?"

The girl nodded again.

"That way," said Rose, pointing at the left-hand path.

"How can you…"

"She knows," said Gavin. "Go on."

Clouds began to obscure the sun as they rode on.

―――――――――

They found three of the children twenty minutes later, hud-
dled together beside the small pool that Rose had recognized
from Elizabeth's description. They looked vastly relieved to
see help arrive. Branwell's lips were blue with cold. Their
other pony cropped grass nearby. Rose let go of Gavin with
a reluctance that unsettled her and slipped off the horse. "So
Emily hasn't returned?"

"We did look for her," said Charlotte. "I wanted to go farther, but Maria…"

"I didn't wish to lose another of my sisters," said the oldest
Brontë sibling. She didn't look so self-possessed today. "Papa
will be very angry," she added, near tears.

Thinking that concern would be more appropriate, Gavin
dismounted. He lifted Elizabeth from her pony, set her down
beside the others, stripped off his greatcoat, and wrapped it
around all four children. "Keep Branwell in the middle to warm
him," he said before turning to Rose. "You could use my horse
to go for help while I search." She knew every path hereabouts.

Rose glanced at the sky. "The storm will hit before I could get back. And certainly before I could fetch anyone."

Gavin scanned the horizon. She was right. And she was more likely to know where they could shelter the children out here.

"We both will look," Rose said. "She can't have gone too far. She's so small. We should walk around this place in circles."

He considered, then nodded. "I will go out fifty yards or so and move inward. You can start close by."

Rose agreed. She left her specimen box next to the children, and then began to search.

The wind tore at Rose's bonnet and cloak as she pushed through the heather. She gathered the folds of cloth close to keep them from catching on the brambles. Far-off rumbles of thunder and the heavy dampness of the air promised a tempest in a while. She moved as quickly as she could while peering under every bush and behind every stone. She feared to find Emily had fallen and hit her head. Otherwise the girl should have heard her family calling and responded by this time, no matter how dreamy she was. Except, if she was in the wrong direction, this wind would carry voices away. Perhaps Emily was forlornly calling for help into its teeth. Rose tried to move faster without overlooking any nook or cranny.

She found no small, crumpled body, only the familiar plants and small creatures of the moor. She made one circuit, and another. The wind grew stronger. On the third pass, when she scanned upward as well as down, a flutter of movement caught her eye. There, thirty feet up on top of a slender tor, was…something. Rose moved sideways, walked closer.

It was Emily. The tiny girl held her arms out like wings and faced the wind, which tossed her hair in wild tendrils. She looked far too close to the edge of the tor. How had she gotten up there? Rose didn't call out for fear of startling the little girl and making her fall. Instead, she walked around the crag, searching for a way up.

The other side was less steep. A tumble of stone formed a rough sort of stair up the side. Very rough. Rose took off her cloak and placed it on a boulder, where she would easily find it again. She weighted it down with another stone so the wind would not take it. She pulled up her skirts and tied them in a knot to free her feet for climbing. And then she began.

It wasn't easy. The wind had grown so strong that it almost seemed it might sweep her off the tor. Rocks turned under her sturdy shoes and threatened to trip her. Rose bent and used her hands to steady her steps. She kept her eyes on the path before her, resisting the temptation to peer up at Emily and make sure she was still all right. It was fortunate that she did, because three-quarters of the way up a whole slab of stone teetered under Rose. She had to lunge forward, grabbing a bush with both hands and jerking herself forward, to keep from being dumped into thin air. The slab fell back with a weighty thump. Rose rested a moment on the other side, shaking. After taking several deep breaths, she went on.

Finally, she reached the top, staggering a little as she came out into the main force of the wind on a small oval of grassy rock above the spreading moor. She walked over to Emily, knelt at her side, and put a careful arm around her. The child wasn't quite as near the edge as it had seemed from below, but close enough.

"Isn't it glorious!" Emily declared. She faced the coming storm, her arms extended, her expression entranced. Her bonnet dangled from its ribbons. Her hair was a tangled mess. She had no gloves. Rose took one of her hands. It was icy. But Emily looked ecstatic.

"A storm is coming," Rose replied. "We must go down." This isolated height would draw the lightning.

"I want to see it." Thunder growled, and Emily smiled beatifically.

Rose wondered how she was to coax this fey child off the tor. It would be best to carry her. But could she manage that with the shifting stones? She didn't think so.

She stood, keeping a hand on Emily's shoulder, and turned in a careful circle. The greater height let her see Gavin in the distance. She began to wave her free arm. It was useless to call in this gale. After several moments, he noticed her and raised a hand. Rose beckoned urgently. At once, he moved toward them.

It didn't take him long to reach the foot of the tor. He came up it with agile strength, and soon his head appeared at the edge of the crag, followed by the rest of him.

"We need to carry her down," Rose nearly shouted over the wind.

Gavin nodded and lifted Emily as if she weighed nothing at all.

The little girl squirmed in his grasp. "I want to watch the storm," she insisted.

"Not from up here," Gavin replied. He looked at Rose, then quickly away. Her skirts were still tied up, Rose realized, and her mud-spattered stockings were visible to an utterly scandalous height.

Thunder rumbled, closer. A drop of rain spotted the stone at their feet. They needed to leave this height at once, Rose thought. And she couldn't unknot her skirts until she'd descended. She made a shooing gesture at Gavin. He turned, holding the reluctant Emily, and started down.

As always, it was more difficult going down than ascending. It was harder to see where to place her feet. The wind blew loosened strands of hair across her eyes. Rose moved as quickly as care allowed. She avoided the teetering slab, but other rocks moved under her. Gavin faltered now and then too, but he kept a firm hold on Emily. A few drops of rain spattered Rose's shoulders, a promise of torrents to come.

Rose was panting a little when she reached the bottom at last. She untied her skirts and retrieved her cloak, Gavin right behind her. And then they ran back toward the other children.

They burst out of the heather by the little pool side by side. The children jumped up, happy to see Emily restored. Maria held out her arms, and Gavin handed the younger sister over.

Maria dropped her as a bolt of lightning crashed to earth not five yards away, a lance of searing light and heat. A bush burst into flame.

Rose cried out and ducked. The children shrieked. The horses plunged and squealed, yanking at their reins. They'd been tied up to a stand of heather as there were no trees nearby. The slender branches broke under their panic, and the three animals raced away. "Damn it!" shouted Gavin.

Thunder clapped. The children screamed again. "Heigh-ho!" shouted Emily from beside the pool.

In the silence that followed the strike, Rose's ears rang. The power of the storm was awe-inspiring and frightening.

"We must get to shelter," said Gavin.

Rose was roused from her shock by the sight of a curtain of rain sweeping toward them from far across the moor.

"Where shall we go?" he asked, deferring to her knowledge of the place.

Rose turned in a circle, taking into account the direction of the wind and reviewing her internal map. "This way." She herded the children before her and headed for a place she recalled from her walks.

The Brontës were chilled and dazed, except for Emily who danced excitedly around the others. Branwell was shuddering with cold. Gavin finally picked him up and carried him. Rain spit at them intermittently. The wind nearly blew Gavin's greatcoat out of Maria's hands. He stopped to put it back on, then lifted Branwell again, pulling the garment around the boy. Rose took a cloth bag from Elizabeth and carried it along.

They made it just before the storm really let loose over their heads. It was not a real cave that Rose brought them to, but rather a large horizontal crevice that ran across a low cliff facing away from the wind. The opening was head height at the front, tapering down to nothing ten feet in. She set down the cloth bag and her specimen box and helped each child up over a two-foot lip of stone into the recess. It didn't keep out all the wind, but it sheltered them from the torrent of rain that now began to pound over the moor.

Gavin set Branwell down. He'd had to bend his head to fit in the crevice. He removed his greatcoat and gave it back to Maria for the children to wrap around themselves. Then he gazed out at the pelting rain. "That will not end soon. We need a fire."

"There is some wood at the end," Rose said, pointing to the pile in a dim corner. "People use this place sometimes, so they leave it here. Shepherds and travelers. Do you have a flint and steel?"

"Yes, but no tinder," he replied. "And that wood looks a bit damp."

Elizabeth stepped forward and took a small notebook from her coat pocket. "You can use this for tinder."

"Not your stories, Elizabeth!" exclaimed Charlotte.

"We can't burn those," said Gavin, touching Rose's heart.

"I don't mind," Elizabeth replied. "It is for the greater good. The children are freezing." She spoke as if she wasn't a child herself, and visibly shivering with cold.

"It is your duty," said Maria with a nod of approval.

"Yes," said Elizabeth. She thrust the notebook at Rose.

Rose accepted it reluctantly. They really did need a fire. Branwell especially had to be warmed and his wet clothes dried. She opened the notebook to a page of tiny handwriting, not readable in the shadows of the crevice. She hesitated, then sighed and tore out the page. Ignoring a small wince from its owner, Rose began to tear the paper into thin strips. She gestured at the wood. Gavin went to fetch some.

Rose made a large, loose nest of paper toward the front of their shelter. Gavin set small sticks in a pyramid over it, and after several tries, he ignited the strips with his fire striker. The flames faltered, then caught and crackled with welcome heat. Gavin carefully fed larger pieces of wood to the fire.

"Sit between the fire and the back wall," Rose said to the children. "The rock will reflect heat. Branwell must take off his wet clothes, and we will hang them on sticks to dry."

The little boy drew his sodden garments closer.

"You can wear Sir Gavin's coat," Rose added. "Here, I will hold it up while you undress. Do you need one of your sisters to help you?"

"No," Branwell declared.

"You can't undo the buttons," said Maria.

"Yes, I can!"

Rose extended the coat like a screen, and when Branwell had managed to shed his clothes, she wrapped it around him. Gavin had already pushed some branches into cracks in the rock beside the growing fire, and she hung the small garments there to dry. The rest of the children were only damp. The flames would dry them. Outside their shelter, the rain continued to pound. Rose folded her cloak into a long pad for them to sit on.

"What will happen to our ponies?" asked Charlotte, looking worried.

"They will return to their stable," replied Rose. She realized that if Gavin's horse did the same, it would go to his home, not Yerndon. That would perplex people.

Thunder cracked nearby. Elizabeth whimpered and cowered. "I am afraid of storms," she said. "I know it is very foolish of me."

"But they're *splendid*," said Emily.

"They're *terrible*," replied Elizabeth.

The other children looked back and forth between them as if trying to decide where they came down on this issue. Thunder rumbled again, and Elizabeth moaned.

"My grandfather told me a tale," said Gavin, drawing all eyes.

He'd settled on the other side of the fire from Rose. Its light danced over the strong planes of his face. He'd removed his hat, and a lock of dark hair fell across his forehead. He looked strong and unworried and utterly dependable.

"He said thunder was the sound of giants playing tenpins," Gavin continued.

"Up in the sky?" Emily half rose as if to go and look. Maria restrained her.

"Yes." Thunder growled, and Gavin held up a hand. "There, you see. All knocked down. I expect that giant is winning."

This didn't explain the lightning, Rose noted. But she didn't say so.

"Giants like in 'Jack and the Beanstalk'?" asked Charlotte.

"He fell down and broke his head," said Branwell with grisly satisfaction. He looked very small swathed in the folds of Gavin's greatcoat.

"A different kind of giant," said Gavin. "Jollier. Fond of games."

"Do they live on clouds?" asked Emily.

"Ah, yes I expect they do." Gavin glanced at Rose. His smile warmed her as much as the fire.

"I would like to live on a cloud," the little girl added. "How can I get up there?"

"You would have to fly," said Charlotte. "But you can't."

"Unless you found a huge bird you could ride on," said Elizabeth.

"There was an old Greek horse with wings," put in Branwell. "Papa told me. Pegasus."

"That was just a story," said Maria. "It wasn't real."

"Papa showed me a picture!"

"I could climb up," Emily replied. "If I found something very tall."

Rose raised her eyebrows at Gavin. They'd already pulled Emily off a tor. She didn't need encouragement to scale other heights. "You wouldn't want to do that," he said in response.

"Why not?"

"Well, uh, it's their home, you see. And they don't like visitors. You don't just walk into people's houses, do you? Without an invitation."

"But they would *like* me!"

"No, they wouldn't," said Branwell.

"Yes, they would!"

"Wouldn't. They'd step on you like a mouse and crunch your bones." The little boy gnashed his teeth.

Emily gave him a large-eyed stare.

"Stop it," said Maria. "You are staying at home with us, of course, Emily. Papa would not allow you to go."

This seemed to settle the matter. It helped that the thunder was receding in the distance.

The rain had slackened a bit, no longer quite a torrent. If they'd had the horses, they *might* have plodded through it, Rose thought. But the children couldn't walk such a distance wet and cold. It would make them ill. They would have to wait a little and see. They were fairly comfortable for now, away from the main force of the wind and warmed by the fire. She peered at the woodpile in the corner. They would run out if they tried to spend the night here. Which they couldn't do for many reasons, though she supposed it wouldn't be a dreadful scandal because the children were with them.

"I'm thirsty," said Branwell. He struggled to his feet, holding the folds of the greatcoat around him. "I'm going to stick my head out and drink some rain."

Emily sprang up as well. "Me too."

"No—" Rose began.

"Need for that," finished Gavin. "I'll fill my hat." He upended it and stuck it out into the rain.

This roused delighted laughter. Emily, Charlotte, and Branwell went to watch the hat fill. It took some time, but after a while everyone got a drink. Gavin left his hat outside for future needs.

"I suppose it will be ruined," Rose murmured to him.

He shrugged. "It's a hat. Not on a par with the child's lost stories."

She gazed at him, wondering what had become of the man who did nothing but argue and blame.

"May we have our picnic?" Maria asked. She spoke as if she wasn't sure they would be given permission.

"Picnic?" asked Rose.

Maria pointed to the cloth bag Rose had carried into the crevice.

Rose pulled it over and untied the strings. Inside she found a loaf of bread, a wedge of cheese, napkins, and five wizened apples. "Splendid," she said. She took the food out and laid it on one of the napkins. Feeling one more item in the bag, she brought it out. There were five oatmeal raisin cookies wrapped in another napkin.

Charlotte stared at Maria. "You brought sweets?" she asked in astonishment.

"Hurrah!" exclaimed Branwell.

Gavin picked up the bread and began to cut it with his pocketknife. As he handed out slices to the children, joking about their unevenness, Rose marveled again at the difference in him. She could not have imagined this scene just a month ago.

Sitting by the fire munching was comforting, almost as if this was a picnic in truth. The steady rain was like a murmuring curtain before their shelter, shutting out the world.

"We must calculate how to divide five apples and five cookies into seven portions," Maria declared after a while.

"Not mathematics," groaned Charlotte.

"Every occurrence is an opportunity for learning," Maria replied with the air of one repeating an axiom.

Branwell glowered. Emily stared out at the rain as if she hadn't even heard. Charlotte sighed deeply. "We could cut them all in half," Charlotte said.

"How many pieces would that give us?" Maria asked her.

"Um, ten." Charlotte frowned. "That's three left over."

"I would eat those," offered Branwell.

"That would not be fair," said Maria.

Rose started to say that she did not require any, but she happened to meet Gavin's gaze just then and was caught by the twinkling fascination she saw there.

"If we divide each apple and each cookie into thirds, we will have fifteen pieces of fruit and of sweets," said Elizabeth. "Each of us may eat two of both. The single piece left over…"

"Should go to you for your successful calculations," said Maria. She looked at her sisters and brother and received nods of approval. Except from Emily, who was easing one finger out into the rain, pulling it back and licking it, and then repeating the process.

The proposed dissections were accordingly done by Gavin, closely supervised by Charlotte and Branwell. Maria doled out the servings, and everyone ate their dessert. They had another round of drinks from Gavin's hat as well.

Branwell's clothes dried out, and he resumed them behind the greatcoat screen. Maria had to assist him this time. Putting on was more challenging than taking off. The oldest Brontë child was looking anxious about the situation, and she seemed more so when Elizabeth bent to whisper to her a bit later. They frowned at each other, looked around the shelter, looked at the rain, and grimaced. Rose was about to ask what was wrong when Gavin stood up. "I believe we need to extend our domain," he said. "My coat will be required again."

The children had all been wrapped in it once more. They shifted and handed it over. Gavin walked along the crevice to the far end. He had already moved all the wood to a spot nearer the fire. Now he bent to pick up a handful of the small stones that littered the floor here. He pushed the collar of his coat into a narrow crack in the ceiling and wedged it tight with pebbles. Extending this process to the shoulders and lapels, he created a barrier, the greatcoat hanging like a cur- tain across the end of the space. "This will be our privy," he said, pulling it back, gesturing at the other side, letting it fall, and smiling as if nothing could be more commonplace.

Elizabeth burst into tears.

For the rest of her life, Rose would count that moment as the one when she knew she was in love with Gavin Keighley. Her view of him had been changing, true. He had revealed unsuspected depths and facets. His kisses had made her dizzy with desire. But this act of considerate tenderness, done without anyone asking, conquered her.

He came back to the fire, and Elizabeth slipped off to be the first to take advantage of the new arrangement. The hiss of the rain covered any sounds from their improvised facili- ties. "How did you know?" Rose murmured.

"I am nearly ten years older than my sisters," Gavin said. "I have some idea of how to care for children."

And others as well, Rose noted. Care was what he did, though she hadn't seen it properly for years. Their families' dispute had distorted her perceptions and all their inter-actions. Rose sat quite still, grappling with a whirl of emo-tion. Why had she listened to all that spite when she'd been acquainted with him as a child? She'd known he wasn't some cardboard demon. She should have objected! Despite the battles that would have filled her home if she had. But one took on opinions from parents. Until the time came to decide for oneself. Perhaps it should have been sooner, but at least it had finally arrived.

The other children made use of the rustic privy in turn, then settled back on top of Rose's cloak. They looked quite contented. Charlotte began to create a tiny cairn with pebbles.

Gavin came to sit beside Rose. "We're running low on wood," he said quietly.

Rose nodded.

"And the rain doesn't seem likely to stop."

"No." The violent storm had passed, but the rain remained steady and heavy. The day was dark and would soon descend into night.

"How far do you make it to Yerndon?" Gavin asked. "Or some other nearer house?"

"With the way we rode, five miles to Yerndon. And no one nearer than that. Unless perhaps a shepherd's hut."

Gavin nodded agreement. "I thought so too. A shepherd would have no mounts for the children."

"No."

"I could walk to Yerndon in an hour or so."

Rose supposed she ought to urge him to go, but she had to tell the truth. "Not in this." She gestured at the rain. "It would be difficult to find your way. We are off the pathways. And it would be even harder to get back here in the dark."

"Yes."

"The Terefords may send out searchers eventually. Phelps might find us. He knows the moors."

Gavin gave Rose an odd look.

"But the duchess is so sensible," Rose added. "She may just assume we took shelter somewhere."

"They must be looking for the children," Gavin said.

"I'm sure they're growing frantic. But Haworth is even farther off. We rode away from there."

Gavin looked out at the rain. "I will leave at first light and fetch help."

Rose nodded. It was the sensible plan. The weather might have cleared by then. And so they would spend the night in this place together.

Ten

Sitting by the side of their small fire, leaning back against the slanting stone of the crevice, Gavin felt an odd combination of contentment and restlessness. The shelter had grown fairly warm. The back reflected the heat of the flames as they had planned. The children were sitting or lying between him and Rose at the other end of the row. Emily had collapsed into sleep like a worn-out puppy or kitten. She'd shown no sign of guilt for causing this misadventure. Indeed, she and Branwell seemed to be having a splendid time. The older girls were more concerned.

It occurred to Gavin that groups like this had sat together, perhaps in this very spot, out of the rain, across years and years of history. Hundreds, thousands of years, if he remembered correctly. There were remains of ancient people on the moor. He and his friends had tried to dig into a barrow once, until Alan scared them off with tales of "ghost wights." Whatever a wight might be. Sheltering here, making fire, caring for children, these things had happened over and over. Gavin felt as if he was staring down a bottomless well into the depths of time. It was disorienting.

His gaze caught on Rose as she bent to add a bit of wood

to the flames. His mother and sisters always sneered at her, the dull and dowdy Rose Denholme, the eccentric collector of plants, the awkward outsider. But she wasn't like that at all. He'd known that once upon a time, and yet had lost track of it under his mother's incessant criticism. Now he was recovering the lost knowledge of his past. Rose was quick, smarter than any of them, Gavin thought. She was also lovely and passionate. When he'd held her in his arms…

Heat ran through him, as if the fire had suddenly roared up. Rose was delectable, and he wanted her, more than he could remember wanting anything else in his life.

She looked up at him, as if his thought had reached her. Their eyes locked. She received his gaze freely and fully. She even gave a small nod, agreeing to…what? They were here, together, in the night.

With five small children in their care.

A man could not explode, Gavin told himself. He was not a cannonball or an incendiary bomb. But right at this moment, he didn't know how to contain his longings. "I'm going to look for more wood," he said.

"Your clothes will be soaked," Rose replied.

He'd want to rip them off. Well, so he would, damn it. "I don't intend to wear them."

"What?"

"I'll leave them here," Gavin told her. "To be dry when I finish."

Rose's mouth fell a little open. Those parted lips! When she moistened the lower one with the tip of her tongue, Gavin sprang to his feet.

"I can help," declared Branwell, starting to remove his small coat.

"No," Gavin replied. "You must stay here and watch over the ladies."

His eldest sister, Maria, looked indignant.

"You won't be able to see much in the dark," Rose said, her voice a little choked.

"Neither will you," quipped Gavin, pleased to have flustered her. He rose and walked behind his hanging greatcoat, tearing at his neckcloth as he moved.

He sat on the stone to pull off his boots, then rose and shed coat, shirt, riding breeches, stockings, and drawers. He was too roused up to feel the chill.

After a brief consideration, he put his boots back on. He couldn't walk through the dark, over rough ground, barefoot. Then he paused a moment to smile at the picture he must make—naked except for his footwear.

He stepped down from the crevice into the rain. The cold droplets pelting his body tamped down the inner fire. It was a bracing sensation. Gavin laughed quietly. He hadn't spent the night on the moor in years. This was something a bit more piquant than those youthful expeditions.

He took a careful step and then another. The fire behind him threw a little light on the bushes. Rain soaked every inch of him. Proceeding slowly to let his eyes adjust to the dark, he moved along the cliff. He'd remembered seeing a downed birch tree not far from its upper end when they arrived.

The crevice dwindled down to nothing. The stone escarpment dipped into the earth, no longer a guide. Gavin narrowed his eyes against the rain and turned from side to side. Catching a pale glimmer in the corner of his eye, he shifted carefully along the rocky ground and after a while found the birch. It had broken off near its base. A few shreds held the trunk up off the ground, so it had not rotted. He took hold and pulled the trunk free.

Turning, he found the light of the fire and started toward it, dragging the small tree behind him. It caught briefly on a bush. He jerked it loose. And then he was approaching the firelit part of the crevice. Rose and the children looked like a painting by Rembrandt, arranged in a row with the firelight gilding their faces.

Gavin doubted they could see more than a pale figure with their fire-dazzled eyes, but he kept the branches between himself and embarrassment. He pushed the birch trunk onto the lip of the crevice and then fed it along to the back. Rose took hold and helped it along, pulling the tree well in.

Slipping back from the light, Gavin returned to the curtained end of the crevice. He used his neckcloth to dry off a bit before redonning his clothes. With a last rub at his wet hair, he pushed back the greatcoat screen and joined the others. He felt Rose's eyes on him as he emerged.

"How did you cut down a tree?" asked Branwell.

"It was already broken," Gavin replied. He edged past the others to the birch. Putting one foot on the upper trunk, he pulled and broke off the slender upper part with its crown of thin leafless branches. He set this aside and lifted the rest of the tree, placing the middle carefully on their fire, so that the wet bark didn't douse the flames. "We can push the ends inward as it burns," he said. "It should last the night."

Rose nodded.

He started to sit down beside her. But that wouldn't be wise. To be so close would be to yearn to touch, and he could not. Gavin returned to his former place flanking the children.

Emily slept with utter abandon. Branwell's eyelids were drooping, and Charlotte had curled up on Rose's cloak ready to drop off. The two oldest Brontës sat close together, their expressions anxious. "I suppose people have been looking for us," said Maria.

"Tabitha probably went to the village for help," said Elizabeth. "I hope worry does not make Mama worse."

Her sister winced.

"Perhaps they didn't tell her," Elizabeth added. Neither girl looked convinced of that.

"Papa will say I have been wickedly heedless," said Maria. Her shoulders drooped. "And I *was*. I know that Emily is likely to wander off in a daydream."

"Branwell fell in the stream," said Elizabeth.

"That too!" Maria answered. She took it as another criticism, though Gavin thought it had been meant to excuse her.

"No harm has been done," said Rose. "We will see you safely home."

"I failed in my duty to watch over the children," replied Maria.

Too heavy a duty for a child of her years, Gavin thought. "This is really no great matter," he said. "My friends and I had many more serious mishaps when we were young.

Youngsters here range over the moor. I will tell your father so." He saw Rose looking at him and gave her a half shrug. It was true that children this age did not go wandering. And they might have been hurt if they'd been caught out alone in the storm. But he wanted to lift some of the weight from the little girl's spirit.

Maria did seem a little comforted, though she said, "I shall be more careful in the future."

"We all begged you to let us go out for a whole day," said Elizabeth.

"And I shan't listen again."

With this the older two lay down, and in a few minutes all the children were sleeping. Fatigue made the rock floor comfortable enough, Gavin supposed. He listened to their even breathing, the crackling of the fire, and the hiss of rain, becoming more and more conscious of Rose a few feet away. Their silence seemed to make her more present rather than less.

"I've never been out on the moor all night," she said softly after a while. "I used to envy you and the other boys when you did it."

She wouldn't have been allowed, Gavin thought. He remembered how it had been. The scattering of girls in their group of youthful adventurers had disappeared one by one as they passed into their teens. A while later, they'd reemerged, like butterflies, in long skirts with their hair up. He'd simply accepted that. He hadn't considered what they missed.

"It's fine but a little... Not as wild as I expected." She sounded disappointed.

"In this way, with a fire," Gavin replied. "It's like being in a house with walls of light."

"Walls?" She looked around.

"The firelight cuts one off from the moor."

She gazed out into the darkness, nodding.

"But without a fire, it's a very different thing." He thought back to those camps. "We would go out before sunset and find a good spot. On a hillock, say, or even the top of a tor. Wrap in a blanket and let the darkness fall. Your eyes become accustomed after a while, and you can see a good deal by starlight. The animals out about their business. Owls hunting."

"But what about?" Rose gestured at the rain.

"Well, we didn't venture out in any storms. A fair night is best, of course. And a full moon even better." Gavin smiled at her.

Rose smiled back. "I would like to see that."

Gavin's heart beat faster. He started to say that he would take her out for a night on the moor when next the moon was full, but then realized he couldn't do that. Tonight was as close as they would come to such an expedition. And when her parents learned she'd been out here... He sighed.

Rose looked away. Emily muttered in her sleep and turned over. The others softly breathed. "They are such unusual children," Rose said quietly. "I wonder what they will become."

"Something interesting, I suspect," Gavin replied.

"I have no doubt. It is an interesting household."

"Young Branwell with four sisters..."

"Five. There's a baby at home."

"Oh yes. Five sisters! He will have a time of it."

"A time?" Rose repeated with raised brows.

"Some sort of time. I can't quite imagine. Two sisters are enough for me."

Rose started to speak, then appeared to change her mind.

Noticing that the birch trunk was burned through, Gavin pushed at the end nearest him, moving another section into the flames.

Emily suddenly sat up. "Scratching at the windows," she said. Her eyes were open but vacant. Gavin didn't think she was fully awake. "In," she said. "Let me in."

"It's all right," Gavin said, keeping his voice low but decisive. "We are keeping watch. You are quite safe."

Emily let out a deep sigh and sank back down. Her eyes closed. She might never have moved.

They were silent for a while after that.

She had never felt safer, Rose realized. What an odd thing that was. She was miles from home, with five children in her charge and no means of transporting them. She ached a bit from sitting so long on stone. She was hungry. Their shared picnic seemed a long time ago. And yet she wasn't worried. Indeed, she was…elated. Because of Gavin Keighley. She glanced at him and found him looking back. His eyes seemed full of messages. She could imagine some of them, but she couldn't be sure. They had things to say, she thought. Not here and now, but…soon. It needed to be soon. Until then she had better look away. "I think the rain is less," she said.

"Maybe a little. It could clear off by morning."

Rose leaned back against the wall. Maria stirred, stretched, and rose to go behind the greatcoat screen. When she returned, she seemed disinclined to sleep again. No, now was not the time for important conversations, Rose thought. She smiled at Maria to reassure her. The fire and the rain kept up their antiphonal melody. At some point in the deep night, Rose sank into slumber.

When she woke, the sky was lightening and Gavin stood at the opening of the crevice. The rain had eased a bit. It was a drizzle now rather than a storm. He turned when she moved. "I will go and bring back horses," he said.

She nodded, blinking away sleep and working stiff muscles.

"What is the quickest route from here, do you think?" He always acknowledged her familiarity with the moors. He didn't make a rivalry of it.

Rose gathered her thoughts and drew the paths in the thin layer of ash on the floor of the crevice.

"Yes, I see," he replied.

When they explained what he meant to do, the children insisted he take the greatcoat. Since it had served its function, and Rose thought the little girls would be more comfortable with her anyhow, she joined in their urging. Gavin took it down and put it on. He insisted on leaving his hat so that they would have drinking water. He bent and stepped down from the crevice into the rain. "As soon as I can," he said to Rose. With a nod, he strode away.

"He'll find help," said Charlotte Brontë.

"Yes, he will," Rose replied without a trace of doubt.

"I wish we had muffins," said Branwell, rubbing his eyes. "Or even porridge."

And a cup of hot tea, Rose thought wistfully. "It won't be long."

The rain soon soaked Gavin. The drops falling on the top of his head and running through his hair and down his face felt strange. The skirts of his greatcoat grew heavy with water.

Yerndon was closest, and he moved along the route Rose had outlined as quickly as he could. In daylight he could find his way without trouble. As she'd said, it would have been another story at night.

Tereford would let him have horses. The children would have to ride in the rain, which was not ideal, but no vehicle could reach them where they were. He would ask the duchess for heavy cloaks as well.

Gavin strode along at his best pace, and at last Yerndon loomed up through the rain. He came out near the stables, and as he rounded the corner of the building, he came upon Phelps leaning in the doorway gazing out over the moor. The man's eyes showed a flicker of surprise. He looked Gavin up and down, taking in his sodden state. Questions were obvious in his expression.

This was not ideal. On the other hand, Gavin needed to deal with Phelps. It would just have to be quick. "Did my horse return here?" he asked.

Phelps shook his head.

"He was spooked by lightning," Gavin added.

"Ha. Likely headed for the stable he knows best then," the man suggested.

And thus would require an explanation to his mother,

Gavin thought. Not that he could have avoided the topic once the story got out.

"Miss Denholme's not with you?" Phelps asked.

She obviously wasn't. And she was. It was too bad Phelps had caught sight of that kiss.

"When you both went missing, I wondered if you might have run off together, like Lucy Trent and that young footman."

This was open insolence. "What did you say?"

"After what I seen the other day," Phelps added.

"Which was none of your affair," replied Gavin.

"It weren't what you'd call private."

"I would call it exactly that."

Phelps shrugged. "It's no matter to me," he said. "But her ladyship does ask for news. Likes to hear all that's going on in the neighborhood."

"I didn't take you for a talebearer," said Gavin coldly. He fixed the man with a hard gaze.

"The thing is, I'm no manner of use here," Phelps replied. "It'd be best if I go along home and see to my proper work."

"And keep your mouth shut."

"If I was back there, I'd be too busy to be talking."

Gavin nodded. It was a clumsy attempt at blackmail, but he was glad for Phelps to go. "Fine. But before you leave, we must ride out and fetch the Brontë children. They were lost in the storm, and I sheltered with them last night. Ready four horses. I must speak to the duke." He turned his back on Phelps and went to the house.

Gavin found the Terefords together in the parlor. The duchess exclaimed over his drenched state. "What has happened?" she asked. "We thought you and Miss Denholme must have gone to a neighbor in the storm."

"We were about to send out inquiries," said the duke.

He told them the story. "I hoped you might lend some cloaks to keep the rain off the children."

"Of course."

The duke rose. "I'll see to it. And of course you must take any of the horses."

"Change into dry clothes before you go out again," the duchess said to Gavin. "You mustn't make yourself ill."

Though he was driven to rush, Gavin took her advice. He also pulled out a thick wool cloak that shed water fairly well. He could shelter the two smallest Brontës under it if they rode before him.

Downstairs, he found four more heavy cloaks waiting. The duke wore one of them. "You needn't come," Gavin told him.

"I wish to."

In the stable, Phelps and the grooms had horses ready. Since Tereford would be along, Gavin told Phelps to remain behind. "You can pack up your things and be off as soon as you like," he told him in a low voice.

They mounted up and rode out into the rain, which continued at a lesser rate. Gavin's cloak helped but didn't keep off all the damp.

The journey was quicker on horseback with the landmarks Gavin had noted as he walked. They reached the crevice before noon. The children jumped up and cheered when they appeared at its front edge.

One by one they were lifted to the saddles. Gavin took

Branwell and Emily, wrapping his cloak around them. They peeked out of the folds like baby birds in the nest. The duke took Charlotte. Maria rode on her own. Rose dowsed the fire with water from Gavin's never-to-be-the-same hat. Then she donned her own wool cloak, mounted from the lip of rock, and set Elizabeth before her.

They rode first to Haworth parsonage, where they found the Brontë household frantic with worry. The ponies had indeed returned there without their riders, and the servants had been out searching the area all night. They greeted the children with glad cries of relief and carried them off in a cacophony of chatter as all the young ones tried to recount their adventure at once.

Of course they would tell the whole tale. Now that the children were home and safe, Gavin realized the story couldn't be kept secret. And it would likely be garbled as it spread. He and Rose would certainly feature in the explosion of gossip that followed. He noticed that Rose had the hood of her cloak up and was keeping in the background. How could he shield her from what was to come? Just now he couldn't think of a way.

The three of them rode back to Yerndon, where Gavin discovered that Phelps had gone. The duchess had hot drinks to welcome them, along with a crackling fire. Rose disappeared into her bedchamber almost at once. A few minutes later, the duchess went upstairs as well. Gavin clasped his hands around his warm cup and wished he was back in the shelter on the moor.

———————

Rose wasn't surprised when the duchess arrived at her bedroom door. Now that the excitement was over and the children safe, there were other things to deal with. She'd been out all night with a man. They hadn't been alone, but her confidence in that protection was waning. Word was no doubt flying around the neighborhood. It might already have reached her parents. On top of Ian's elopement, this was more excitement than this place had seen in years.

The duchess came in.

"I don't see what else I could have done," Rose said before her hostess could speak. "I went out walking. *Alone.*" Just looking for a bit of peace, Rose added silently, and with a strong sense of irony. "I encountered Sir Gavin. Briefly." And did *not* kiss him again, she added silently. She wouldn't be granted any credit for *that.* "I was going on my way, *alone,* when Elizabeth Brontë came riding up and said Emily was missing and begged for help."

The duchess sat down in the armchair by the fire. She said nothing.

"I suppose I could have let Gavin go with her and come back to fetch the others. But we wouldn't have known where they were." And without Rose, Elizabeth wouldn't have found her way back to her siblings. Also, it wouldn't have felt right to send the girl off alone with Gavin. And the truth was, Rose had wanted to go with them.

"You may say I should not have been out walking on my own at all." Her mother certainly would have. Rose sat on the bed, reaction to the end of the adventure washing over her. "But I was."

"And so you were in place to do a good deed," the duchess said.

"And now I will pay for it," Rose replied. She was relieved not to be scolded, but she felt very tired suddenly.

"There will be talk."

A humorless laugh escaped Rose.

"But I think Maria Brontë is of an age and level of understanding to assure people that there was no impropriety. We will simply be surprised that anyone might imagine there had been." The duchess raised her golden eyebrows and looked haughtily astonished.

Rose laughed again, more naturally. She was filled with gratitude for this unusual woman. If only the duchess was the chief authority in her life. "That won't matter to my parents. They will only care that I was with Gavin." Rose grimaced. "They will order me home, I expect. In disgrace of some kind or another, no matter what Maria says."

"But if they act as if you had done wrong…"

"I know," Rose put in. "Everyone will assume there must be something to it. But this enmity with the Keighleys always takes over. Everything! In the stupidest way."

The duchess shook her head. "So you don't wish to go home?"

"No!" Surprised by her own vehemence, Rose blinked. "I wish I never had to." It was a melancholy realization.

"Sir Gavin has said something similar to James," the duchess told her.

"He has?" Rose blinked. "But he is the owner of his house."

"Not the only inhabitant, however."

Rose nodded. Lady Keighley would be raging about their rescue of the Brontës. She too would care more about their joint action than for the children's fate. "Why can't there be an end to this stupid feud?"

"Sir Gavin gave James the idea that he is happier here," the duchess went on.

"Because you make a real home," Rose replied with sincere admiration.

Her hostess smiled. "Thank you. I believe your presence has been important to Sir Gavin's feelings."

"Mine?"

"Yes."

"He said that?"

"It is my observation." The duchess's blue eyes twinkled. "I am rather good at noticing things."

It was almost as if she knew about the kisses. Which she couldn't, of course.

"It seems to me that you are fond of each other."

Under the other woman's steady gaze, Rose admitted it. She was more than fond. She cared deeply for Gavin. If he felt the same... She was shaken by a sense of danger. "We can't be."

"No?"

"Our families would never permit..." Anything. She didn't have words for the opposition that would erupt.

"Would you let that stand between you and happiness?" asked the duchess.

"I wouldn't!" Rose exclaimed defiantly. "Except..." Her father held the purse strings and authority over her in the eyes of society. And she simply couldn't run off the way Lucy and Ian had. She didn't want to marry that way. Also, nobody had asked her to. What might she dare if…someone did?

"We must see what can be managed."

It was easy for the duchess, a happily married noble-woman, to say such things. Rose smiled politely and wished she was back out on the moors with her beloved landscape around her.

Eleven

"IT IS MY OPINION THAT THERE IS NOT ENOUGH ENTER-tainment available for the inhabitants of this neighborhood," said the Duke of Tereford to his wife the following day. Water dripped at the windows of Yerndon Manor. The April day offered not waving daffodils but damp and fog. They sat cozily in the parlor together, however, with a pot of tea and a plate of scones. Their guests had retreated to their respective rooms after another spate of familial notes, which had been extended rants, by report. "I believe this feud lends excitement to their mundane routine," he added. "With no plays to attend. No local assemblies. Rather long distances to make calls."

"I think you may be right," said the duchess. "It is a rather lowering reflection that people will take pleasure in fighting with each other."

"Perhaps not pleasure so much as stimulation," he replied. "They seem to find it as exciting as a bare-knuckle boxing bout."

His wife made a face at the comparison. "Our guests' parents seem such irascible people. The Reverend Brontë too. His note of 'gratitude' for the recovery of his children was the most grudging thing."

"Do you think our houseguests have been ordered home?"

"I suspect so, as if they were errant children themselves."

"And yet they don't seem to be going," the duke pointed out.

"They don't want to."

"We cannot keep Miss Denholme against her father's wishes."

"We are not keeping her," the duchess said. "She is of age. It is her decision."

Her husband raised one dark brow.

"And yet still under her father's authority as far as society is concerned," she acknowledged with a sigh.

"I'm not certain why the Denholmes and Keighleys haven't arrive in force to haul their offspring away. It seems like something they would do."

"They're awed by your rank," said the duchess.

"And the setdown you administered to those twins," he replied.

Her smile was half-hearted. "Perhaps." The duchess was surrounded by letters and documents that had come in a packet from London, full of news of friends and matters of business that required attention. She picked up a fat document and put it down again.

"I will deal with those," said the duke.

"Yes, all right."

"Not even a mild protest? Your spirits seem low, Cecelia."

"I do miss London," she admitted. "I will never be a lover of the moor. The rain seems somehow…bleaker here."

"Not to be repetitive, but we can set off for home whenever you give the word."

"I think I am ready to give it, James." She gestured at the papers. "Some of this can only be dealt with in town. But even more..."

"Friends. Shops. A softer springtime."

"Yes."

"And I would very much like to settle you in Tereford House, with the doctor nearby."

"I feel quite well."

"Which is splendid. Though you have admitted that you are more tired than you are accustomed to being."

"Yes."

"And a long journey by coach..."

She acknowledged the point with a nod.

"Shall I make the arrangements?" he asked hopefully.

"I would like that." The duchess looked regretful. "But how can we leave our new friends caught in their dilemma?"

"Dilemma?"

The duchess gave him an impatient look "You have talked to Sir Gavin, I to Rose. They are clearly enamored with each other."

"Well on the way to being, yes. But hampered by what their families have taught them."

"Pounded into their heads, you mean."

The duke nodded.

"I wish we could do something. It is so silly."

"I did have an idea."

"What?"

He explained. He was barely halfway through his plan when the duchess began to smile.

"Amused?" he said.

"That is outrageous, James."

"Well, yes. A bit."

"But I was mainly smiling because you took the time to think of it on your own. With no prompting from me. It was very kind of you."

He half shrugged, almost shy. "Do you want to suggest it to them?"

She thought a moment, then nodded. "But whatever will they think? Or do?"

"That is up to them, of course."

The duchess bit her lower lip in contemplation.

"You could speak to Miss Denholme and I to Sir Gavin?"

"They will refuse," she concluded. "They'll think we've gone mad."

"Perhaps."

The duchess shook her head. "I think they will, James. With all the weight of family history on them?"

"But if they had an escape?"

"I don't know."

"Well, it is up to them. And we will have done all we can to help. We will go home with a clear conscience." Again, he raised one eyebrow to inquire whether this was enough.

"I suppose you're right."

"Just occasionally I am," he teased.

"Quite often really, James," she replied with another lovely smile.

Before they could communicate his plan, word came that Ian and Lucy had returned from Scotland, duly married and quite pleased with themselves. An old uncle of Lucy's was taking them in on his farm. He would teach Ian to run it and eventually pass it along to them. "And they will settle down to live happily ever after," the duchess suggested to Rose when they heard this latest bit of news.

"I hope they do," Rose replied. She wondered if farm life would satisfy Lucy's love of drama. But she could do nothing about that. They were fortunate to have a relative to turn to. She certainly felt the lack of any sympathetic family just now. "The farm is a ways off. And I believe I have convinced my parents that making trouble for Ian is beneath them. At least, I had before..." She waved a hand to encompass the current fuss.

"Oh, good."

"Is it? Why should they have considered doing so? Over Ian's choice of a wife? A respectable girl of his own rank and station." Rose bit back further complaints. She was feeling battered by her family. The rescue of the Brontë children had exposed a level of bile and pettiness that depressed her spirits. She wanted to admire her parents. Their behavior was making that difficult. Worse, she would have to go home soon. She couldn't keep dodging their demands for her return. That would anger them further and put the Terefords in an awkward position.

"Indeed," said the duchess. After a pause, she added, "I wanted to talk to you about something."

Her tone made Rose perk up her ears.

"It is time for us to go back to London. We want to be home well before the child is born."

"Of course." Rose hoped she hid the way her heart sank at the idea of losing her new friend Cecelia. Naturally they wanted to be at home for the birth, and naturally they wanted to leave this contentious place. Who wouldn't?

"We have mainly set Yerndon to rights."

"You have done very well." They would find a tenant from town, Rose supposed. Some stranger would come to live in this house where she had been…so surprisingly happy. Perhaps it would be a very pleasant and interesting family, she told herself. But her parents would only resent them. Reason seemed to have flown out the window in recent days.

"We are leaving the day after tomorrow."

So soon? Rose exclaimed silently. She nodded. "I have enjoyed my visit with you very much. Thank you for inviting me." She would have to begin packing her things. Guests did not stay on after their hosts departed.

"We will go to Leeds first to reach the main road south."

"Yes." That was the most efficient route, though Rose was not certain why the duchess was telling her this.

"And we had an idea. Or James did, to give proper credit."

She proceeded to lay out a plan that made Rose's eyes grow wider and wider. By the end, her mind was reeling.

At the close of their conversation the duchess led a dazed Rose to a parlor at the back of the house. They hadn't been using this room, but today a bright fire burned on the hearth. The duke escorted Gavin into the room on their heels. Then the Terefords walked out together, shutting the door firmly behind them.

Rose stared at Gavin. He stared back, looking as startled as she felt. "Did the duke tell you?" she asked.

At the same moment, he asked, "Did she tell you?"

"Yes," they said in unison.

They stared a bit more.

"It is out of the question, of course," Rose said finally. She heard her voice rise at the end, as if this was a query.

He didn't reply.

Rose wondered if she looked as stunned as he did. She wondered if he felt anything like the mixture of astonishment and uncertainty and...ridiculous, tremulous hope that roiled in her.

"Our families would..."

She threw up her hands. "Can you imagine the uproar?"

"It would be ten times worse than it is now."

"More!"

"But." Gavin looked down then up to meet her eyes. "We wouldn't be with them," he added slowly.

She wouldn't have to go home, Rose thought. Sad that the idea should draw her.

"Also, there would be no more point of contention," he added.

"Over Yerndon."

"Yes. The...issue would be resolved."

Was he actually considering the Terefords' mad plan? Rose couldn't decipher his tone. Did she want him in favor? She wanted. Intensely. What? "That's not a reason to take such a mad step," she pointed out.

"No." He gazed at her again.

"We would have to have other reasons," Rose went on. He must know that. "For *ourselves*."

"Yes. And that is the crux of the matter." He moved a bit closer to her. "When we first came to stay here, we made a bargain."

"To pretend to get along," Rose replied.

"But pretending has led to reality, wouldn't you say? We do get along."

The phrase seemed pallid to Rose. *Get along* sounded like something one would say to a recalcitrant horse.

"Don't we?"

Was that a tinge of anxiety in his tone? Did she dare hope so? She couldn't seem to find words.

"This visit has certainly changed the way I look at you."

"You look at me as if I was a puzzling oddity," she said.

"No." He moved closer still. "As if you were a marvelous surprise."

He was riveting, powerful. He smelled intoxicatingly masculine, just as he had those other times when they had...

"We could change everything," he said.

"Things should be changed." Her voice wavered. There was no doubt about that. Just about other factors. The ones that truly mattered. The ones that buzzed in her blood and filled her heart. Rose found she'd taken a step, raised her chin, and offered her lips.

There was no hesitation in the way he took them. His arms slid around her and pulled her close. Her senses whirled as their bodies pressed together and his mouth tantalized her.

She couldn't think. She could only feel. She loved him. He... liked her? He found her a marvelous surprise. What did that mean? Was it enough? He certainly liked kissing her. She had no doubt about that. And she felt she belonged in his arms. Could she throw caution to the winds, take what she wanted, and leave the future to unravel itself?

Gavin looked shaken when they separated. "Rose," he murmured.

His voice pulled at something deep in her. He looked like a man in the throes of some...profound emotion.

"So shall we?"

It wasn't the sort of question that should settle one's fate. It wasn't the way she'd wanted to be asked. Rose felt as if she was standing on the edge of a cliff poised to dive into an unknown sea. There was a rush of exhilaration, a surge of triumph, and a fear of being dashed to pieces on unseen rocks. She shouldn't. She mustn't. Wildly, crazily, she leaped. "Yes," she said.

And so when the Terefords' luxurious traveling carriage set off from Yerndon not long after this, driving east toward Leeds, Rose sat with the duchess inside. The duke and Sir Gavin rode beside it. Most of the servants followed in another comfortable vehicle, Rose's maid, Sue, among them. The stablemen had started south with the extra horses the previous day.

The Terefords had not announced their departure to the

neighborhood. Indeed, they had taken some care to disguise their intentions. The manor was left in the charge of a taciturn older couple, the Smithsons, who had come highly recommended. They had few connections in the area, did not approve of gossip, and would have no patience with questions. No callers were expected, but if they came, they would be put off. The ruse would not last many days. But as the duchess had pointed out, many days were not required. The blizzard of written complaints would probably continue. But there would be no one present to read them.

Leeds was an easy journey of twenty miles and a world away from the sweep of the moors. Each time Gavin came to the city, there seemed to be more warehouses and mills, more smoke in the air, and more people and vehicles thronging the streets. Industry was burgeoning in Leeds, bringing great wealth to some and grinding toil to others. Gavin didn't care for the place and usually completed any business he had as quickly as possible. Today, however, the city offered a newfound sense of freedom. No one at home knew where he was. It would take time for them to find him. Complaints and admonishments wouldn't reach him here. He could forget all that for a while. It was a great relief.

They found three rooms awaiting them at the town's finest hotel, along with accommodations for the servants. A groom had galloped off as soon as the decision was made and alerted the hostelry to his employer's arrival. He'd also carried letters that went off south by fast courier. Gavin had nothing to do, except to hazard his whole future on a lunatic roll of fate's dice.

They settled in their chambers. They shared a cordial dinner in the hotel's dining room. It was like being in a dream, Gavin thought. He moved through familiar actions automatically, his mind floating, disconnected. He didn't want to draw back, but he felt almost as if he was two people—a determined daredevil and an aghast man of property lured into a high-stakes gamble.

In the morning, the Terefords were fully occupied with letters to write and a business appointment. They urged Rose and Gavin to go out together and enjoy the city. As it was a sunny April day, and they had nothing else to occupy them, they took this advice and at ten set out walking in the busy streets. Rose had been to Leeds numerous times, accompanying her mother. But Mama came for one reason only. She loved to shop. She could spend hours in pursuit of the perfect length of cloth or hat or shoes. She enjoyed examining every possible choice of whatever item she was seeking. She insisted on visiting all the most exclusive shops before settling on her purchase, often back at the first place they'd tried. And discovery of a new emporium delighted Mama as much as undiscovered countries did a bold explorer.

Rose did not share this zest. She was more likely to settle on the first thing that was good enough and bring the shopping expedition to a close. This had led to friction with her mother on almost every trip. Rose's walks through the streets of Leeds had been punctuated by a stream of complaints about her sulky attitude that spoiled her mother's enjoyment and took the fun out of everything. Thus, for the first few minutes in the bustling throng, Rose felt stiff and uneasy. But no complaints came. Gavin's comments were soothing.

Gradually, she absorbed the difference and began to relax and look around as herself, not the eternally disappointing daughter. "It's interesting," she said over the surrounding babble of voices. "It's almost like being on the moor."

Gavin looked down at her in surprise.

"Not the scene but the…situation. None of these people care about me or think I ought to have a better attitude." She gestured as the bustling townspeople. "No more than if they were stands of gorse and heather."

He laughed at the comparison. "A better attitude?"

"Mama adores shopping. That I do not is just another example of my…failure to meet her standards."

"That's ridiculous. Shopping is a chore to be gotten through. I detest standing about while people look over all the offerings in a place."

"So do I!"

Gavin smiled down at her. "We will do none! We must avoid the areas where our neighbors would be likely to do business or shop anyway."

"Yes. It would be harder to dodge them here than in the heather."

Gavin laughed again, and Rose felt her spirits lift.

They strolled away from the main thoroughfares into smaller avenues. The crowds grew less and changed a bit in character. Around the next corner they came upon a small square that held rows of market stalls. Stopping at the edge, they looked over it. "We used to go to a place like this on our days off when I was at school," said Gavin. "There was a fellow who sold really splendid hot pies."

"Did your school keep you hungry?" Rose asked.

"They fed us well. But I was always hungry at that age."

"You grew several inches while you were away." He looked startled, and Rose flushed. Yes, she had noticed, even though Gavin had become a forbidden connection by that time.

They walked through the aisles on their way across the square. Some of the stalls offered early vegetables or household necessities. Others had handcrafts. There was a tinsmith repairing worn pans. A flash of color caught Rose's eye, and she turned to discover a row of lovely handwoven scarves tied around a rod and stirring in the breeze. "How beautiful." She was drawn irresistibly closer. The hues were soft but striking—sage green, pale pink, amber gold. The threads were exceedingly fine, so that the scarves were almost filmy, and the weave was perfect. "I make all me own dyes," said the old woman who sat behind the display.

"Beetroot for the pink?" asked Rose.

"Yes, miss. You're one who knows, I see."

Rose ran her fingers over the one in shadings of green. The cloth was beautifully soft.

"You should buy it," Gavin said. "Take several of them. The duchess might like one." The old woman perked up.

Rose longed to buy. She might be no enthusiastic shopper, but beauty like this captivated her. She had no money, however. Her father had an unalterable position on this issue. He provided for all her needs. He had even ordered her specimen box when she requested it. And fresh notebooks whenever one was full. But he did not give her coin.

They had accounts in the village to cover household requirements, and all bills went to him, as part of his "system" to monitor expenditure. Rose drew back her hand, conscious of Gavin's gaze. It was too humiliating to admit this. "I have scarves," she muttered to the cobblestones.

"The green would become you right well, miss," said the old woman hopefully.

Rose started to turn away.

"Do you like that green one best?" Gavin asked her. "The pink is pretty too." He reached into his pocket.

"You can't buy them," said Rose.

"Of course I can."

"It isn't…"

"The least improper," he interrupted. "Under the circumstances."

They brought their strange situation out in the open. Rose felt her cheeks heat up.

"The green," Gavin said to the vendor. "And the pink. That heathery one too."

Looking very pleased, the old woman untied these three scarves from the display rod and folded them. When she named a price, Gavin didn't bargain very hard, and Rose was glad. This vendor was an artist and deserved a generous payment for her work.

The old woman brought out a piece of paper and started to wrap up the scarves. Gavin reached over and picked up the green one. "You must put this one on," he said to Rose. He draped it around her neck and tied it over her cloak. When his fingertips brushed her skin, Rose trembled.

"There," said the old woman. "Didn't I say it would look well?"

"Lovely," said Gavin, his voice uneven.

Rose met his gray eyes as she touched the soft fabric. Was that tenderness she saw there? At least it wasn't pity; she was certain of that. "Thank you," she said.

"There's no need of thanks between us," he replied.

"What?"

"This was not a case of largesse or…patronage."

His tone made Rose realize that her father's "careful" habits were known in their neighborhood. Of course they would be. People talked about that sort of thing. And Gavin had remembered, in that brief bit of silence, that she was kept penniless. The surprising part was his response.

"This is just a gift, as between equals," he went on, indicating the scarves.

"I think that would be all the more reason to acknowledge it," Rose replied with similar gravity.

"He's a fine lad," said the old woman. "Don't let go of him, miss."

Rose smiled.

The other scarves were wrapped in paper and tied with string. Gavin put the small parcel under his arm, and they walked on.

They moved through bustling streets and leafy lanes. The day remained fine. They strolled around other small markets, though none had things as lovely as the scarves. Rose felt wryly vindicated. Her mother's shopping habits wouldn't have turned up any better choices.

In the early afternoon, they paused before a tea shop. A plate of small cakes was displayed in the window, fancifully decorated with tiny flowers and curlicues made of sugar icing. Gavin and Rose looked at each other, smiled, and turned to go in.

Appetites sharpened by the walk, they ordered a lavish tea with small sandwiches of ham and cucumber and an ample selection of the iced cakes. These tasted as good as they looked.

"Just one more of the chocolate ones, Mama, please," begged a little boy at a nearby table.

"You've had three, Lionel," his parent replied.

"I know but they are *heavenly*."

"*One* more. Do not ask again."

"Yes, Mama." The boy took his cake and bit into it with an ecstatic expression.

Rose met Gavin's smiling gaze. "Do you remember how Edward would bring cake from home out onto the moor?" she asked.

"He told his mother it was to share with the group," Gavin answered. "But then he ate most of it himself." Edward had been pudgy as a boy, though he had grown out of that.

"He would like this place."

"He would. Perhaps we can bring him someday."

Rose blinked. Gavin watched her consider this possibility and discover vistas opening for the future. He'd had similar moments himself today, which had held more laughter than any other he could remember. Things they might plan and decide without constant interference. "He would enjoy the indulgence," Rose said.

"Indulgence indeed."

Rose blushed delightfully. There was that too, Gavin thought. More than kisses. Life was suddenly offering so much more than he had anticipated for years.

They finished without hurry and then rose and moved slowly onward through the city. Gavin had a map of Leeds in his mind, and he had taken them in a rough circle. Now they were walking back toward the hotel. At the top of a slight rise, Rose stopped and pointed. "Look. Is that a fire?"

Gavin saw a column of pale smoke in the distance. Beneath it, a line of heavy wagons lurched slowly along. "I believe it is the steam locomotive," he said.

"The what?"

"It is a horseless cart powered by a steam boiler. Used to haul coal from the mines in Middleton down to the landing near the bottom of Salem Place. To feed the power looms and other machines in the cloth mills. The first of its kind, I think."

"Oh yes, I have read about that," said Rose. They watched it lumber along. "It doesn't seem much faster than horses."

Gavin nodded. "It doesn't require rest though or become ill."

"Nay, it just blows sky-high," declared a raspy voice behind them.

Turning, they saw a grizzled old man standing nearby. He was neatly dressed, leaning on a tall staff. "Didn't ye hear about the *Salamanca*?" he asked.

"The battle?" Wellington had won a great victory at Salamanca in 1812, but Gavin didn't see what that had to do with this.

"Nay, they named the engine of that infernal machine after it. And then the thing exploded a matter of two years ago. Killed the driver stone dead." The old man shook his head. "Flung him a hundred yards. Like he was no more than a rag doll."

"Oh dear," said Rose.

"They claimed he messed about with the safety valves. But what I say is, a horse don't blow up on you like a bad piece of artillery." The old man gave them a decisive nod and stomped away.

"Thank goodness," said Rose. "An exploding horse would be a dreadful thing to see." She shuddered.

It was a grisly picture. They walked on as if to leave it behind.

"The lamplighters are coming out," Gavin said as they approached their hotel. They'd seen these men last night, igniting the rows of gaslights that made the streets almost as bright as day.

"Leeds is changing," Rose answered. "I wonder what it will be like when we are old?"

"Very different," Gavin said. He had no doubt of that.

"But the moor won't be."

"No." They exchanged a glance of perfect understanding.

They paused a moment before going inside the hotel, as if they both felt an impulse to prolong the walk. "This has been a splendid day," said Gavin.

"It has." Rose put a hand to her new scarf. She still tasted icing on her lips. But it was not the things that had made the day memorable. It was the company.

"I've never enjoyed myself so much in the city."

"Nor I."

"Are we surprised by that?" Gavin asked.

Rose smiled at the laughter in his tone. "A bit?"

"Though not nearly as much as we once would have been."

"Not nearly," she replied softly.

"Which is a good omen?"

She nodded. They gazed at each other. Rose felt as if a current of heat passed between them. But there couldn't be kisses in the public street. Those would have to wait. She felt a shiver of delicious anticipation.

Looking regretful, Gavin turned away. They went inside together.

The duke and duchess awaited them, and they enjoyed another convivial dinner. The Terefords' business had gone smoothly, and they enjoyed hearing about the day's adventures. When they separated to go to their beds, the duke said, "My courier should return tomorrow."

Rose went very still. She looked at Gavin. He couldn't tell if she was more startled or excited. He smiled. After their day together, he was certain they had made the right choice. Her answering smile was a tremulous agreement.

Twelve

IN FACT, THE DUKE'S MESSENGER ARRIVED VERY LATE THAT night, having ridden hard from London. They were given the packet he had brought at breakfast. And so, that very morning, Gavin and Rose were married by a clergyman who had been forewarned, using the special license the courier had fetched. The Terefords stood up with them in the church, and the servants observed. Rose's maid stared as if she couldn't believe her eyes. In a surprisingly short time for such a revolution in one's life, the vows were spoken, the marriage lines signed, and the union sealed.

There was no time for Rose to mull over her new status. The Terefords and the Keighleys had an appointment immediately following the ceremony with a local solicitor. "I have the conveyance you requested ready," the man said to the duke when they arrived at his offices. He took them into a room with a large table, ushered them all to seats, and laid a document before the duke. Tereford read it, passed it to his wife, and waited until she nodded approval. Then he took up a pen and ascribed his signature at the bottom.

"There," he said when the ink had dried. He placed the pages before Gavin and Rose, who sat side by side opposite him. "We have settled the estate of Yerndon on the two of you. Jointly. Ownership not to be alienated from either."

Rose stared at the document. She had known it was coming, as part of the plan, but the reality was still astonishing.

"You have done what your families wanted," said the duchess with a smile. "Yerndon now belongs to the Keighleys *and* the Denholmes."

"Not exactly what they wanted," murmured Gavin.

Rose nodded. Their families wanted sole possession. And, strictly speaking, she was no longer a Denholme. But she'd been one all her life up to now. Surely this would end the silly war. Strangely, she felt as if a rug had been pulled out from under her. The dispute that had shadowed her whole life was gone. "You're sure you wish to do this?" she asked the Terefords. Both she and Gavin had asked before. It was such a generous act.

"We have many properties to manage," replied the duchess, as she had before. "We would never use Yerndon. I see your love for the moor, but I cannot really share it."

"But the money," said Rose. "You might have sold the place. Or earned rent."

Gavin nodded.

"I consider it an investment in amity and friendship," said the duke. "Things I have learned a great deal about in the last year." He looked at the duchess, tenderly amused.

His expression made Gavin remember their first meeting. He'd thought that Tereford sneered, that he was effete and incompetent. He couldn't have been more wrong. The world turned upside down since then.

"And there is some reason to argue that it should return to your family holdings," the duke added. "Both of them, that is."

"As you have repeatedly heard," murmured Rose.

The four of them smiled at each other.

"We know you will do well by Yerndon because you care for it," said the duchess.

"You are a fine estate manager," her husband said to Gavin.

"Thank you," Gavin replied. He desired no greater compliment.

"Also, should an opportunity arise, you can do a service to someone else. In some different form. My wife has made me a great believer in…roving kindness."

The duchess laughed at the phrase.

"Yes indeed," said Rose. "We certainly will."

Gavin pushed the document toward her. "You can keep this safe."

"I?"

She seemed stunned, and Gavin had some idea why. Her father would not even have thought to let her read such a paper. Gavin had quite a different philosophy. He nodded.

Rose picked up the pages as if they were terribly fragile. She put them into an envelope the solicitor provided and held it to her chest.

They returned to the hotel, but the rush of events did not slow. The Terefords were ready to go now that the business was concluded. They were packed, and their luggage was brought down and loaded. After final farewells, they and most of their servants set off for London.

———

Gavin watched the carriages drive off down the busy street, then turned to Rose—his wife! She gazed up at him. Her maid and two of the Terefords' servants who had elected to stay in Yorkshire for a time to help out stood beside her. Those three seemed to be anticipating the next act in this headlong drama with relish.

But events seemed to have skidded to a halt now. Passersby walked around them as if they were stones in a flowing stream. Carts and carriages went by in the street.

"Shall we go back in?" Rose asked.

They shouldn't stand here like blocks. Gavin ushered the group into the hotel.

"I think we should stay here one more night," Rose said.

Their wedding night, Gavin thought with a flash of yearning. He would do whatever Rose wished, of course. What would she wish? It was better to find out here than at Yerndon, where their families would be wondering where they'd gone. They might already be lying in wait for them. Gavin hid a wince. They would endure the uproar that was coming. Just not right away. "A good idea," he replied. He went to speak to the hotel staff and found it easy to engage their rooms for another night. The servants were dismissed to do as they liked for the day.

This left the newly married couple alone together. They had made the leap into the unknown, and now here they were in it. Gavin wished they could walk out onto the moor together. They knew themselves best there.

"Could we go back to that tea shop?" Rose asked. "It was such a pleasant place. Can we find it again?"

"Of course." He knew where they'd rambled on a day that had been relaxed and carefree—unlike this one. Perhaps Rose wanted to recapture that mood? It was another good idea. She was full of them.

"We can declare its pastries our wedding cake. And toast each other with cups of tea."

Gavin surveyed her expression. She looked merely amused. "Do you wish you'd had a more festive wedding?" Ladies cared about such things.

Rose cocked her head at him. "Festive? With our families in attendance, you mean? And our neighbors in the church pews waiting for…metaphorical bloodshed? No."

"Forget I asked."

He offered his arm, and they walked back along the route they'd taken yesterday. More swiftly, as the weather was not as fine. Scudding clouds passed overhead, and it was cooler. Coming to the tea shop, they went in and sat at the same table as yesterday. "We should order one of every kind of cake they have," Rose declared.

"Even that anise one you didn't like?"

"It was…a strong flavor," she admitted.

"You screwed up your face like a cat sniffing lemon peel."

She laughed. Heartily, gaily. Gavin felt something in his chest ease and expand. It would be all right, he thought.

"Not that one then," said Rose. "Just all the others."

When they had been served, she held up her cup. "We actually did it," she said. She tapped his cup in a salute and took a sip. "The morning went by in such a rush. My brain is still reeling."

He felt the same.

"It's sinking in, though. I'm a married woman. I have my own house. Signed and sealed. Not to be taken away." She laughed. This time she sounded giddy. "Do you know what that means?"

"Beyond the fact of it?" Gavin didn't think she was referring to the changed nature of their relationship. The spark in her gaze was almost militant.

"The 'fact of it' means I can do what I like. I'm no longer some sheltered miss who isn't to know anything or decide for herself. Such a ridiculous creature. I can…" She stopped short and looked at him with narrowed eyes.

They were the eyes of the youthful Rose who'd been in the forefront of their adventures, who'd shone with daring, who'd disdained obstacles. Until she'd been driven into hiding by a clamor of scolding voices. Well, he wasn't one of those. Not anymore! "You can do what you like," he echoed. He could hope that what she liked would be…him. She wouldn't have married just to get free of her parents, would she?

His tone had obviously not convinced her. "If I am half owner of Yerndon, I should be entitled to half the estate income," she said.

Gavin nodded. "It isn't large at present, but it will rise as the place is improved."

"I have some ideas about that," Rose replied, a clear challenge.

"Splendid," he answered, though he did feel he was much more skilled at estate management than she could be. Her father would not have brought her into the process. And even if he had, Denholme wasn't very good at it. "Much of the income will need to go back into the land for a while," he said. He wished this didn't sound like bargaining. "You will be in charge of the household accounts, of course."

"Of course," she repeated as if she'd expected this. Gavin saw the flicker of surprise in her eyes, however. "Also, I shall walk on the moors. Every day, I imagine. On my own."

Gavin nodded. She was a creature of the moor.

"I am telling you about it," she went on. "Not asking permission."

"Why would you?"

"I shall want a room of my own at Yerndon for mounting specimens and keeping my record books."

"Any room you like."

"The front parlor? The dining room? Both of them perhaps?"

"If you wish." This was easy as he knew she wouldn't want those. She'd prefer something more private.

"The corner bedchamber at the back would work well," she said. "It has windows on two sides."

"A good choice." And if they were speaking of bed-chambers... But they weren't, not in the truly interesting sense. Could he inquire about sleeping arrangements for tonight? He couldn't decide how to frame the question in this context. It was certainly not part of any bargain. He wouldn't ever have it so. "A cake?" he asked instead. "You liked these pink ones." He picked up the small pastry and held it out to her.

Meeting his gray eyes, Rose noticed both warmth and uncertainty in those depths. He wasn't fighting her. Or pointing out her flaws and shortcomings as her parents liked to do. He'd given that up. She thought of all the ways he'd changed since they first arrived at Yerndon to stay. As she had too. He'd given the deed to Yerndon into her care. He'd made this daring change *with* her.

And something else had changed today, Rose realized. Kisses were now allowed. Encouraged even. Rather than forbidden. Kisses and much more. She was…authorized to explore realms of sensuality that had been hidden from her. On impulse, she leaned forward. Instead of taking the cake from him, she took a bite.

Gavin dropped it.

A current of wild laughter ran through Rose. She wanted everything, all the pleasures society's rules had withheld. All the powers a wife, a householder, might wield. Sugary icing melted on her tongue. She savored the sweet taste. She enjoyed the flush on Gavin's cheeks and the hope in his expression.

He retrieved the bitten cake and put it on the small plate in front of her. "You know, Rose," he began. And stopped.

"I know a good many things," she answered. "I hope to learn many more." Her tone was suggestive. Yes, it was. She hadn't even known she possessed such a tone. Gavin raised his eyebrows. She nearly giggled. He was afraid to ask. She smiled at him and thought his breath caught.

"You." He stopped again.

"I?"

"You…have a crumb." He touched one corner of his mouth.

She licked it away, slowly. The effect was gratifying. "Thank you."

His hand dropped. "What do you hope to learn?" he asked.

He'd found his suggestive voice. It felt as if the shop had suddenly gotten warmer. "So many things." Her giddiness was overtaken by a more serious ambition. "Joy," she said. "Contentment. Triumph."

Gavin stared. "You can't expect me to know those things," he said with a catch in his voice.

"How would either of us know them after the way we've been reared? But can't we discover them together?"

"Rose." He reached over and took her hand. She closed her fingers around his. "Do you really think we could?" he asked.

"I do," she replied. It was another wedding vow, a promise between the two of them.

He looked moved. His grasp was warm and strong. He nodded. Then he seemed to become aware of how closely they were leaning, of the chattering strangers around them. He sat back, released her hand, touched his teacup, then cleared his throat. "I did want to say. About the…intimacies of marriage. We can take things slowly. I would not do anything…"

"I should have said passion too," Rose murmured. "I want to learn all about *that*."

Gavin went very still. "You…"

"I indeed. And thoroughly."

The air seemed to crackle between them. The others in the café ceased to exist for a moment.

"Shall we go back to the hotel?" she asked.

The effect was all that Rose could have wished. The remaining cakes were put in a box to take away, their coats were resumed, and they'd stepped outside. The walk back to the hotel was much faster than the stroll out had been, but not because of the thickening clouds that covered the sky.

Gavin moved in a fever of anticipation. He would not, of course, sweep Rose up in his arms and carry her down the busy street, into the hotel, and up to his room, as part of him wanted to do. That was out of the question. And it was too far anyway, a more practical part of him pointed out. He would be panting with exhaustion by the time they reached a bed, and that would not do at all. He wanted to be panting with something else entirely. He thought of telling Rose. She would probably laugh. But perhaps it was too soon. She might be embarrassed. And he wasn't looking for laughter just now in any case.

Leeds seemed frustratingly crowded suddenly, with mobs of people in his way. It felt as if the hotel continually receded into endless distance.

At last they reached it, however, and went inside, where Gavin was annoyed to find Rose's maid lurking.

"Oh, Sue," said Rose.

"I didn't know if you might want me, miss."

The girl wasn't lurking, Gavin acknowledged. That wasn't fair. But right now she was one more obstacle to be got round.

"Not just now," Rose replied.

Sue nodded. "Only, there's a play on right nearby here. A comedy, they say. The others thought of seeing it."

"Go, by all means," said Rose. "Take the evening off."

"May I really, miss?"

Yes, thought Gavin. Go, go.

"We'll be busy enough when we return to Yerndon," said Rose. "Do you have money for a ticket?"

"Yes, miss."

Gavin dug in his pocket and brought out a handful of coins. "Treat yourselves to dinner. All three of you." He held them out.

The maid hesitated.

"To celebrate the wedding," Gavin added.

Sue seemed to recall that they now had a new relationship. She took the money. "Thank you, sir."

"Have a good time," said Rose.

The maid gave them a sly look. "You too, miss," she dared before hurrying away.

Rose's muted gurgle of laughter was adorable, and somehow as enflaming as any seduction Gavin had ever known.

"Will you come to my room in twenty minutes," she said a bit shyly.

"Twenty," he repeated. It was not an eternity. It just felt that way.

They walked up the stairs together and then separated. In his old room Gavin shed his greatcoat, hat, and gloves and wondered how to prepare for a wedding night that he must reach through a public hotel corridor. He decided he would dare to take off his neckcloth. Shave? Wash up certainly.

When the time had at last passed, he went and knocked at her door.

Rose opened it and stepped back. She was wearing a clinging, skimpy garment of satin and lace that he would not have thought she possessed. His expression must have said as much because she gestured at it. "The duchess gave me this." Letting a ribbon trail through her fingers she added, "I asked her to." A blush traveled down her cheeks, her neck and onto the enticing curves revealed by the low bodice. "It's lovely but…"

"Breathtaking," Gavin interrupted. He stepped in and shut the door.

Rose shifted under his heated gaze. "It's odd wearing so…little when you're fully dressed."

"That is easily remedied." He shed his coat and shoes and stockings and stood before her in breeches and open shirt.

Rose took one step, another, and then was in his arms, offering her lips, twining her fingers in his hair.

She was fragrant and pliant and eager. The nightgown was mere gossamer under his hands. He felt the heat of her skin as if it was bare. They kissed as they had before, and yet differently. The barriers were gone, in every sense.

As a countrywoman, Rose knew the basics of mating. But it was one thing to know and another to feel the rush of sensation that came with caresses. Longing flooded her, arched her up to meet his touch. He teased and roused each most urgent part of her, making it obvious that he had done this before, while she had not. She didn't care.

They threw off their clothes and climbed into the bed Rose had daringly turned down. She let her hands roam as well now, discovering him, exulting when she made him moan. She would learn passion by the thrilling sounds she could draw from her new husband. She would create a map of desire from his pleasure.

And then Rose forgot every plan and ambition as Gavin took her to the taut peak of longing and over it, into a bright, dissolving ecstasy. When he entered her, there was a little pain, soon gone as he moved, first gently and then with an urgency that thrilled her. She held him as he found his own release, delighting in the power of giving it.

They panted together. Gavin raised his head and dropped quick, butterfly kisses on her cheeks, her lips, her eyelids. When she laughed, he smiled tenderly.

Afterward, they lay side by side, her head on his shoulder, encircled by his arm. "Are you...well?" he asked.

"Very," she replied. "Happy to have begun my study of passion."

He laughed. "May it be rich and satisfying," he said.

"Oh, I think it will be." She rose on one elbow to kiss him.

There was a rattle of rain on the window. It felt inexpressibly cozy to lie here in his arms in the inclement evening.

"Do you want to go down to dinner?" Gavin asked a bit later.

She didn't want to rise and dress and mingle with a dining room full of strangers. She could think of much better things to do, in a bit. But she was hungry. Rose was reluctantly conceding that dinner might be in order when she remembered the box they'd brought back with them. "That is unnecessary," she answered. "We will eat cake in bed. Naked and thoroughly dissipated."

This time Gavin's laughter was uproarious.

Thirteen

GAVIN WOKE IN HIS WIFE'S LAVENDER-SCENTED BED AND under the bright gaze of her blue eyes. They reached for each other at the same moment, and he fell headlong into the delights of his new marital state.

"Perhaps we could stay here forever," Rose said in a dreamy voice when they had sated each other and lay languorously intertwined.

"Live at the hotel," he replied, not as a question.

"Send out to the tea shop and subsist on cake."

"Instruct the staff here to deny our existence to any who might ask."

"After we move to a suite of rooms on the very top floor."

"Where we can watch the locomotive pass in the distance."

"And think of nothing but…" She ran her fingers down Gavin's side, making him catch his breath.

"Nothing," he murmured.

"We'll send the duchess's servants back to her in London. With a note pledging the Terefords to secrecy as to our whereabouts."

"But there is your maid," said Gavin, and then cursed his literal mind.

"Oh." The whimsy went out of Rose's tone. "Yes, of course. There is Sue. She will probably be knocking on the door soon, wondering when we leave for home." She sighed.

"We have to go," said Gavin.

"I know."

The fantasy thoroughly dissipated, they rose and began to make ready.

Gavin hired a post chaise for the ride back to Yerndon. He hadn't been able to bring his own carriage as his family would have wanted to know where he was going. They would soon find out now, and the results would descend on their heads.

By one o'clock, they were on the road west. Rose and the servants filled the chaise. Gavin rode beside it. There would be no chance for private talk until they reached Yerndon again.

Rose watched the busy streets of Leeds pass by the carriage window, newly washed by the overnight rain. It was a lively scene, full of interest. The April day was temperate with a gusty breeze. She was at once glad and sorry to leave the city. She had been very happy here. She nearly hugged the delicious memories to her. But the moors would be burgeoning with spring, and she could walk them now whenever she liked, as much as she liked. Her husband fully understood that need, as he did a number of others, she thought with a secret smile.

She had a husband. Rose contemplated this fact, turning it in her mind like a gleaming stone found in a streambed. She'd observed husbands often enough. She'd expected, in an abstract way, to have one at some point, though never had she imagined it would be Gavin Keighley. The duchess seemed to find hers eminently satisfactory. But what was it like, day in and day out?

The nights, well, she had no worries about *those*.

"Whatever will the master say?" asked Sue.

Rose started, thinking her maid meant Gavin, and that she had somehow sensed Rose's sensuous thoughts. Then she realized Sue was referring to her father. He would have a great deal to say, she imagined. As would her mother. She didn't want to speculate, particularly before the two other servants, whom she barely knew. She simply shook her head.

The journey was soon done. They pulled up before Yerndon in late afternoon, carried in the sparse luggage they'd taken to Leeds, and paid off the post chaise. Sue took Rose's case upstairs, and the other two servants went to the kitchen. At long last, Rose and Gavin were alone in the front parlor. "We must let our families know what we've done," Rose said. She hadn't meant for it to sound like a transgression. "Before they hear the news from someone else. My maid will tell her friends at the first opportunity." The weight of the family dispute descended on her like a heavy pall. She'd thrown it off in Leeds, but it had not gone away.

Gavin nodded. The set of his mouth was grim. More like the Gavin of weeks ago than her tender partner of last night and this morning. Just this morning? Yes.

"I suppose we should go and see them," Rose said reluctantly.

"We can write to them. They bombarded *us* with letters."

"Doesn't that seem cowardly?"

"I don't care."

He seemed distant, perhaps angry. Though she knew those impulses weren't directed at her, Rose's heart sank. Would the old frictions and habits of years and years pull them down? Apart? "They'll come to see us as soon as they hear."

"And we will receive them in our home rather than theirs. Thus, we can tell them to go away."

"Your house belongs to you," Rose had to point out.

"Indeed, but Mama rather...fills it."

That was easy to believe. Lady Keighley tended to dominate. The dowager Lady Keighley, Rose realized. That title belonged to her now, a Denholme. Gavin's mother would be enraged by that, whether she was expected to relinquish it or share it. And she was very good at being angry.

Rose nearly quailed. She told herself that she had her own establishment now. Whatever anyone else thought, she owned Yerndon. Co-owned, all right. But no one could take it away. It was her bastion, her sanctuary, a place she could order just as she liked. Even Gavin could not stop her. Of course he wouldn't want to.

"We'd best write the notes together and send them off," he said. It sounded like a curt command. "I think we should say..."

"I can decide what to say to my parents," Rose put in.

"We don't want to give the wrong impression. We must take charge, present a united front."

"Front? Is that like pretending to get along?"

"What's wrong with you?" Gavin asked. "You know this is a delicate matter."

He said it in the impatient tone so familiar from all the years they had been snapping at each other. The voice that put her into a flame. She resisted, but the habit of argument came so easily. "Nothing whatsoever is wrong with me. I will go and compose the note."

"And show it to me before it's sent off."

Rose gritted her teeth. "Do you intend to do the same?"

"Of course," he replied.

"We will exchange copies then?" Like warring nations drafting a treaty, Rose thought.

"That is what I said."

"Very well." She turned and walked out.

Gavin remained where he was, struggling with his temper as he had not needed to do for some time. What had happened to the sweet, confiding Rose of last night? Had regrets overwhelmed her on the ride back from Leeds? Was she wishing him at Jericho? Had they been utter fools to think that things could change between them in a few weeks? Now that they were back to the reality of their lives, was Rose sorry she'd married him?

He gazed out the window at the cloud shadows passing over the moor. The April afternoon was waning to gold. As always, the sight of the country he loved held peace.

Memories of their visit here at Yerndon came back to him—the honest talk, the tender kisses. They weren't the same fractious people who had first come here. They'd had reasons for their plunge into the unknown. Or had the duke and duchess created a fantasy world that disappeared with their departure?

Gavin hadn't really understood the phrase *blood ran cold* until this moment. If Rose regretted their marriage, that was...insupportable.

What had gone wrong?

They'd reached Yerndon. They'd faced up to the next step. He'd been thinking of what to say to his mother and of her certain outrage. She would rail at him. At Rose too, perhaps more at her. She would be full of vitriol. As she had no right to be. His temper had flamed at the idea. He'd wanted to hit something. And so he'd snapped and growled like a baited bear.

Gavin walked closer to the windows. He breathed in the sight of the sun gilding the heather. As soon as their families came into it, things tried to go bad. Engrained opinions—and insults—were like a great wave, trying to sweep his feet out from under him, insisting that rage was the only thing to feel.

But it wasn't. Rose had taught him that. And the Terefords had too. He should apologize.

He headed for the stairs, but before he had taken three steps up, Mr. Smithson rushed out of the back premises. "That daft girl has set the kitchen on fire," he cried. The caretaker was no longer the silent, self-contained servitor. His face was covered with soot.

Gavin ran back with him and found one of the servants the duchess had left screeching and flapping ineffectually at a row of flaming dish towels. Somehow, the drying rack had been lowered into the edge of the coals on the hearth.

He eased the girl aside, pulled the cloths off the rack, and stamped out the fire. Mr. Smithson raised the drying rack out of danger.

The room was filled with smoke.

"Where is Mrs. Smithson?" Gavin asked. The older woman had seemed calmly competent.

"Went to the village, didn't she?" Mr. Smithson wiped his face with one of the charred towels, which didn't do much good to either. "Had to, if there's to be any dinner tonight."

Rose's maid, Sue, came in just then, gawked at the mess, and exclaimed, "I'll tell my lady." She ran out again before Gavin could object.

A few minutes later, Rose arrived and looked at him as if the fire was his fault. Or so he felt.

"I didn't mean anything, my lady," said the servant responsible. Gavin ought to know her name, but he didn't. "I needed a cloth to wipe up the eggs," she added. There were three broken eggs on the floor by the kitchen table, Gavin noticed. "And then I–I don't know how it happened."

"Ham-handed flibbertigibbet," Mr. Smithson muttered.

The girl burst into tears.

Gavin backed away. Frantic sobs were among his mother's tactics when she wished to get her way. They usually led to outright hysteria. "Perhaps you can deal with this," he said to Rose. It was a plea, but came out surly. Why could he not speak to her as he had last night?

"Certainly," Rose replied, biting off the word. "Do slope off."

"I am not…"

"Go!" She made a shooing motion.

Gavin went for a walk.

He took deep breaths, filling his lungs with the bracing air of the moors. The sun was setting, the birds exchanging their last calls before settling to rest. He saw a fox slip over the rise behind the stables. "No chickens for you here," he murmured. They'd need a sturdy henhouse before they installed any, which he intended to do. He'd bring more of his horses over tomorrow. Or, soon, once the new situation was…made clear to his family. His mind shifted to the improvements he meant to make in the acreage. Those were practical and satisfying. Soothing. He knew how to do that. He was less certain how to make amends to Rose. He would, though, in a while.

In Yerndon's front parlor, where she had lately sat with the duchess and enjoyed lively, amusing conversations, Rose crossed out a sentence on the page before her and frowned at an ink blot. Sending letters to their families rather than calling on them was actually a good idea, she admitted. They could explain what they'd done without the constant interruptions that would certainly fill any face-to-face conversation. She could so easily imagine the horrified exclamations and disbelief. The criticism and blame. Which would cause digressions and degenerate into excuses for things that hadn't even happened. Much better to tell the whole story in writing first. But every word she chose seemed fraught. She'd even wavered over using *the* rather than *a*.

The door opened, and Gavin came in. "There you are."

In her prickly mood, it felt like an accusation. "Where else would I be?"

"Ah, well…"

"I am composing a letter to my parents, as we agreed." She hadn't meant it to sound so militant. Gavin—her husband!—frowned and came farther into the room.

"It will be best to simply set out the facts," he replied.

"Simply. Oh, I hadn't thought of that. It's such a simple matter after all."

"I didn't mean…"

"Have you made the attempt? Have you considered the reactions?" He winced, and she was glad of it. "Perhaps you would like to prepare a model if it is so *simple*?"

He took a breath, swallowed. "Pardon my poor choice of words, Rose," he said. "I seem incapable of finding the right ones. Or a good way of saying them. The problem has plagued me since we returned here."

It was what she had just been thinking about the letter. "Trying to put it…plausibly has made me cross." What they had done was so *implausible*, really.

"The old dispute rears up to make us so," Gavin replied. "I think it *tries* to, Rose."

"An abstract…situation cannot *try*."

"You wouldn't think so. But when my family comes into it, it feels like a great weight pushing me to snap and snarl. Call it old habits, if you like. They rush in before one can stop them."

"When we think of our families? Of getting in touch, or seeing them."

He nodded.

Rose thought this over. "Because we weren't having such...difficulties in Leeds."

"When they were far away and we didn't have to... include them."

"Are you saying Yerndon is tainted?" she asked sadly.

"No," he said.

"I won't have it," Rose declared at the same moment.

"We will not allow it to be," Gavin added. He came closer and offered his hand. "We will take care that it is not."

Rose grasped his fingers. "We have been different. Here in this house. Things began to change here."

"Yes. We have shown that we can fight off the past."

"Rather than with each other?" She remembered their walks in Leeds, their tender caresses. Those had felt so easy. "I thought we were done with that."

He looked regretful. "I wish we were. Anger seemed to sneak up on me when we returned and considered how to present ourselves."

Rose sat straighter. "Present ourselves. As if we were criminals arguing our case."

"Which we are not."

"We are the opposite," Rose declared.

Gavin smiled slightly. "What would the opposite of criminals be?"

"Those who look to mend instead of tearing down or tearing apart."

He looked much struck. "That is… That is lovely, Rose. That is exactly…"

"What you most like to do," she finished. She knew that about him. It was part of what she adored.

"Yes. As you revere and preserve."

She loved those labels, and that he'd seen this in her.

"We will work together," he added.

"We *are* together, and we won't let anything come between." She pressed his fingers as a seal to the promise. He squeezed back.

They were still for a moment, determined, happy. And then the scatter of crumpled, blotted pages on the desk in front of Rose seemed to grow more visible, as if trying to intrude on their pact.

"May I see what you've written?" Gavin asked.

Once, he would have just picked it up without permission, Rose thought. Still, she was reluctant to hand over her messy page. Usually, she wrote neatly and concisely. She never produced such wild daubs, and she was not at all satisfied with her attempt. But she let go of his hand and gave him her messy letter, watching him as he read. The lines of his face were so familiar—stark and strong. And lately, she'd seen softer expressions there, tenderness in those gray eyes. It was true. They had changed. They were a…an island of affection in a sea of discord. He looked up. Her pulse accelerated when their eyes met.

"Perhaps we could say 'made the determination to marry'?" he asked. "Would that imply a considered decision?"

Which it had not been, Rose thought. More of a wild leap

into the unknown, hopes flailing like loose cloaks in a gale. She raised her eyebrows.

"Yes, but it sounds…legal," Gavin said, responding to her expression.

"Legal?"

"Not the right word. Except that our marriage is quite legal."

"Signed and sealed," Rose agreed.

"Here's an idea. What if we begin our letters with the transfer of Yerndon to us? First thing, right up front. Before we mention anything else. That should disarm them, eh?"

As if their families would be charging in with weapons raised, not a vision one wished to conjure on announcing a marriage. But it was a good thought. "That is the most important fact, to them," Rose said.

"It was the point of our visit," he replied. "At least to my mother."

"And my parents," Rose said.

"So, they read that first and are filled with triumph." He made a fist and shook it in the air. Then he paused, looked at his raised hand.

Rose was gazing at it too. She saw him notice. A fist seemed like a symbol of their two families' enduring feud. And a bad omen? Gavin grimaced, let his fingers open and his hand drop.

"We tell them about our ownership and then perhaps congratulate them on the achievement of their lifetime aim. Make it sound as if they'd done something."

"Yes. That's very good. Should we note this down?"

She had the pen and ink out before her, Rose acknowledged. Gavin was still standing, though now he went and sat in an armchair. It was natural that she should write. She was not taking dictation. She refused to let that small sliver of irritation emerge.

"Then something about Yerndon," Gavin continued. "How good to have the borders restored."

"That is a bit deceptive from the Denholme side," she pointed out. "Yerndon will be no part of my brother's inheritance."

"You are as much part of the Denholmes as he is."

"Not in my father's eyes."

"But his grandchildren," Gavin began, then stopped.

Their eyes met. Rose felt her cheeks grow warm. Children came from the sweet intimacies and dizzying passions that had just begun for them.

Gavin cleared his throat. "Perhaps talk about increasing the sheep herd," he said.

A choked laugh escaped Rose. Lambs rather than children? No, both, she told herself. She wanted a household full of youth and laughter.

"The acres can support quite a few more," he added, as if she'd argued.

"I'm sure my father will agree with you."

"It would be the first time."

"Well, there must be one, if things are to change."

There was a short silence as they contemplated the unpleasant alternative.

"So, begin the letters with the conveyance of property and congratulations to them," Gavin said.

"Because they are very unlikely to congratulate *us*," Rose couldn't help but say.

Gavin's sympathetic look comforted her.

"And then sheep." Rose actually wrote down the word. She omitted the hollow laugh. "Followed by some sort of transition to announcing our wedding."

Dinner that evening was eaten in the parlor as they continued to wrestle with recalcitrant phrases.

"It is difficult to explain a marriage without any reference to feelings," Rose said at one point.

"Our families won't care to hear about those," Gavin replied.

"No. *They* won't." She looked at her husband, then realized she'd sounded sarcastic. For no real reason. He was trying very hard. As hard as she was. And this difficult letter writing was not a time to be speaking of...love. That would come—surely it would—when they'd dealt with their families and grown more settled. She gestured at the rising pile of blotted pages that surrounded them. "Onward."

They toiled on. It seemed to take forever, but at last they produced a draft that satisfied all the concerns they could raise. "I think this is the best we can do," Gavin said.

Rose nodded.

"We should each write out a clean copy."

"You don't want me to do yours as well?" Rose held up the pen with which she'd been taking notes. She wanted to kiss him, but also to box his ears. No, she didn't. Not the second thing.

"It must be in my handwriting," he replied, looking puzzled.

If she'd asked him to take the notes, he would have, Rose told herself. She was nearly certain he would have. But she hadn't asked. She was being unreasonable. This must stop. She pulled out fresh sheets of paper and another pen. They sat opposite each other at the table, carefully wrote the letters, and sealed them, ready to be sent off first thing in the morning. Before their families heard about their return, they hoped.

"I feel as if I've been hauling sacks of coal," said Gavin when they were done.

"Oh, are feelings to be mentioned now?"

"What?"

She'd sounded angry. But she wasn't. Not really. Not exactly.

"It's been a long day," Gavin replied. "You must be tired."

"Must I?"

"*I* must be choosing the wrong words again," he said. "I don't mean to offend you, Rose."

"You aren't. I just…" Rose bowed her head. "I suppose I am practicing for the family discussions ahead."

"Gathering your courage and resolution," he said as if he understood the impulse only too well.

She wished she didn't need those traits to confront her parents. She wished she didn't anticipate a battle. But she did. Rose sighed again. "And when I can scarcely put one thought with another."

"We have done our duty." He gestured at the letters. "We don't have to think anymore tonight. We can forget about all that."

"Can we?" She looked at the sealed pages. "You were very right. History does…impinge, even when you don't want it to."

"Let us leave it behind. Come." He rose and went to the sofa by the fire. When he beckoned, she joined him. "Let us imagine what would be worse," Gavin suggested.

"To keep our tempers."

"As you taught me."

And he had taken that lesson from her, Rose thought. That had been just one of the surprising developments of the last few weeks.

"We could each be back home," he went on. "We might not have been given Yerndon."

Rose didn't want to think about that. She shook her head. "I don't want to do the 'worse' just now. Let's name the happy times we've had here instead."

"A new habit forming," he replied.

"Yes."

"A good idea."

He acknowledged that she had them. Another change. Shifts *were* possible. "There was the duke surrounded by the Brontë children," she said.

"Looking all at sea," said Gavin. "I enjoyed seeing him at a bit of a loss."

"I know."

"Well, he's so very…" Gavin made a vague gesture.

"Polished, but not toplofty. Assured, but not vain. You liked him in the end."

"I did. Despite every effort to the contrary." Gavin smiled.

Rose smiled back. "And the duchess..." She broke off. She'd thought of the day her hostess routed the Keighley twins as a happy time, but mentioning that would spoil what they were doing.

"There was that time on the stairs, when we made our original agreement, and I nearly kissed you," Gavin said.

"Did you? I thought you might have..." Rose had certainly yearned toward him in that moment. It had been the beginning of...everything.

"I came so close I shocked myself."

Rose laughed. She'd felt the same. "Was that actually a happy time?" she asked him. "Or more an unsettling one?"

"It was the beginning of all the rest." He looked around. "And then I did kiss you. For the first time. Right here in this parlor."

"It was." Rose gazed at the pleasant room. "But I believe I kissed you. Actually. That time. You pointed that out."

"And offended you." He looked apologetic. "But I couldn't just..."

"What?"

"Sweep you into my arms. I didn't know what you wanted."

Rose met his eyes. Desire burned there. She gloated over it. "Then," she said.

"Then?"

"You couldn't sweep me into your arms *then*."

"Ah. But now." He did so, to Rose's immense gratification, and kissed her with that gentle intensity that drowned her senses. Kisses had not been the problem, she thought, while she could still think. Only their implications.

"I had our things moved to the bedchamber the Terefords were using," Rose said breathlessly when their dizzying embrace paused. "It is the best in the house."

Desire burned in his gaze. "But is it? Shouldn't that notion be tested?"

"You're right. It really should be."

Gavin stood, pulling her to her feet. They snuffed the candles, taking just one along to light their way. With his arm around her, they left the parlor and climbed the stairs. It was late. Everyone else had gone to bed.

They entered the grandest bedroom side by side. Gavin went to light some other tapers before setting the candle-stick down.

"Our first night in our new home," Rose said. Would they live here happily and prosperously for years? Or would outside pressures crush their hopes? She shook her head in denial.

"What?" asked Gavin.

"No one can come between us," she replied fiercely. "We *will not* allow it!"

And then they were shedding garments in a laughing melee, tumbling naked into bed. The caresses and endearments that drowned her then gave Rose hope.

Fourteen

Rose's parents arrived at Yerndon two hours after her note had been dispatched to them, which was still quite early. She was sitting in the front parlor making a list of tasks to do when their carriage pulled up. Gavin had gone out to ride the bounds of the estate. Each of them was beginning to put their mark on the place, Rose thought. They *would* change things together. Her lips still tingled from his farewell kiss.

She got up when she saw the carriage and went to the front door to greet her family, watching them step down like wary scouts entering enemy territory. When her mother saw her standing in the doorway, she rushed forward to envelop Rose in a tight embrace. "Oh, my darling, what have you done?" she cried. Then she stepped back, still holding Rose's shoulders, and shook her a little.

Her father, coming up behind, waved a sheet of paper. "What is this ridiculous tarradiddle?"

Rose assumed he was holding her note. It could be nothing else. She moved away from her mother. "I explained things clearly."

"Clearly! There is nothing clear about this."

"What don't you understand? I am now the owner…"

"How do we know you haven't been duped?"

"Because I am not a fool?" responded Rose. But quietly. Because she didn't want to have a shouting match with her father. She found she was not inclined to ask them to come into the parlor and sit down, which was a lowering reflection.

"This may be a conspiracy to ruin you," said her father.

Here was an accusation she hadn't anticipated. And she thought she had imagined them all. "How?"

"With a false marriage ceremony, a playacting parson."

He could make a conspiracy out of anything. "The duke and duchess were there and witnessed the wedding, Papa."

"I must speak to them immediately."

"They have gone back to London."

"Gone? After creating this havoc? How dare they? And how do we know those people weren't imposters?"

"Papa."

"I want to see marriage lines."

"Of course you may do so. And go and speak to the clergyman who presided as well, if you wish. In his perfectly legitimate church in Leeds." Her tone was acerbic, her fists closed. Rose gritted her teeth. She had been lured into defending herself over something silly. Again. She wished this conversation could be over. "You may see the document that signed Yerndon over to me too."

"To your husband." Her father spit the final word. "*Wives* don't own property."

Rose glanced at her mother to see how she took his apparent contempt for the word *wives*. Mamma didn't appear to notice. "They can when it is set forth and guaranteed," Rose said. "It is a joint ownership, not to be taken away. The legal gentleman explained it to us."

"And who is he?" muttered her father. "Some charlatan."

"You cannot actually think that."

"Why did you sneak off and keep all this secret if it is not a fraud?"

"Because I didn't want to argue!"

Rose's parents blinked and stepped back. Had she never shouted at them before? Perhaps she hadn't. Rose groped for the rags of her composure. "Mama. Papa." She waited until they both seemed to be paying attention. "You got what you've wanted all these years. Don't you realize that? A Denholme owns Yerndon. You should be happy now."

"We didn't mean you should sacrifice yourself to Gavin Keighley," cried her mother.

"I did not sacrifice myself." This was not the time to explain her feelings. They'd never believe her.

"Where is the fellow?" her father demanded. "I have a deal to say to him."

At least she was spared that, Rose thought. "He is out looking over the fields."

"To think of you yoked to that evil man," her mother moaned.

"He is not evil!"

"He is known all over the neighborhood for his dreadful temper," her father said. "Just like his virago of a mother."

"He has often been goaded into losing it," Rose replied. "By us."

"You have gone over to the side of our enemies?" Her father looked more distressed than angry now.

Rose was sorry for that. "There are not two sides any…"

"What are we going to do?" Her mother wrung her hands.

"I don't see that there is anything for you to do. Except give up your suspicions and accusations."

Her father bridled.

She tried once more for calm reason. "You sent me on this visit to win Yerndon, and I have achieved what you wanted." It was true, Rose thought. Perhaps not as they'd planned, if they'd actually had a plan. But it was true. "Can't you be pleased with me now?

"We did not know you would lose your mind!" replied her father.

"Could you ever be pleased with me, I wonder?"

"Of course we are pleased with you," said her mother. "It is just that you…"

"Always do things wrong," Rose finished.

"I did not say that." But Mama's expression admitted it.

"We thought that you would…"

"What?" Rose asked when her father's voice trailed off. They'd had no specific ideas. They'd flung her into an absurd situation, left her to it, and now they didn't like the result. And here she was, arguing again. Rose bent her head briefly. This feud was like one of those maelstroms that captured ships and dragged them to the bottom of the sea. It grabbed every phrase, every gesture, and pulled them into the dispute. "We are all one family now. The Denholmes and the Keighleys."

Her parents stared as if her words made no sense.

"There's nothing to fight about anymore. Yerndon is ours." Or mine, Rose thought. Not theirs. Hers. And Gavin's of course.

Her father looked quite bewildered.

"You must come home with us," her mother said. "You can't stay here alone with…"

"My husband?"

"We will deny…" Again, her mother couldn't complete her sentence.

"Sue was at the wedding. I'm certain she's told all her friends."

"Servants' gossip," snapped her father.

"Which everyone listens to," said Rose. "And in this case, it is perfectly true."

"What is wrong with you?" asked her mother.

Something in Rose snapped. She had tried to talk to them and gotten precisely nowhere. "You know, Mama, nothing. Nothing is wrong with me. Except that I am very busy. I'm sorry to cut your visit short, but I have a great deal to do."

"Here?"

"In the house you wished me to acquire, yes."

"You'll stay, on your own?" Her mother didn't seem able to believe it.

"I am quite capable of running a household. You've trained me to do it."

"Do you wish us to wash our hands of you?" asked her father in an ominous voice.

"No, Papa, I don't. I wish you would consider the changed situation and adjust to it."

He stared at her, open-mouthed.

"We will invite you to dinner when…things are more settled." And you can be more reasonable, Rose did not add aloud. She'd said her piece. She moved forward, herding them back toward their carriage. They were so flustered that they went.

She opened the vehicle's door, handed her mother in, and waited for her father to follow. Then she nodded at the coachman. He gave her a wink as he signaled the horses to start off.

Rose's father stuck his head out the window as the carriage moved away. "We will have more to say about this," he declared.

She was sadly certain that he would.

As soon as the vehicle was out of sight, Rose fetched her specimen box, put on sturdy boots, and started to sneak out of the house. Then she realized that there was no need for stealth. No one could tell her not to roam the moor for as long as she wished. Yes, she needed to set her new household on order. But she could do that in her own time. She took a deep breath, and another. Her life had changed. It didn't feel quite like freedom yet, with her family looming just over the horizon. "I'll find it though," she said to the air, and set off walking.

———

Gavin spotted his sisters near the northern border of the Yerndon property, the one that marched with Keighley land. They were riding along it, staring across as if they were patrolling soldiers planning a raid. Their backs were to him, and momentarily, he was tempted to slip away. But that only put off the meeting. It had to happen sometime. And it was better to begin with the twins. He urged his horse out of the lane and across a field. His sisters turned at the sound of hoofbeats and watched him approach, two identical pairs of accusing eyes.

"What have you done, Gavin?" Jillian asked when he drew near.

"That letter you sent. It was absolutely incomprehensible," said Janet.

"I would have thought it rather easy to understand," he replied.

"We thought at first it must be some idiotic joke," said Janet.

"Not the least bit amusing," said Jillian. "The opposite really."

He simply looked at them with eyebrows raised.

"You have actually married Rose Denholme?" Both twins stared as if they wanted to drill through his skull and see his thoughts.

"I have." And he wasn't sorry. Not the least bit.

"And Tereford indeed signed Yerndon over to us?" Jillian asked.

Not "us," Gavin thought, silently. "To me and Rose," he answered.

"Was the marriage the duke's price for handing it over?" wondered Janet.

Jillian looked at her twin. "Why should he insist on that? Or care?"

"It is really quite outrageous. She must have cajoled him into it."

"But who knows by what means," Jillian said darkly.

"Don't be daft." His sisters' antiphonal nonsense could go on and on. "It was not a price. It was…" And here he was arguing a ridiculous point that had been thrown out like a lure. He'd vowed to stop that. "It was an equitable solution," he finished.

"That's an odd thing to call a marriage," said Jillian.

He'd meant the ownership of Yerndon, not the match. He had not made a marriage of convenience, no matter how convenient the union was in terms of Yerndon. He'd wanted Rose. And she'd wanted him. He'd seen it in her eyes, felt it in her wholehearted kisses.

"I suppose you actually *are* married?" asked Janet as if she still didn't quite believe it.

"Yes," replied Gavin firmly.

"Well, you must come home with us and explain to Mama. She is beside herself."

"There is nothing to explain."

"Mama does not agree," said Jillian.

"Not about any of it," said Janet. "She smashed the best teapot."

He was not in the mood for one of his mother's rants. It was always best to let her cool off for a while before trying reason. "She wanted the Keighleys to own Yerndon. Her wishes have been fulfilled. Perhaps you could remind her of that?" He had tried to do so in his letter.

"*We* don't want to," said the twins in unison.

"And she didn't mean for you to marry Rose Denholme!" Jillian exclaimed.

"Couldn't you have found a better way than being stuck with a boring wife?" asked Janet.

"Rose is not boring," said Gavin.

"She proses on and on about plants," said Jillian.

"Until one is ready to scream," agreed Janet.

"When have you talked to her long enough to be bored?" Gavin asked. "You aren't really acquainted with her. Only with the criticisms you've been taught. And her knowledge of what grows on the moors is fascinating."

"Fascinating?" His sisters stared at him, then at each other.

"Surely he doesn't..." began Jillian.

Janet waved her concern aside. "He is always going on about the moors." She turned back to Gavin. "Mama thinks you can have the marriage set aside," said Janet. "What is it called? Not a divorce, which would be shocking."

"Annulment," said Jillian.

"That's the word. I mean, it's hardly been any time at all."

"We are married and will remain so," said Gavin. His tone brooked no argument. He was tired of this conversation.

"Your whole *lives*?"

"Indeed." It was a rather satisfying idea. If they could just get past this stupid feud.

"Mama won't have it."

"Mama has no choice in this matter," Gavin replied.

"She doesn't like that." Janet looked apprehensive.

"You may tell her..."

"Not me." Both twins raised hands in protest. "She will *insist* that you end this marriage."

Their mother's insistence was difficult to endure, Gavin

thought. Yet he would do so. "Why?" he asked. "What is so terrible?"

"She's a *Denholme*," said Janet.

He shook his head. "This has to end."

"Oh well, Rose might die in childbirth," said Jillian as if in response to his statement.

A horrified shock ran through Gavin. "What did you say?"

Jillian blinked as if startled by her own words.

"Women do," said Janet, automatically supporting her sister. "It is a sad thing but..."

"Is this what we have come to?" Gavin asked them. "Such a depth of venomous spite?"

"I didn't mean I wished it to happen," said Jillian in a smaller voice.

"Of course she did not," said Janet.

"You will not ever say or even think such a thing again." Gavin glared at his younger sisters.

"I shouldn't have said it." Jillian frowned. "I don't know why I did."

The twins were even more deeply enmeshed in the feud than he had been, Gavin realized. They'd been kept closer to his mother, heard more of her complaints. He should have done something about that.

"Come home with us, Gavin, and..."

"My home is at Yerndon now," he interrupted.

"But Keighleys have lived at the manor for hundreds of years."

"You cannot leave Mama all alone," added Jillian. "You know she hates that."

"We are going to Brighton in three weeks, to stay with our aunt and enter society," said Janet.

Gavin hadn't precisely forgotten this plan, but he'd had quite a few other things on his mind.

"We've started packing," Janet said. The twins stared at him with identical anxious eyes.

"Mama will withdraw her permission now that this has happened," Jillian whispered.

It would be good for them to get away. "I'll see that she doesn't," Gavin replied, without knowing how he could fulfill that promise.

"Come and do so now," Jillian urged.

He still wanted to give it time. This was not sheer cowardice. His mother was incapable of listening when she was in a rage. "Tell her I will call in a few days," he said.

"Call?" repeated Janet. "As if she was a stranger?"

"Don't be overdramatic," said Gavin. "I am very weary of Cheltenham tragedies."

"Is that why you married dreary old Rose?" asked Jillian.

Gavin swung around in the saddle. "Listen to me, Jillian. Janet. You are not to speak ill of my wife. Inform Mama as well. I won't stand for it."

"What has happened to you?" Janet asked. "Has Rose Denholme poisoned you against your own family?"

"Remarks like that are just what I mean," Gavin answered. "They must stop. Now."

"Mama will not be told what she can say."

"Then I suppose she could go live with Aunt Mary," Gavin interrupted.

"You would throw her out of her *home*?"

"No, I would not. Though many sons would expect her to move on the occasion of their marriage. But there is no need in this case, if she will stay friends with me."

"Friends?" The twins looked at each other, then back at him. "She's your *mother*."

"And I will treat her with tenderness and respect. As long as she accords my wife the same. I would appreciate it if you could pass along that message. But I understand if you cannot. I will tell her myself." It needed to be soon, Gavin realized, before his mother spread her complaints through the neighborhood. He must balance the timing carefully.

Fifteen

ROSE RETURNED FROM THE MOOR CALMER AND HAPPIER, as she always did, and with a very gratifying new specimen for her collection. Sue caught her ascending the stairs and told her she had more visitors. "Who?" Rose asked unenthusiastically. She did not intend to face Gavin's family without him. If they'd called, she would have them told she was still out.

"Ian and Lucy," her maid replied with the air of a magician revealing a trick.

"Ian and Lucy," Rose couldn't help repeating. She hadn't expected the eloping couple to return here.

"They're sitting in the kitchen, brazen as can be," said her maid. "Shall I send them packing?"

"Is that what you wish to do?"

Sue looked startled to be given a choice. "Well… I don't know."

Rose thought of her parents' reaction to her own hasty marriage. It had not been an elopement, of course. Still, she felt even more sympathy for the errant couple than she had before.

"Their behavior was shocking," Sue added.

She seemed to be working something through in her mind, and Rose let her.

The maid waggled her head between no and yes. "Ian was sorry, I think. That Lucy though, she *will* do just as she likes. You know?"

It would be a good thing to know, Rose thought. Perhaps she did, really. More and more.

"It's…something to see," Sue finished. There seemed to be a tinge of envy in her voice.

Rose made up her mind. "Send them to the front parlor after I have taken off my things."

"You'll see them?"

"Yes."

Sue looked doubtful, and thoughtful as she walked away.

Twenty minutes later, Rose received tall blond, broad-shouldered Ian and pretty, dark-haired Lucy—Mr. and Mrs. Daniels now—by the fireside in the front parlor. They were clearly dressed in their best clothes. "Hello," said Rose. "I…"

Lucy surged forward, fell to her knees before Rose, her skirts spreading around her, and raised her hands in supplication. "Oh, my lady, have mercy on us!"

Rose blinked. "Ah."

"'The quality of mercy is not strange,'" Lucy continued. "'It droppeth like a blessing from heaven to them as gives and them as takes.'"

"'Strange,'" repeated Rose. That wasn't right, was it?

Ian looked both embarrassed and proud. He held out a hand. "Now, Lucy, stand up."

She did so, gracefully, looking pleased with herself and not at all self-conscious.

"Her granny was an actress on the stage in London town,"

Ian said. He gazed at his new wife as if he couldn't quite believe she was his.

Lucy tossed her head. "A fine one too. Before she met Grandad and settled down." She cocked her head at Rose, bright-eyed, looking for encouragement.

Rose, fascinated, couldn't help but give it. "Was she indeed?"

The girl nodded. "She had a book of Shakespeare, and she read it out to us of an evening. It was like our own play right there in the house." Lucy made an expansive gesture as if she was onstage herself. "Granny always said I was the most like her of all her family. My uncle Ritchie got the book when she died. But it should rightly have come to me."

"That is the uncle you are staying with?" asked Rose.

"Oh no. That's Uncle Collum, my mother's brother. Uncle Ritchie is on my dad's side." Lucy's smile was lovely. She looked as if she would happily enumerate all her relatives at the least excuse.

Rose was tempted, but said only, "You have come to see me?"

Ian shifted from foot to foot. "Miss... My lady, that is, we're in a bit of a fix. We find we aren't well suited to farm labor."

"It is horridly tedious!" Lucy exclaimed with another wide gesture. "'Tomorrow, and tomorrow, and tomorrow, creeping at a pretty pace till you're fretted half to dusty death.'"

Ian couldn't hide an appreciative smile, and Rose liked him for it. "It's not that we don't wish to work hard," he went on. "We will! But we're not trained for the farm, you see. Not like we are for our old posts. So, when we heard that you and Sir Gavin had wed and came back here to Yerndon…"

The news had spread even faster than she expected, Rose thought. The tide of talk must be rising all over the neighborhood. Gossip was surely one of the speediest things on earth.

"We thought we'd ask if we could come back and work for you," Ian finished in a rush. "As you'll be needing staff."

"Ah," said Rose again.

"I can cook," said Lucy without the touch of drama. "My ma taught me some, and I was learning more from Mrs. Jenner."

That was the Keighleys' cook, who was quite skilled, Rose had heard. Not that she'd ever been asked to dine there.

"And Mrs. Redding as well," Lucy added.

The Terefords' cook had been superlative.

"And Ian can do anything a butler could."

"Lucy," the former footman said.

"Well, you could." Lucy might have seemed impudent or coarsely heedless, but she didn't. Rather, her raised chin and steady gaze simply refused to be cowed by others' opinions. "We may as well *ask*, now we're here," she added, angling not only to be reinstated, but for promotions.

Rose had to admire her spirit. She contemplated the two young people. They were trying to make their way in the world. Could they be blamed for that? They'd been rash, but they would not have been given easy permission to marry, as servants and with the families at odds as they were. Rose had been rash too, if it came to that. And oppressed by the feud as well.

She did need staff, and Ian and Lucy had done well when they worked here. It was not so easy to find trained help in this widely scattered neighborhood. But hiring them would brand her household as unconventional. At the least. Did she care?

Did she?

What was her household to be like? She could make her own choices now.

Ian looked braced for a refusal and ready to face the consequences of his actions. Rose respected that. Lucy was brightly expectant. "Very well," Rose said. "We will give it a trial and see how we get on."

Lucy clapped her hands.

"A trial," Rose repeated.

"Yes, my lady," said Ian. He looked at Lucy. She nodded.

"You know Sue," Rose said.

"She's a friend," said Ian. They had worked together at Rose's parents' house.

"We get on well," said Lucy.

Rose wondered if they really did, or if Lucy just thought so. Sue had seemed ambivalent. "Two of the duchess's staff stayed on temporarily to help, Gemma Varley and Annie Roush."

"Gemma'll be wanting to go back to London, I'd think," said Lucy.

Both the maids had already expressed that wish, after the kitchen fire. Rose had expected it, though not so soon. And the Smithsons would be returning to their cottage. They were willing to help temporarily, but not join a regular staff.

Yerndon was in danger of having no servants at all soon. "Do you know anyone else who is looking for a post?" she asked.

"I might, my lady," said Ian.

"There's Rafe," added Lucy. "And Nelly."

"Not Rafe," Ian replied. "He drinks. And Nelly…" His voice trailed off.

Perhaps she shouldn't have asked, Rose thought. "We can see how you get on with the cooking, Lucy."

"If you like it, I'll be Mrs. Daniels in the end," Lucy replied with a grin.

Cooks were usually given that mark of status. Lucy really was irrepressible. Rose had to admire that, but she would be the one in charge. "We'll see," she said.

"We'll be loyal to you to the very end," Lucy added. She put a hand over her heart.

"That isn't really—" Rose began.

"Us having the same star-crossed matches, like," Lucy continued. "Only *we'll* not end up like Romeo and Juliet."

"Dead," said Rose.

"Yes, my lady. We won't."

"Certainly not." Lucy would certainly make Yerndon interesting. She wanted interesting, Rose decided.

"Not being so foolish as to drink down some bally potion without being sure *you* knew the wheeze," Lucy added, looking at Ian.

He nodded as if he'd heard something like this before.

"Make your plan together, that's our motto." Lucy said to Rose. "Don't go haring off on your own."

It seemed to Rose like quite good advice.

"I'll go and take charge of the kitchen, shall I?" Lucy smiled cheerily.

Take charge indeed, thought Rose. "Not until I've talked to the others. Do you know the Smithsons?" And would Mrs. Smithson, older and rather stiff, object to the presence of the runaway couple?

"Course we do," answered Lucy. "Or I do, at any rate. Jem Smithson's father was a cousin of my granny."

"The actress?"

"Yes, my lady."

That might be good or bad. Lucy didn't seem concerned, but she clearly wasn't one to worry. "You could go and fetch your things from where you're staying," Rose suggested.

Ian looked sheepish. "We brought them," said Lucy. "Just hoping, you know."

She seemed very good at that.

"We could take that room Mrs. Redding was in."

The Terefords' cook had used the best of the servants' quarters. "Just stay here for a bit," Rose replied, refusing to be rushed. She went to assemble the current denizens of Yerndon and inform them of her decision.

When Gavin returned to the house late in the afternoon, he was surprised to be greeted by Ian at the door. "Ah, hello."

"We've come back, sir," the footman said.

"Oh, have you?" Who was "we"? Gavin wondered.

"Yes, sir. Lady Keighley is sitting in the front parlor."

"My mother?" His pulse sped up. Was she confronting Rose?

"Miss Denholme as was," said the footman with an odd look.

"Oh." He must become accustomed to that. "Of course. Thank you." He went upstairs to change out of his riding clothes.

When he came back down, he paused at the parlor door. It was ajar, and he saw Rose before she noticed him. She was sitting at the writing desk with papers and an inkwell before her. She'd lit a branch of candles on this gray afternoon, and they threw golden light over her face and blue cambric gown. She dipped her quill and made a note on a page. She looked intent but peaceful, softly beautiful, and all he desired.

He was a lucky man, Gavin thought. Against all odds—very high odds—they'd discovered each other. If the Terefords had not decided to visit this far-flung bit of their properties... That didn't bear thinking of. He pushed the door farther open and walked into the room. Rose started and stiffened in her chair. The peace drained out of her expression, then was replaced by relief. "Oh, it's you."

"I hope I am not interrupting," Gavin said.

"Of course not. I was just... When the door opened, I didn't know... My parents were here earlier."

They had upset her, Gavin saw. "Not a pleasant visit?"

"The fact that we own Yerndon, as they always wanted, seemed to make no difference to them," Rose said. "They were still angry and dissatisfied. They didn't listen to me." She grimaced and murmured, "They never have."

"I met my sisters when I was out riding. They were the same."

"And your mother?"

He said nothing as the answer was obvious.

"I'm a little frightened of her," Rose said.

"I won't let her disturb you."

"How? Am I to shut myself away here and avoid seeing her? I have no wish to be a hermit like old Mr. Cantrell."

"Of course not. My mother will become reconciled—"

"Reconciled," she interrupted. "A rather sad word."

"Are you regretting our marriage, Rose?" he asked bluntly.

"No. I do not. I will not." Her expression softened. "I could not."

The relief that coursed through him was profound. "Neither do I. That is the important thing."

"I do regret the brangling that surrounds us. And will not seem to end."

"We will deal with our families together. They will come round."

"Do you really think so?"

"I do."

This echo of their wedding vows seemed to reverberate in the room.

Rose took a deep breath. "I am getting organized." She gestured at the pages before her. "Thinking what servants to hire."

With that, Gavin remembered who the footman was. "Was that one of the runaways at the front door?"

"Yes, Ian and Lucy asked to come back," said Rose. "I agreed to a trial."

"That won't be…a problem?" The neighborhood would have comments.

"I don't intend to let it." She leaned forward. "I have been thinking, Gavin. About how people treat each other."

Her parents' visit had sparked that as well, Gavin assumed.

"I want to have a household where everyone is happy to be here, and servants are well paid for their work as well as appreciated. Like the duchess's."

"Amity," said Gavin. They had not seen nearly enough of that in their lives. He liked the idea.

"If I can manage it," Rose added.

"You can."

She looked at him. "The place feels so empty with the Terefords gone. As if we don't fill it."

"They had more people with them."

"That's true. I think, though, that even just the two of them would create a home." She emphasized the last word as if it held deep meaning. "What if we can't?"

"Why shouldn't we?" Gavin asked.

"We are two people who have been at odds for all of our adult lives."

"Until lately," he hastened to point out.

Rose nodded. "Until lately. But we were taught to be that way, in homes full of friction, by families who don't want to give up their misguided anger."

"And will try to goad us back into it," Gavin replied. Ironically, the idea irritated him.

She nodded.

"We will refuse."

"We will. But what if we don't know how to be any other way?"

He went over to take her hand. "We've already proven we can change. And dare. We went off to Leeds and got married."

"We did."

"So we will create whatever sort of household you want."

"You will help me?"

"All I can, though I think you are better at amity than I am," Gavin teased. Rose laughed, as he had hoped she would. He bent to drop a kiss on her lips. "I will take on any task you assign me, of course."

"You will obey my commands?"

"Aye, captain." He sprawled on the sofa. "With the utmost pleasure."

She laughed again, her cheeks pink. "I suppose the income from Yerndon is small."

"For now, yes. The estate has not been kept productive."

"I'm sure it will be under your management," Rose said.

He enjoyed her confidence. "In time. But hire whomever you like. I can provide funds."

"It wouldn't be right to use the income from your old estate."

"Why not? It is my money."

"Indeed." Rose frowned. "Well, I have never had any," she added, so quietly he barely heard.

"I…" Gavin stopped. With the way things had been in the past, it was important to think before he spoke. Rose had made that point already. "You should take charge of everything Yerndon yields."

She blinked at him, astonished.

"We wouldn't have it without you, Rose." He gestured at the room "This all began with your suggestion that we make a show of getting along. I would have blundered along sniping and complaining in the old way. And probably stamped off home in a few days after offending everyone."

"Your innate kindness would have emerged," she said.

"My...?"

"As it did when an opportunity came along. With the Brontë children." She left the writing desk and came to sit beside him. "And at the Milsomes' ball. And long ago, with the fishhook."

Gavin didn't even know what she meant by the last one. But he forgot to wonder when she leaned forward and kissed him.

His arms went around her, and she laced hers around his neck. Each of their kisses had been more intoxicating than the last, Gavin thought. How was that possible? He let his hands roam. Rose pressed against him, sending fire racing through his veins. His knee slipped between hers.

It was late afternoon. The night was yet to come. But did they have to wait for night? Couldn't they go upstairs right now? This was their house. They could do as they liked. Who would stop them?

A dark-haired girl wearing a large apron over a plain gown came into the room. Without knocking. Anyone with the least sensibility would have withdrawn when she saw what they were doing, Gavin thought. But this girl just stood before them, grinning. She was holding a large wooden spoon, he noticed. Why? Rose pulled away from him, lamentably.

"'What light through yon window breaks,' eh?" asked the interloper. "But not from up on a balcony? Bit better than *that*."

Gavin wondered if she was touched in her upper works. What was that supposed to mean?

"What is it, Lucy?" asked Rose.

With the name, Gavin realized this was the eloper, the *footman's* new wife. He recognized her now. That didn't explain the spoon, however.

"It's about dinner. What it's to be, or not to be."

Rose laughed. "As long as it doesn't involve any slings and arrows."

Gavin frowned at her.

The girl's grin widened. "What does it mean, slings? I always wondered about that."

"I think it has to do with throwing," Rose replied. "Like spears. Or perhaps catapults? Those siege engines that hurl rocks at castle walls?"

"Hurl," repeated Lucy. "That's a fine word."

Rose looked at Gavin. "He can't have meant slingshots, can he?"

"Slingshots?" What the deuce were they talking about? And why wouldn't the girl go away so that they could return to their previous pleasures? "He who?"

"Shakespeare," replied Rose.

Vague recollections of declaiming actors stirred in Gavin's mind.

"'Slingshots of outrageous fortune,'" said Rose. And giggled.

Lucy laughed outright. She had no trace of deference.

"It's hard to figure what he's saying sometimes, ain't it? Like shuffling off a mort of coil. Is it wiggling out of a wound-up rope, do you think? I seen a man do that at a fun fair once."

"That's a good question," said Rose. She turned to Gavin. "What do you think?"

The girl looked at him too, with happy heedlessness. She did not intend to leave, clearly. "Did you actually work for my mother?" escaped Gavin. Mama would never have tolerated this sort of conversation. She would have labeled it insufferable cheek and squashed this girl like a bug.

"Matter of three months," said Lucy. "I reckon she was about to turn me off when she sent me over here."

To be rid of her, Gavin was sure. And perhaps to stir up trouble for the visit. That would be like his mother.

"She'd heard about Granny," the girl added.

"Granny?"

"Lucy's grandmother was an actress," said Rose. "On the London stage."

The girl nodded proudly.

"Before she met Lucy's grandfather and settled down," Rose went on, her eyes dancing.

Gavin gave her a look.

"Lady Keighley... *Old* Lady Keighley didn't approve," said the girl. "Turned up her nose, she did, and was glad to be shut of me. She wouldn't have taken me back. Not that I wanted to go. She's a right shrew. Not a tamed one either."

Gavin suppressed a snort of laughter. He couldn't let it out. One didn't encourage such disrespectful remarks, whatever grains of truth they might contain.

"Begging your pardon, sir," added Lucy. "No offense meant." She bobbed a curtsy.

Intercepting a quizzical glance from Rose, Gavin shrugged. Apparently, this was a sample of the sort of household Rose wanted. It couldn't be more unlike the one he'd grown up in. As the idea sank in, Gavin realized that was a good thing.

"What was it about the dinner?" Rose asked.

"Right. There's a chicken Mr. Smithson fetched, if we was wishful to kill it. Only it looks like a good layer to me, my lady. So we might want to keep it for the eggs. For a bit anyways, to see how she goes."

"Foxes will be after it if you put it in the stables," said Gavin.

"That'd be a waste," replied Lucy. "We need a proper coop and a flock of birds."

"I know," said Gavin dryly. It was a new experience, being told his business by a maid, and should have been offensive. But this girl's cheerful cheek was disarming.

"Perhaps I'd better come and look over what we have." Rose gave him a wistful glance as she went out. Gavin's regret at losing her company was only mitigated by the certainty of what tonight would bring.

Sixteen

ROSE WAS STILL TINGLING WITH AROUSAL AND BUBBLING with amusement as she went though the supplies available and plans for their dinner. It was a distracting combination, further complicated by the squawking chicken. Fortunately, Lucy seemed to know what she was doing and only needed a bit of guidance.

The noise and closed doors obscured the sound of horses outside. So Rose was not prepared to find Gavin's mother in the front parlor when she returned there. She wouldn't have returned if she'd known.

The older Lady Keighley was sitting on the sofa where Rose and Gavin had recently embraced. She wore her outdoor garments and a sour expression. "A fine thing," she was saying. "When my only son does not come to me. Forces me to drive through the cold to speak to him."

The April day was really rather clement, Rose thought.

Their visitor spotted her in the doorway. Her expression grew grimmer. She turned her head away. "I do not know why you wished to humiliate me in that way," she went on.

Gavin sighed audibly.

Rose had to do her duty. More, she had to support him.

"May I take your bonnet and cloak?" she asked. "And offer you some refreshment."

"No," replied the older woman without looking at her. "I won't be staying long."

Rose supposed she ought to urge her to stay for dinner. It would not then be the cozy meal she had anticipated. Still, here she was. And she was Gavin's mother.

She and Lady Keighley had never had much to do with each other. As a child, Rose had been a creature of the moors. Later, the quarrel between their two families had made easy relations impossible. Gavin had inherited his strong features from his mother, Rose noted. The broad forehead and square jaw that looked so good on him made his mother forbidding and reinforced her daunting reputation. Or perhaps it was her stony glare.

"Perhaps you might go away, so that I can talk with my son," Lady Keighley said. Her icy tone implied that she was addressing a negligible person.

"No," said Gavin. "Rose will not be ordered out of her own parlor."

"Hers!"

"Ours," said Rose.

"Ours," Gavin echoed. He moved to stand at Rose's side.

The older woman glared at them. "This…arrangement is entirely unacceptable," she said.

"We were sent here to…acquire the estate from the Duke of Tereford," Gavin replied. "We are now the joint owners of Yerndon. You *got* what you wanted, Mother. Can no one comprehend this?"

"Joint!" Her mouth pursed up as if she'd eaten something rotten.

Just like her parents, Rose thought. Nothing was ever good enough. "They're all angry because the matter was resolved by us and not in the way they decreed," she said, half to herself.

Lady Keighley reared back as if she'd been slapped. "I beg your pardon!"

Gavin nodded thoughtfully.

"Why does the method matter so much?" Rose asked. "If the outcome is favorable?"

"It is not favorable for you to be married to my son!"

She seemed fond of those two words, Rose thought. They made Gavin sound like a possession.

"I shall apply for an annulment," said Lady Keighley. "It is the only proper course of action."

"You don't have the right to do that," replied Gavin. "Marriages are not set aside because you don't like them."

"We will see about that!"

"We would oppose you, of course. You will only make a fool of yourself."

"How dare you speak to me in that way?"

"Like a reasonable man? Trying to make a reasonable point?"

Lady Keighley rose with a swirl of her cloak. "I shall not stay here to be insulted!"

"I have not insulted you, Mother."

"We would like to—" began Rose.

"Insult me?"

"No, I was going to say—"

"Don't speak to me, you conniving little minx!"

"No," said Gavin. "You will not speak in that way to my wife. Ever."

"You would side with a *Denholme* over me?"

"You are being ridiculous, Mother. Will you let that go?"

Lady Keighley's face contorted. She bared her teeth in a rictus of rage, shook her fist at them. She made a frightening sight, and Rose couldn't help shrinking back a little. Gavin put a sustaining arm around Rose's shoulders. His mother made a low rasping sound. Then she clutched her chest and groaned, sinking to her knees.

Gavin started forward and bent over her. "Mama?" She grasped his coat lapel with one hand, crushing the fabric as if she would never let go.

"Help her onto the sofa," Rose said.

Old Lady Keighley shook her head emphatically. Pulling so hard on Gavin's coat that he nearly toppled into her, she struggled upright. "Home!" she ordered, swaying on her feet. "Take me home! At once! I will not stay here!"

"You should lie down for a…"

"No, no, no!" she cried, her voice rising to a shriek by the end.

Supporting her tottering figure, Gavin looked at Rose. "I had better take her."

"Should she be jostled in a carriage?" Rose asked. Even though it would be a strain to have Lady Keighley as a guest, she didn't want her to grow worse.

His mother made a slashing gesture. "I won't stay here!" she repeated.

"Send word to the doctor," Gavin said. "Ask him to come to Keighley Manor as soon as may be."

Rose nodded.

He held out his free hand. Rose took it. His fingers were strong and warm around hers. "I'll return as soon as I can."

Lady Keighley emitted a growl. The sound couldn't be called anything else.

Rose squeezed her husband's hand and let go. He tightened his arm around his mother and helped her out.

Her carriage was outside. The coachman had been walking the horses up and down. He pulled up when they emerged, and Gavin half heaved his mother inside. "The manor," he said to the driver, then joined her.

His mother leaned back against the cushions as they drove, her head tilted back, eyes closed, jaw tight. Gavin asked what was wrong, how she felt, was there pain, but he received only stark silence in answer. After a while, he gave up and settled for bracing her against bumps and jolts.

The journey seemed long, but at last they turned into the lane and stopped before the stone house where Gavin had been born and lived until recently. He sprang down and helped his mother from the carriage. She leaned heavily on him. The door was opening by the time they reached it. "My mother is ill," he said to Franks, the butler. "The doctor has been sent for." He trusted Rose for that. "We must get her up to her chamber. Summon her maid."

His sisters appeared as they were making a halting progress up the stairs. "What has happened?" asked Jillian.

"What's wrong?" said Janet.

"Mama is not well—" Gavin began.

"As if I could be," their mother croaked. "After what you have done."

Gavin's sisters looked reproachfully at him. He continued helping their mother up the steps.

They left her with her maid to be put to bed and gathered in the drawing room to await the doctor.

"What did you do to her?" Jillian asked Gavin.

"I didn't do anything."

"You *married* Rose Denholme," said Janet. "She's mad as fire about that."

"As she often is, about any number of things," Gavin replied. But he felt a stirring of guilt.

"Not like this," said Jillian. "What did you say? What did Rose do? Did she insult Mama?"

"No, of course she did not. She never would."

"Her father did," said Janet.

"That is irrelevant."

"How can you say so?" asked Jillian. "You joined up with our enemies."

"They are not—"

"And driven Mama into a decline," said Janet. "You must have been an absolute beast. I've never seen her like this."

"I…" Under a rising tide of guilt, Gavin groped for words to defend himself. He had spoken to her calmly. He'd wanted reconciliation. What should he… A memory surfaced from years past. "I have," he replied.

"What?" His sisters gazed at him.

"She took a turn when our father died," Gavin remembered.

He'd been grieving himself, taking on new responsibilities, and there had been some disagreement about… He couldn't recall what exactly. But his mother had had a similar attack in the midst of their dispute. The same dreadful contorted expression and sudden collapse. She'd taken to her bed, though she'd issued a stream of orders and complaints from it that had made his tasks more difficult.

The twins looked at each other. "She did?"

"You were too young to recall," Gavin suggested.

"The house went quiet," said Jillian. "We crept about like mice."

Janet gazed at her sister. "As if all the life had gone with Papa."

"Yes," replied Gavin as Jillian nodded. His mother had been…furious at her husband's loss. He remembered that quite well. When the man who'd found Papa out in the fields brought the news of his death, Mama had almost hit him.

Dr. Baring arrived and was taken straight upstairs. He spent nearly an hour with their mother before joining them in the drawing room.

"Lady Keighley is unwell," the small, plump man told them.

This was obvious, and unhelpful. "What is wrong?" Gavin asked.

The doctor avoided his gaze. "An excess of choler."

"Collar?" asked Jillian. "What do you mean?"

"It is one of the bodily humors," the doctor began.

"And signifies irascibility," Gavin put in. He remembered that after his father died, Mama had risen from her bed whenever there was anything she particularly wished to do. And experienced renewed attacks when she was contradicted. He'd been young and woeful. He hadn't made the connections.

"Will she be all right?" asked Janet.

"I have advised her to take things more calmly," replied Dr. Baring.

"But that does not seem to be her nature," said Gavin. His sisters frowned at him.

The doctor avoided his eyes again. He was definitely shifty, like a man who'd received dubious instructions. "She should not be upset. You must take care not to agitate her."

"Do whatever she wants, you mean?" Gavin asked. He was beginning to suspect that his mother was feigning illness.

"Of course we should," said Jillian.

Dr. Baring chose to address the twins. "I've given Lady Keighley something to ease her. You should let her rest for a while. I will call again tomorrow to see how she goes on."

"Thank you, Doctor," said Janet.

With a relieved nod, the man departed.

As soon as he was gone, the twins turned on Gavin. "You can't leave," said Jillian.

"I'll stay here tonight." He'd already made up his mind to that. He would write a note to be taken to Rose at Yerndon.

"You must return home for good," said Janet. "You must stay with Mama." She gazed at Jillian and then at Gavin. "Brighton," she said.

Her sister nodded. "I know it is selfish to think about that now. But we have never been *anywhere*."

They both looked near tears.

"Of course we are worried about Mama."

"We are not very good nurses, though."

"The doctor said so when you had that fever, Gavin."

"He threw us out of your room."

"Said we made you worse with our fidgets and chatter."

And an antiphonal flow rather like this one, Gavin thought. The twins always seemed to have a larger impact than two mere individuals. "There is some time yet before you are to go."

"But…"

"I suspect Mama will recover quite soon." He would need to discover the true nature of her complaint, or pretense. He went to write his note and give it to a groom to take to Yerndon. He tried not to indulge in wistful thoughts of Rose and the very different sort of night he'd been anticipating.

Later in the evening, Gavin went to see his mother, taking a chair beside her bed. She was sitting up, wearing a nightdress and a lace cap. Her eyes were bright and her cheeks rosy. She didn't look at all ill. "There you are," she said. "Now we are settled again. We can do what needs to be done."

"And that would be?"

"You must see, now that I have got you away from that hussy."

To describe Rose as a hussy was so ridiculous that Gavin nearly laughed. But the situation was too sad for humor.

"You can't have lost all your wits," his mother added. She used the sarcastic tone that was designed to make one feel dim. Gavin was quite familiar with it. He felt his temper stirring. He bit off a sharp reply. She was ill—perhaps. There was no sign of it now.

His mother counted on her fingers. "Set this farcical marriage aside. How you let yourself be...cajoled into it, I will never understand. Idiocy, Gavin!"

His anger grew.

"Dispute this 'joint' ownership of Yerndon in the courts," she went on. "The idea! A chit who knowns nothing of estate management to hold land? Ludicrous. It is an insult to you. A calculated snub. It's as if those London people set out to make a mockery of the Keighleys."

"They did no such thing," snapped Gavin. And then, catching a sly, sideways glint in his mother's eyes, he realized that she wanted him angry. Furious even. Too irate to think or analyze. It was the emotion she knew best. And knew best how to make use of.

He sat back, anger diverted by...dismay.

Suddenly he saw his mother in a different light. Being away from the manor, as he had not been since his school days when things had been very different here, had altered his point of view. She hugged anger to her. It was her friend, her defense, her tool. She'd cultivated it in him, like some sort of internal gardener.

"Yerndon will be ours, as it always should have been," Mama continued. "The Keighleys will not be scorned."

Which no one had done, Gavin noted. But the word was designed to enflame. "And Rose?" he asked.

His mother made a dismissive gesture. "She has a home to go back to."

"There would be talk," he replied, testing how far she would go with this.

"Well, she shouldn't have behaved like a lightskirt if she didn't wish to be talked about. Spending the night with you on the moor!"

"Along with five children."

"Too young to understand scandalous behavior."

Did his mother actually imagine that he and Rose had indulged in improper acts in front of the Brontë brood? The most sharp-eyed, intelligent youngsters he'd ever met? That was ridiculous. And…he was letting himself be steered toward an irrelevant argument.

"In time you will bring a bride here," his mother went on, with the air of one offering a treat. "A nice respectable girl."

"Someone you can dominate, you mean?"

"What a word!" She gave a false laugh. "Nothing of the kind. But I suppose my advice and guidance are not wholly worthless."

"You are not really ill, are you, Mama?"

"What?" She fell back on the bed and clutched her chest. "Dr. Baring—"

"What did that quack say to you? I told him—"

"To order us to do whatever you say?"

"To let you know that my health requires your—"

"Absolute obedience? How could you pretend that way, Mama? You must know how it worried us."

"I had to do whatever was necessary to bring you to your senses! Am I to hold back when people conspire to humiliate me?"

"You know, Mama, I don't think anyone actually does that."

She didn't seem to hear him. "I am not some meek little mouse."

No, she looked for battles so that she could blame others for her troubles. Gavin didn't like this observation, but he couldn't help seeing it. Had she been this way before his father died? He didn't think so. "And you are not truly ill," he said.

She bared her teeth. "You have no idea how I suffer!"

"I don't suppose I do." He didn't know how to help her either, though he would have been glad to. "I am going home tomorrow," he added.

She looked bewildered. "You are at home."

He shook his head. "Yerndon is my home now. With my wife."

"But we will have that false marriage—"

"There is nothing false about it." He met her glaring eyes, carefully not angry. Which was a fierce inner battle.

"She is a Denholme!"

"I am so tired of that fight."

"You cannot care more for her than for your own mother?"

Gavin started to struggle with the question. How could he possibly choose? Conflicting impulses and loyalties threatened to overwhelm him. Then he realized that he didn't need to answer. This was another argument he was not required to have. He could care for both of them, as deeply as he was able, more than he now knew, and not stint either one. "It is not a contest," he said, half to himself.

"Contest? What are you talking about?"

"Simple good sense?" Gavin murmured. He was entranced with the idea—arguments one need not have.

His mother's fingers twisted the cloth of her nightdress. "You will leave me here to die alone?"

"No, Mama, I will not. I will visit you quite often."

"Visit!"

"And if you should ever be truly ill, I will move heaven and earth to aid you."

"I am ill," she declared in a petulant tone that was not the least convincing. "Are you calling me a liar?"

"But I will not be chivied into needless debates." He stood up.

"That Denholme chit has ruined you!"

"Or redeemed me," Gavin said as he went out.

Seventeen

THE MARRIAGE OF SIR GAVIN KEIGHLEY AND MISS ROSE Denholme was the wonder of the neighborhood. Over the next few days, they received a stream of callers, come to view this marvel after all the years of feuding. Some were looking for tidbits of gossip, wondering how in the world it had happened. Others were merely observing social forms. Some were glad to think the long enmity was at last over and they might look forward to a more cordial local society. Rose wished she could agree with that last group, but their families were making that impossible. They still refused to accept the change.

When Rose sent for her things, her parents refused to send them, including her precious shelves of specimen books. That bit of petty spite really hurt her. They knew how much she cherished those records. Gavin sent a pair of men to retrieve his possessions, and they reported that his mother had railed at them and threatened to have them forcibly ejected. Fortunately, the manor servants were well acquainted with the messengers and had not attacked them. Gavin's sisters had prevented their mother from firing a shotgun.

"What if they will never live peaceably together?" Rose asked Gavin when they heard about this incident. "I am so weary of the fighting."

He merely nodded.

"At least your mother doesn't sound ill."

"No, she appears to be in fine form," he answered dryly.

He offered to dispatch the same men to wrest Rose's things from her old home. She refused for now, not wishing to provoke her father even more.

Their work on the estate was satisfying, and their nights together were tenderly glorious. But the situation remained unhappy. And each of them found it harder because they understood the other's pain.

One bright spot for Rose was setting up a room devoted to her plant collection efforts. She'd emptied the back corner bedchamber, sending the bed to the attics, and brought in a large table set up for pressing specimens, as well as oil lamps to supplement the light of the two windows. She would order shelves built on all the available wall space and have all the storage she could desire. It was a joy to have a room all her own, dedicated to the work she loved. She would never again have to cram items into awkward piles or squeeze out a few inches by discarding other possessions. Gavin, brought in to admire her progress, was full of admiration. When things grew particularly fraught, Rose went and sat in her room and savored it.

At breakfast on a fine late April morning, Rose found a folded note by her plate. When she had opened and read it, she told Gavin, "The Brontë children want to come to call."

"I thought they were confined to quarters since their night on the moor."

"Apparently the ban has been lifted." She held up the

note. "This comes from their aunt. It seems their mother's sister has arrived to help."

"Well, they are welcome to come, of course."

"It will be pleasant to see them," said Rose wistfully.

"Less complicated."

"Yes." He understood with no more words than that. It really was a miracle to be grateful for.

The following afternoon the Haworth party arrived in a hired gig from the village inn, and Rose and Gavin went to the door to greet them. The children tumbled out in a chattering mob, the older ones carrying bundles. They were followed by a dignified, dark-haired woman with a picnic hamper. Maria Brontë introduced her as their aunt Elizabeth Branwell. "We've come to have a celebration," said Charlotte. "Because that's what one does for a marriage, only we don't get invited to such things since we are too young."

In their case, there hadn't been one, Rose thought, unless she counted the wedding day in Leeds.

"So we will make our own," declared little Branwell, who lugged a box that seemed nearly as large as he was. "And we brought a gift too!" He thrust the box at Gavin.

"I am to open it?" Gavin asked.

There was a chorus of assent.

He did so and drew out a man's hat.

"Yours was spoiled by the rain," said Maria. "When you let us drink from it. So we bought you another. Well, Aunt Branwell did."

Gavin put it on and bowed to a round of admiring applause.

"We have cakes too!" said the sole Brontë son. "And surprises."

They went inside and settled in the front parlor. The cakes were unpacked and added to the refreshments Rose had provided. "This is lavish," said Elizabeth Brontë.

"What is lavish?" asked little Emily.

"Bounteous," said Charlotte.

Emily did not look enlightened. Rose marveled again at these children's precocity.

"A special treat for a special occasion," added Maria. "Not an everyday indulgence."

As the children dug into the food, Rose sat down beside their aunt. "It was kind of you to bring them to visit," she said.

"They very much wanted to come, and I could see no harm in it."

"And you purchased the hat." Rose wondered what the Reverend Brontë had thought about this expedition.

"I have my own income and can do as I like to some extent."

"All the more admirable that you have come to help during their mother's illness."

"My sister is dying," said Elizabeth Branwell baldly. "I could not turn away."

Rose made a sympathetic sound.

The other woman shook her head. "Six children. Mr. Brontë is not up to the task."

This might have put a damper on the occasion for Rose, but the youngsters were too lively for that. Their animation and imagination could help carry them through the sad times ahead, Rose thought.

When the cakes and other treats were eaten, Maria unfolded a small easel and set it on a table. Elizabeth brought an oblong package wrapped in a scarf and set it upright there. "This is our other gift," she said. "We made it for you."

"I helped," declared Emily.

"So did I," said Branwell.

"We all did," said Charlotte. "But it was mainly Maria and Elizabeth who..."

"Don't spoil the surprise," her eldest sister interrupted.

Maria stood on one side of the easel. Elizabeth Brontë on the other. "Behold the Annals of Haworth Parsonage," said the latter. Maria pulled the scarf away.

A homemade book was revealed, covers of cardboard bound together to enclose a stack of pages. The front was decorated by a watercolor of the crevice where they'd sheltered from the storm. The place was clearly identifiable. "Oh, that's well done," said Rose.

"Maria painted it," said Charlotte. "She's an artist."

"She is teaching me to paint," said Branwell.

The eldest Brontë blushed and looked down. "Everyone did their part," she said. "Elizabeth wrote the words, and Charlotte did some drawings too."

"When I'm older, I shall write a story about you," Charlotte replied.

Smiling, Elizabeth Brontë opened the book. The title was in large lettering that could be seen across the room— THE NIGHT ON THE MOOR. The lettering was bordered by tiny drawings of moorland creatures like an illuminated manuscript. Emily and Branwell made muted fanfare noises. Elizabeth turned the page.

"'One of us was lost,'" she read. This was accompanied by a drawing of a tiny figure on a tor, arms extended, hair streaming in the wind. Storm clouds massed on the horizon.

"That's me," said Emily. "I told Maria what it looked like." She waved her arms. "*Whoosh, whoosh.*"

Elizabeth turned the page. "'And one was shivering,'" she read. Beside these words, there was a sketch of a small boy being pulled from a stream by three girls.

"The rock tipped," Branwell muttered softly, as if this was a sore point. "Wasn't my fault."

"'None knew what to do,'" Elizabeth continued. She had clearly been appointed narrator. She turned another page. "'And then rescue came!'"

Emily and Branwell provided more fanfare sounds.

Rose had to suppress a laugh. This page showed two heroic figures on horseback, standing at the top of a rise, surrounded by beams of light. Like knights of old and quite an enhancement of the actual circumstances, but very well executed. She met Gavin's gaze. His gray eyes were dancing.

Elizabeth turned another page. "'They found the youngest lostling. And guided all to shelter.'" A series of small drawings here showed the descent of the tor and ride across the moor.

"'Only just in time,'" said Elizabeth dramatically, turning the next page to reveal a watercolor of a cliff beaten by a storm. "'Thunder, lightning, lashing rain,'" she said, shuddering.

"*Boom!*" exclaimed Branwell.

"*Whoosh, whoosh,*" added Emily. Carried away by excitement, they jumped up and danced around the room.

"Crash, smash," cried Branwell, waving his arms.

"'The horses wouldn't endure it,'" Elizabeth continued. "'They fled, leaving the little band at the mercy of the elements.'"

She turned a page. This one showed another view of the crevice including seven crouching figures. Rain sheeted down before them. Lightning slashed across the sky. It was a grim scene. More so than the reality, Rose thought.

"'The rescuers made fire!'" The next page had several small pictures of increasing coziness. "'They drew water.'" Gavin's hat featured here. "'They made a refuge in the wilderness.'" The hanging greatcoat partition was skillfully rendered. "'And guarded our rest.'" Sleeping children lay in a row by the fire.

Elizabeth gave her audience time to appreciate the details of this sequence before she turned the next page. "'And when the morning came, they brought succor.'" She looked proud of the final word.

"Ta-ra-ra," cried Branwell.

Strictly speaking, Gavin had brought the succor, Rose noted. This drawing showed a mounted troop arriving at the crevice, with rather more members than had been involved. It might, in fact, have been an entire regiment. The effect was striking. Artistic license was not to be disputed.

"'And returned the errant pilgrims safely home,'" said Elizabeth, turning the final page. A watercolor of Haworth parsonage in the sunshine graced it, again very well done.

Elizabeth gestured at the picture, then put a hand to her breast and bowed her head.

The group erupted in applause. "You were splendid!" declared Charlotte to her sister. "Much better than at home."

Emily let out a long happy sigh. She shook her head as if emerging from a trance. "Splendid," she echoed. "Tremendous. Oh, let's do it again!"

"One time is enough," said the children's aunt. "But I'm sure our hosts enjoyed it."

"Hugely," said Gavin.

"It was wonderful," said Rose. "Amazing." It really was. These children built on each other's imaginative flights, she thought, and were far more creative than any one of them could be alone.

Their guests beamed at the praise.

Another round of treats seemed in order. Rose summoned her reserves from the kitchen. Maria Brontë came to sit beside her. "That was extraordinary," Rose told the girl. "You are all very talented."

"You don't think it was a frivolous endeavor?" She looked slightly anxious.

"Not at all. It was a wonderful gift."

Maria ducked her head. "I knew you and Sir Gavin were going to wed," she said.

Rose blinked, surprised. "You did?"

"Yes."

"How?"

"The way you looked that night. I expect you will be very happy."

"You do?" Somehow Rose didn't feel as if she was talking to a little girl. There was something almost oracular about Maria in this moment.

"You are like a fairy tale."

"Those are just stories."

"People are stories, and stories make people," said Maria. "Stories make the whole world." She looked up at Rose and blinked as if surprised by her own words.

Lucy, who had just entered with a tray and heard this, said, "That's the truth. It's what we do, eh? Tell stories. From Shakespeare on down. And you have to tell your own before somebody else does. And makes a right hash of it. 'Cause they *will*. That's for certain sure."

Rose looked from the maid to the child. Their phrases had struck a chord somewhere in her mind. Or her heart. Something significant had been planted just now, though she didn't yet know what.

The renewed treats were consumed. Gavin offered a toast to their guests. Emily sang a song. Charlotte recited a poem, not one of her father's. Branwell attempted a handstand and nearly knocked over a table. And with that, their aunt declared it was time for the visitors to go. She stood, quelling a flurry of protests with one stern look. The children subsided and began putting on their coats.

It emerged that the book they'd created was to go with them, not remain as a gift. It was to be part of an ongoing chronicle at the parsonage. "But you can come and see it whenever you like," Charlotte assured Rose and Gavin. They thanked her solemnly.

Their aunt herded the group to the gig in a hubbub of farewells. Branwell hung over the side of the vehicle, waving, as it started off. "Wasn't that a grand celebration?" he asked.

"It was," called Gavin.

"Thank you," said Rose. They watched, waving back, until the gig was out of sight.

The house seemed quiet and empty when they had departed. "Those children will do great things," said Gavin as they returned to the parlor. "That was quite a feat."

Rose nodded. "And they are so young. Think what they'll be like when older."

"If they don't lose that spark. The world will try to take it away from them."

Rose thought of the bereavement ahead of them and their father's rigid rules. "Perhaps they will find refuge in stories," she murmured.

"What?"

"Maria said something. Lucy too."

Gavin raised his eyebrows. "I wouldn't have put those two in the same category."

"About stories. They set me thinking."

He waited, attentive.

"The tales we tell," Rose continued slowly. "About ourselves and each other."

"Umm?"

"They shape." Rose frowned, frustrated. She was not quite catching this elusive concept. She bit her lip. "We were the story of Gavin and Rose. Hereditary enemies."

"Until we retold it," Gavin said.

"Yes!"

"Amongst ourselves, at least." His expression was wry.

Rose nodded. "We have to do more."

"What do you mean?"

"I'm not... You remember my grandmother's idea about imagining what could be worse?" She was working things out as she spoke.

"Of course," he responded "A very useful practice. Even if one's blood runs cold at the possibilities that crop up."

"But...what if...instead of thinking what could be worse, one...imagined a story that could be better."

"Imagined?"

"Told? Insisted upon?"

"I don't quite understand you, Rose."

"I don't either. But I might have an idea."

"You always have good ones."

She loved him so. "We will have to puzzle it out together."

"Those are the best kind of ideas."

———

One fantastically busy week later, Gavin and Rose stood ready to greet their friends and neighbors to a party at Yerndon to celebrate their marriage. They had invited everyone they knew and some people they were barely acquainted with. They had sent for special provisions from Leeds, as well as a rainbow of flowers, and recruited helpers from around the neighborhood. There was a luscious buffet set out in the dining room. A trio of musicians, also from Leeds, had set up in a corner of the front parlor and were tuning their instruments. Fortunately, May had begun warm and dry. If people overflowed the house, they would be comfortable outdoors. Chairs had been scattered about the garden for this eventuality.

Their families were attending. Gavin's mother was being fetched, rather against her will. The twins had helped push her on when Gavin recruited them with the bait of the Brighton trip. Rose's parents had yielded to talk of appearances and what people would think if they stayed away. Gavin trusted that the public occasion would at least give them a bit of time to try out Rose's clever idea.

"That is the Milsomes' carriage," said Rose at his side. "I told you they would be among the first to arrive."

Gavin squeezed her hand, which was trembling slightly in his. "Here we go then."

She turned to look up at him. "Oh, Gavin, do you think…"

"Nothing ventured, nothing gained. It is a good plan."

She gave him an uncertain smile. He hoped he was right.

Forty minutes later, Gavin and Rose sat in the middle of a row of chairs set out in the back parlor, which had been cleared of other furnishings for this occasion. Gavin's mother was at his other side, his sisters just beyond. Past Rose sat her parents. They were arrayed as if they were two families celebrating their union through marriage. Guests could circulate through to congratulate them and then move on to refreshments and conversation. If only their families didn't look stiff and reluctant, Gavin thought. Not to say sullen. Only his sisters were smiling.

As time passed and the press of good wishes thinned out, the older generation began to look restive. They were plotting escape, or worse. It was time to begin. Gavin caught Rose's eye. They exchanged a nod and turned toward their respective parents.

"You are looking very fine tonight, Mama," said Gavin.

His mother's frown eased a bit. She sat straighter.

"Is that a new gown?"

"Isn't it lush?" said Jillian.

"It certainly becomes you, Mama," said Gavin.

"Mr. Milsome's brother, who is visiting, thought she was our older sister," said Jillian with a giggle.

"Him!" Their mother tossed her head.

"He was much struck," said Janet. "He said she is a fine-looking woman."

"Not surprising," said Gavin. "She is."

Their mother made a shooing gesture, but she looked pleased.

"He said he was very sorry he had missed the dance," added Jillian.

"He still wants you to walk in the garden," said Janet.

"Pish," said their mother. But her eyes gleamed.

"You know, Mama," said Gavin in a musing tone that he strove to make casual. "It just occurs to me. Didn't Aunt Mary invite you to go to Brighton with Jillian and Janet?"

The twins nodded. Gavin had not dared prime them lest the plan get out, but he'd hoped they would support him.

"Go?" his mother replied. "How could I go?"

"By carriage with my sisters," he answered. "Quite easily."

"And leave you all al…" She broke off, since this point was obviously specious. He was not alone. "I have far too much to do," she said instead.

"You are always busy," Gavin acknowledged. "You deserve a rest, and a holiday. I think I might manage to care for the estate."

"The one you have abandoned?" his mother asked sourly.

Gavin ignored this gibe. "You know," he repeated. "I have wondered. Did you never think to remarry?"

"What?" Her exclamation brought heads around.

"Our father has been gone for years now. And you are in your prime. As the gentleman said, a fine-looking woman."

"I have devoted my life to my children," she answered. "However ungrateful *some* of them may have been."

"And now the youngest of us are to be launched into the world," Gavin said. "Jillian and Janet will go off to their own homes soon, I daresay."

"You would certainly know about *that*," replied his mother. She looked less grim, however.

"I daresay you would enjoy the company in Brighton," said Gavin. "With people of taste and discernment all around you."

"Unlike here," she replied.

"Very true," said Gavin. There was a spark of interest in her eye, he was certain.

"You would need more new dresses," said Janet. "More fashionable ones."

This idea did not repel their mother, Gavin thought.

"Brighton is full of fine modistes," said Jillian. "Some move from London for the summer."

"Aunt Mary would know all about that," said Janet. "She could advise us all." The twins exchanged a conspiratorial glance. They were hoping for a new wardrobe themselves out of this idea, Gavin thought. And so they had become allies.

"Mary has no eye for color," grumbled his mother.

Gavin suppressed a spark of triumph. He had gotten her arguing on his ground. "You could set her straight," he said. "I daresay the Keighley ladies would create a sensation at the seaside."

"We could stroll along the shore together," said Jillian.

"I expect you would *often* be mistaken for the twins' older sister," Gavin told his mother. "Fine-looking indeed."

"Do you imagine I don't see what you are doing?" his mother asked in response.

"Suggesting that you enjoy yourself at the seaside? With the cream of London society? And Aunt Mary to present you to her wide acquaintance."

"And so many charming gentlemen," said Janet. Her expression suggested that she was imagining herself the object of their attentions.

"A change of scene," said Gavin. He decided to dare. "A fresh start?"

His mother looked out the window, past the guests in the garden and over the moor. "I will…consider it," she said in an uncharacteristic meditative tone.

For her, this was agreement. Gavin sat back, satisfied.

On his other side, Rose had opened a conversation with her parents. "Wouldn't it be lovely if Daniel were here," she said.

"Your brother does not care to have anything to do with us," replied her father with a frown.

"Oh no. He would have come. But he was engaged with a party of friends for a walking tour of Offa's Dike. Very historical."

"You invited Daniel?" Her father looked thunderous.

"I don't know why I let you discourage me from writing him," Rose said in a musing voice. "Of course I had to let him know about my marriage."

"You dared?" Her father's exclamation brought heads around.

"He thought it was a fine solution to the Yerndon problem," Rose went on. "And rather a good joke, actually."

"Joke!"

"He said he'd always liked Gavin as a boy. And he thought I had too. He'll come and visit another time."

"He can't come here instead of staying with us," exclaimed her mother. "What would people say?"

"He can do what he likes," snarled Rose's father. "He always does."

"I wonder where he got that from?" asked her mother with a sharp look.

"You should go and see him," said Rose.

"He does not care to receive us," replied her father with the air of one closing a case once and for all.

"Because you were always fighting about Yerndon," said Rose. Her brother had thought the feud ridiculous. It had been the chief bone of contention between the two Denholme men. "Now that the matter is *resolved* and need not be mentioned again, I daresay he would be glad to see you."

"Do you think so?" asked her mother longingly.

"I do. You could hear about what he's up to in Oxford."

"Scholarship," muttered her father as if it was some illicit pursuit.

"It might be quite interesting. He was telling me about Offa's Dike in his letter."

Her father looked at her as if she'd run mad.

Rose's mother wrung her hands. "Without Yerndon to argue over, couldn't we be reconciled with Daniel? It is *so* long since we've seen him."

"I won't..." began Rose's father.

"Won't *what*? Rose is right."

Rose had never seen her mother look so fierce. It was rather lovely. And so she didn't twit her parents over the phrase, "Rose is right." She would just enjoy the novelty of it, she decided. And believe that it might be used again sometime. Even frequently.

"I shall invite Daniel *home*," said her mother with a finality that allowed no argument.

"You will do no such—"

"I shall! And you will welcome your son as a father ought."

Rose turned to Gavin. He smiled and offered a small nod. Rose took it for success. They'd agreed they couldn't show any outward sign of triumph. That might undo any progress they'd made. Nor did they expect that one brief talk would change everything. It was just a seed. They would have more work to do. It was a good beginning, however, to a new story.

After their guests had all departed, Rose and Gavin walked out onto the moor together, hand in hand. The sun was at the horizon, throwing golden light and long shadows across the beloved landscape. The birds chirped evening calls as they settled for the night. Fresh scents perfumed the air. The heather would be blooming in another month, a purple carpet over the earth, driving the bees mad with joy. They were both filled with deep contentment here in their heart home as they reviewed their family conversations.

"Charming gentlemen," said Rose with a smile.

"That point did seem to strike Mama," replied Gavin.

"I would like her to be happy."

"As would I. It has been so long since she seemed so. And I would like to see Daniel again as well."

"I think you two could be friends."

"So do I. I always admired him."

Rose looked up at her husband. "Did you? Even though Daniel was a scholar and not an adventurer on the moor."

"Because of it. He reads ancient Greek as if it was a London newspaper."

"Does he?"

"He helped me with some knotty passages during a school holiday."

"I didn't know that."

Gavin smiled. "You don't know everything, even though your idea was a stroke of genius. You are brilliant, Lady Keighley."

"You are discerning, Sir Gavin."

They laughed together.

He raised her hand and kissed it. "You don't know how much I love you."

"I don't, do I?"

He looked surprised. "How not?"

"Well, you haven't actually said so before."

"Of course I have."

"When?" Rose asked him roguishly.

"Well, after we wed. Or when I held you in my arms."

She shook her head.

"I'm sure I must have," Gavin insisted.

"Not as such," Rose told him.

"Are you sure?"

She nodded.

"Well, I have been thinking it for weeks."

"Oh, thinking." She dimpled. "How many weeks?"

"Many more than I understood until lately."

"What happened lately?" she asked.

"The Rose I had nearly forgotten, and the youth who admired her, came out of hiding."

She blinked back a sudden tear.

Gavin sank to one knee. "I love you with all my heart, Rose. Will you be my wife?"

"I am your wife," she pointed out.

"With all your heart?"

She waited a moment so as not to seem flip. "With every part of me. And all my hopes and dreams."

"And so?"

"I love you very, very much, Gavin."

He stood and pulled her into his arms.

About the Author

Jane Ashford discovered Georgette Heyer in junior high school and was captivated by the glittering world and witty language of Regency England. That delight was part of what led her to study English literature and travel widely. Her books have been published all over Europe as well as in the United States. Born in Ohio, she is now somewhat nomadic. Find her on the web at janeashford.com and on Facebook at facebook.com/janeashfordwriter. You can sign up for her monthly newsletter on either site.

THE DUKE'S BEST FRIEND

The Duke's Estates series continues with a sparkling new Regency romance from beloved author Jane Ashford!

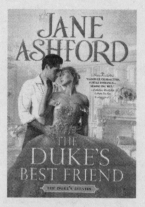

Henry Deeping and Kate Meacham seem to clash every time they meet. Kate is frustrated by the change in her status following the death of her grandfather, a legendary figure in diplomatic circles. As a lone single woman, she is now effectively nobody, even though she has made important contributions to diplomacy in the past. Henry, just joining the Foreign Office, is wondering how to make his mark.

They make a deal—Henry will serve as Kate's escort to important events to which she is no longer invited, and Kate will introduce him to the important people she knows so well. But when they spot a foreign agent, they decide to investigate on their own, enlisting a motley group of friends and relying on each other to uncover the truth...

"Superbly executed...
a daringly different kind of Regency historical."

—*Booklist* for *A Duke Too Far*

For more info about Sourcebooks's books and authors, visit:
sourcebooks.com

CURLED UP WITH AN EARL

A sparkling new sexy Regency romance series
from award-winning author Amy Rose Bennett

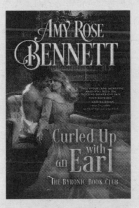

A covert inquiry agent for the Crown, William Lockhart, the Earl of Kyle, is on the hunt for a ruthless killer—and Sir Oswald, a rare botanical poisons expert, is the prime suspect. Posing as a groom in the baronet's household, it shouldn't take Will long to unearth the evidence Scotland Yard needs. If only the beguiling Miss Lucy Bertram wasn't so damn distracting.

Miss Lucy Bertram, daughter of the eccentric botanist, is content to spend her days either writing scientific articles or curled up with a Gothic romance novel. But when her father insists she accept the suit of the wealthy industrialist to save the family from penury, Lucy decides to embark on a search to find her disowned brother and enlist his aid. But she will need a bodyguard, and that handsome Will fits the bill nicely...

"Bursting at the seams with delicious drama."

—*Library Journal* for *Up All Night with a Good Duke*

For more info about Sourcebooks's books and authors, visit:
sourcebooks.com

ANY DUKE IN A STORM

Historical romance takes to the high seas in
this steamy enemies-to-lovers romp by
USA Today bestselling author Amalie Howard

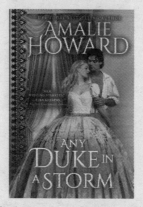

Lady Lisbeth Medford, Countess of Waterstone and famed international spy, is caught between the devil and the deep blue sea. She's
determined to infiltrate a notorious smuggling ring in the West Indies
while on a covert mission as a ship's captain. But her identity is com-
promised and she's forced to flee with the enemy hot on her heels.

The trouble in front of her, however, might be even worse. Raphael
Saint, the Duc de Viel, is her ship's aggravating and dangerously charming sailing master, who might very well be part of the smuggling ring
Lisbeth must bring to justice. But when a new deadly threat on the high
seas looms, the only way out of danger is to face it...together.

**"[Howard's] prose is delightful, her writing
masterful, her characters unforgettable."**

Kerrigan Byrne, *USA Today* bestselling author

For more info about Sourcebooks's books and authors, visit:
sourcebooks.com

THE LADY HE LOST

Sparkling historical romance delivers
friends-to-enemies-to-lovers in the start of
a sexy new series from Faye Delacour

When Lieutenant Eli Williams turns up in the middle of the
London social season after being lost at sea for two long years ago,
his first move is seeking to redeem himself with Miss Jane Bishop.
Her only interest is in making her own way in the world by estab-
lishing a ladies' gambling club. Luckily for Eli, he can help.

As Eli works to regain her trust, Jane's defenses begin to crum-
ble, But when Eli faces a court of inquiry on suspicion of desertion,
Jane must decide if she will let go of the past to build a future with
Eli, or risk losing him for good.

**"Refreshingly charming with a feisty,
resilient heroine worth fighting for."**

Amalie Howard, *USA Today* bestselling author

For more info about Sourcebooks's books and authors, visit:
sourcebooks.com

AN INCONVENIENT DUKE

When the duke starts searching for
answers...no one's secrets are safe

Marcus Braddock, former general and newly appointed Duke of
Hampton, is back from war. Now, not only is he surrounded by the
utterly unbearable ton, but he's mourning the death of his beloved
sister, Elise. Marcus believes his sister's death wasn't an accident,
and he's determined to learn the truth—starting with Danielle, his
sister's beautiful best friend. He never thought Danielle might be
keeping secrets of her own...

**"As steamy as it is sweet as it is luscious.
My favorite kind of historical!"**

—Grace Burrowes, *New York Times* bestselling author,
for *Dukes Are Forever*

A GENTLEMAN OUGHT TO KNOW

A sparkling new Regency romance from
beloved author Jane Ashford!

Charlotte Deeping needs something to keep her occupied now
that she's back home after her first London season. She misses
solving local intrigues with her school friends, but they've all gone
off and gotten married. Then Laurence Lindley, the Marquess of
Glendarvon, comes for a visit, and drops a mystery right into her lap.

In an effort to uncover his past, Charlotte contrives subtle ways
to get close to the mysterious marquess—a closeness they find they
both enjoy. That is, until Charlotte's digging rouses an old vendetta
and Laurence has to delve into his own history to help the young
lady he's come to love.

**"An utterly delightful tale of deception and masquerade
that sets a new bar for the Regency romp.**

—*Historical Novel Society* for *Earl on the Run*

For more info about Sourcebooks's books and authors, visit:
sourcebooks.com

THE ROGUE STEALS A BRIDE

Enter the glittering halls of Regency England with *New York Times* and *USA Today* bestselling author Amelia Grey

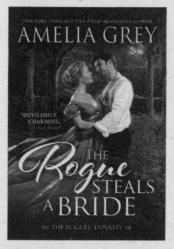

Matson Brentwood has finally met the woman of his dreams. The lovely, red-haired Sophia Hart heats his blood like no other lady. But no matter how attracted Matson is to Sophia, there's no way he can get involved with anyone who is under the watchful eye of the man he's sworn to hate.

"Amelia Grey never fails to entertain."

—Kat Martin, *New York Times* bestselling author

BLAME IT ON THE EARL

A delightfully scandalous Regency romp
from beloved author Jane Ashford

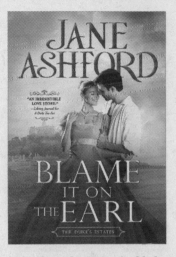

Sarah Moran might be the only unmatched lady relieved to return
to the country after a busy London season. But when she saves
Kenver Pendrennon from nearly falling into the sea while reveling
in the fresh air of Cornwall, the rising tide forces them to seek shelter for the night. By the time they return in the morning, rumors
have already begun to spread, and Sarah and Kenver—who is heir
to an earl—must marry quickly to keep scandal at bay...

**"Sweetly romantic Regency romance
expertly spiked with danger."**

—Booklist for Earl's Well That Ends Well

For more info about Sourcebooks's books and authors, visit:
sourcebooks.com